The Lavende

Chrissy Smith

Cover illustration by Hayley Smith

For Kath and Alan, who loved, lived, and breathed-in Lowestoft.

Note from the author:

I was inspired to write this book following the sad death of my mother in law, Kath, who lived in Pakefield, Lowestoft and the discovery of an old suitcase, full of family diaries, which she'd kept hidden in her loft for many years. The earliest was written in 1942 and I decided to transcribe the diaries for the family to read. They quickly became a window to another time, another world, and they taught me how different life was back then. This story is my own interpretation of the daily events portrayed in the earliest of those handwritten time capsules.

THE LAVENDER DIARIES

PROLOGUE:

The telephone call came one sunny spring day in April, a call always half expected when someone reaches the impressive age of ninety four, but somehow the news still managed to convey an air of shock and finality. There was nothing more that could be said or done for Alice Brown, who had fallen asleep for the last time in her favourite wingback armchair.

The funeral was a perfectly choreographed affair, silent tears were shed by respectful mourners and a moving tribute organised, a slide show of poignant memories, of children and grandchildren, of sunny beach days, of giant snowballs rolled in a wintry garden, of Easter eggs hidden and gleefully found behind a row of majestic flower pots, so many happy smiling faces and all accompanied by the haunting melody of Al Jolson's Anniversary Waltz, a thoughtful nod to Alice's dancing days.

After the service and with hearts full of sad resignation everyone filed away from the crematorium, to be reunited once more at the house, where the atmosphere changed to a much more celebratory occasion.

'Here's to Alice' everyone cheered joyfully, as they raised a glass or two. She'd had a good innings after all and now they only wanted to remember the good times, the happier times, the kind lady who'd given her time and money to so many different causes, who'd volunteered at regular church fetes, a Mothers' Union committee member and Chair of Pakefield

Ladies who'd valiantly bumped up and down the aisle on various coach trips in her efforts to raise a collection for the driver, but also they remembered the young girl, the teenager who'd lived through that dreadful war, the war that no one knew very much about these days, apart from the stories she'd told them of course, particularly her favourite, about her husband Keith, the handsome sailor she'd met at the end of it.

When all the proceedings were over and the guests had finally departed, the clearance of the house began.

Every room was to be cleared, ready for the house sale; wardrobes, cupboards, garage, shed, and most arduous of all, the loft. A lifetime of memories had been stored up there, packed into the farthest rafters, and all of it was to be mulled over and distributed amongst family and friends, or disposed of in some way, a heart wrenching decision sometimes difficult to make. To most onlookers the contents of the bulging bags and boxes might be considered an assortment of junk, fit only for the flea market, but hidden inside were many items of deep and sentimental attachment to those nearest and dearest. There was Alice's Wedgewood collection, sage green in colour and not particularly rare but one which had taken her a lifetime to acquire, a multitude of paintings from Keith's exhaustive hobby, though he'd been gone twenty years now, plus various Victorian tea sets all carefully wrapped in ancient brown-edged newspaper and passed down through the ages, every piece delicately gilded and hand painted. Finally there were a number of dolls and teddies, kept devotedly for many years, all old and worn out, but well-loved nevertheless.

It seemed a daunting task and emotionally overwhelming at times, with tears shed upon each discovery, and yet a home was needed for it all.

The couple's south facing garden had been a joy and a blessing for well over fifty years but this had been no happenstance! When the houses were being built Alice and Keith had waited patiently for the builders to arrive at their favourite plot, the one in the middle, on the sunny side of the street, and when that time came they had rushed to the sales office to reserve it. From that moment on their modest three-bedroom semi with its sunlit lounge and generous garden, had indeed been a place to call home.

Sadly, when Keith passed away, Alice lost her enthusiasm for the garden, in fact for pretty much everything, 'I've lost my compass,' she declared to her children plaintively, 'I'm adrift on an open sea,' she'd sigh, but after a while she decided to head out there, it was somewhere to go after all, away from the house and the photographs. Once outside, she'd wander around aimlessly looking for something to do, perhaps lifting out an unwelcome dandelion, or cutting off a meandering branch grown too long over the path, she'd always find a little job, that small something to keep her occupied, until eventually the garden became her sanctuary and as it turned out she began to look after it surprisingly well.

The garden had always been Keith's province, some unwritten law had decreed it, and he'd always watched Alice like a hawk if ever she ventured outside with the vague notion of pulling up a weed or perhaps to use her secateurs in such a way he considered reckless, but after his death she became free, free to nurture the flowerbeds in an unrestricted fashion, free to grow copious amounts of tomatoes, cucumbers and grapes in the greenhouse, and to plant her own favourite plants in any of the flower beds, in any way she liked, with gay abandon.

The electrics had been cleverly installed by Keith, a practical man, who could make or mend anything as long as he had the tools and materials. He'd worked loyally for the coachworks for forty years and on occasion he'd helped himself to a few off-cuts here and there because he hated to see waste and he knew they would never be missed. With the electrics in place Alice could switch on the water fountain from inside the garage and watch it spurting and cascading prettily into the ornamental pond. Keith had designed the pond himself not long after they'd moved in. He'd dug it out with his own bare hands, and a shovel, making it square and deep in the middle with a ledge around the outside for plants to sit on, and above the water line he'd decorated it, just to be different from other ponds in the street, with attractively coloured tiles of blue and yellow which glazed and glistened at the water's edge. He was extremely proud of his achievement, particularly his decision to place the pond on the left hand side of the lawn, which meant it would benefit from both light and shade. But for most of the day it was flooded with sun and Alice could sit and relax by the side of it, in quiet contemplation, leaning back in her comfortable sun chair while allowing her old bones to warm up, lifting her head every now and again to watch the frogs, goldfish and newts swimming contentedly beneath the water lilies. If the breeze picked up she would hear the sound of Keith's homemade weather vane, a fishing trawler fashioned out of discarded sheet metal, spinning gently on top of the washing line, and only then would she allow her memories to flow freely, as she sat in peaceful reflection, enjoying her own little piece of heaven.

The garden always contained an abundance of flowers, from snowdrops in early spring to asters in the autumn, but Alice had two particular favourites. Firstly, she adored sunflowers and every year she'd plant a row of them in front of the old shed at the bottom of the garden. Their golden brightness would bring her some cheer but they were also a temporary camouflage for the shed's scruffy exterior. From her lounge window she'd watch them growing tall and strong and when the flower heads began to bloom she'd hold a secret competition as to which one would be the biggest and the best, purely for her own amusement of course, it seemed her adult grandchildren had lost interest in such trifles.

Secondly, and perhaps more importantly, she loved lavender and her house would always smell of it! Even in her later years she'd hobble out to the front garden, supported by her father's trusty old walking stick, and head over to the large lavender bush growing next to the front gates. She'd delve deep into her apron pocket for a pair of large kitchen scissors and then she'd cut off a few sprigs ready to fill a pair of matching flower vases which were always perched at each end of the mantelpiece, above the gas fire. Sometimes she'd cut off more than she needed and so she'd crumble the extra flower heads into the toe-end of a pair of old tights. The hazy netting would bulge out into a soft brown ball which she'd tie off with a pretty ribbon to hang in the bathroom or wardrobe or occasionally she'd tuck one secretly inside her knicker drawer!

On the last day of ownership a small gathering of immediate family took place, the house was now completely empty, except for one ancient leather suitcase which had been discovered and retrieved at the last minute from the darkest corner of the loft. As the family gathered round, they wondered what treasures might be found hidden inside?

When the rusty locks were gingerly released and the fragile lid prized carefully open, their curious eyes beheld that sadly there was no treasure, no gold or precious stones to speak of, but surely what was inside might be considered treasure nonetheless, but perhaps of a more sentimental kind, for within the musty interior they discovered copious handwritten diaries, small bundles of tiny well-thumbed notebooks, all bound together with ribbons and remnants of lace, and the oldest of them was dated 1942.

When the family members had finally loaded up their cars and hugged each other goodbye, a last tearful farewell was bid to the childhood home they'd known for many years, for, in all honesty, they knew in their hearts they would never return.

When the black wrought iron gates were clanged shut for the last time and locked resignedly into position, the family took one last look at the house and garden. Their eyes seemed strangely drawn to the lavender, sitting in its familiar place by the front gates, but unusually quiet. The familiar hum of insect life, the countless bees and butterflies constantly hovering and crawling over its purple perfumed spikes, had gone! Now it sat, silent and wooden, as if, like Alice, the lavender had suddenly withered and died.

CHAPTER ONE

A stark white letter flapped and fluttered, like a trapped bird, battling against a gusty wind which threatened to remove it from its risky moorings.   As Ellen turned the corner into Walmer Road she couldn't resist a smile of pure delight at the sight of the war department notice, attached rather precariously, to her old front door. How small and insignificant that piece of paper was, she realised, but as she continued to walk along the road towards it her heart began to sing in the sure knowledge that the words printed upon it would alter her life dramatically.   Her modest family home, requisitioned by the Government when the nonsense of another war finally became a reality, was now to be returned to her at last. It was the long awaited sign which proved to her, without a doubt, that the war was well and truly over.

She removed the notice gleefully from the nail upon which it hung and read the typed words greedily.

'With reference to the occupation for naval purposes of the above mentioned property, a claim for compensation has now been assessed in accordance with the Defence Act 1939, and will be payable as from the date of occupation. Forms will be required in duplicate to be returned to the Chief Surveyor'

Ellen folded the letter carefully and tucked it deep inside the pocket of her heavy woollen coat.

She stood back to survey her once beautiful home, sighing resignedly as she took in its shabby exterior, the rotting window frames and the overgrown, sadly neglected, front garden, whilst acknowledging, with a heavy heart, that a huge amount of work was needed both inside and out. After feeling a little overwhelmed at the thought, she wiped away a silent tear of longing and loss. Drawing in a deep breath of resolve, she pulled the warmth of her woollen coat tightly around her slim frame and fastened her belt a little more firmly. With the cold draught shut out, as best she could, she began to walk briskly away from her old home and head towards the small terraced house where she now lived.

The house in London Road had been rented to them by Mr Algar, a pious man of property in the town, who knew the family quite well due to their regular attendance at chapel before and after the war. The rent they paid him was fairly low in comparison to other places in town and she conceded that Mr Algar had indeed been very good to them. Of course he had, of that there was no doubt, but more recently she'd begun to feel that her landlord's constant interference in her affairs, together with his overtly friendly manner, was becoming rather bothersome to her.

She swiftly endeavoured to push those unkind thoughts away with almost instant mortification, her Christian values constantly reminding her that any ill feeling towards another person was sinful. Mr Algar was not a bad man, she relented, he'd always kept a watchful eye on herself and her two daughters while her husband, Frank, was away working and he was frequently on hand to help her with any chores that needed to be done or indeed to assist her with any paperwork.

She did miss Frank though, in fact she missed him so much that it hurt, not only in an emotional way, it also pained her that she had to deal with almost everything herself. She wondered if perhaps that was the reason she felt resentment for Mr Algar's meddling. If Frank had been there with her she wouldn't need any help at all from that man. Without Frank by her side she felt unprotected, vulnerable even, and very alone. He seemed to be away more and more these days. But of course he needed to go where the work was, she understood that, and there was not much reliable work to be found locally at the moment, or at least not at the same level of pay and so he'd been enticed to travel far, journeying by train to many different parts of the country.

The wire she'd received from Frank the previous day had delivered some bad news, he'd told her in a few brief words that he was sorry but he wouldn't be able to come home that weekend. This news had disappointed her dreadfully; she always looked forward to the weekends when Frank returned home, but now she saw those few days stretching ahead of her, yawning and empty.

Frank was in Leeds, working on a housing project, and although he would try to return home at least every other weekend, when he did manage it, he'd often arrive in the early hours of Saturday morning, dog tired, and pretty much 'out of it' for much of the day. He'd remind Ellen that she should never rely upon it, that he could never promise her faithfully he would be there. If the work demanded it he would have to stay away.   Ellen understood that, of course she did, she knew for the time being that this was the way it must be, and of course the extra money came in handy for the girls and their needs, but she was continually optimistic, always ready for his return. She would clean and bake all day on the Friday; buns, patties and tarts, in preparation for his homecoming. She wanted to feed him up as best she could while he was home and whatever they didn't eat she'd parcel up for him to take back with him. Sadly, the only special time they had was on a Sunday, after chapel, because on that day Frank would be fully rested and more himself, they would have their Sunday lunch together and in the afternoon they'd spend real quality time together as a family, walking along the promenade, going out for afternoon tea, or just sitting on the beach, now that the mines had been cleared, playing racquet and ball, but that day was always over too soon because the very next morning he'd have to head back north to Leeds.

Frank often described to Ellen what he'd seen on his travels. Across the country, he'd witnessed the devastating effect of war which had decimated so many towns and villages and, because Frank was adept at a multitude of tasks, he was always in demand. A shipwright by trade, he could turn his hand to anything; woodwork, metalwork, mechanical engineering, whatever the job required, Frank could do it.

On the Monday morning, after his visit home, Ellen would accompany him to the station, doing her best to make the most of every minute they had together and even when the train finally left the station she'd stand on the platform, waving her handkerchief wildly in the air, hoping and praying that he might still have sight of her from his seat by the window. In fact she wouldn't stop waving until the train became a mere speck of grey smoke puffing aloft far into the distance and then afterwards she'd walk back home, feeling dejected. She understood of course that every pair of hands was needed to rebuild the country, there'd been several unrelenting air raids by the Luftwaffe on many Yorkshire towns and she knew she mustn't begrudge his usefulness up there. It also meant they could eat well and have a relatively decent standard of living, compared to many other families in the town, but their constant separations seemed interminable.

She should be grateful, she chided herself, what about those poor families living down on 'the grit,' now they had it really bad, their reliance on the fishing trade had been severely tested throughout the war, their flourishing fishing fleet had been dramatically reduced for the war effort, and they'd also suffered regular bombings across their ramshackle houses which had eventually turned the area into not much more than a slum. Sadly, it seemed, the 'town below the cliffs' was dying and their main catch of herring, one they'd relied upon for more than a century, was now diminishing rapidly.

Ellen tried to shrug off her sudden feeling of melancholy, patting her hand over the precious letter tucked safely inside her coat pocket, and then she smiled broadly, she couldn't wait to write to Frank that very day and share with him her happy news and her joy that soon they would be back together again and living in Walmer Road once more. She imagined seeing Frank in his beloved garden, watching him tilling the soil through the kitchen window, as she used to do, before the war came and ruined everything. The house would need to be renovated of course, she'd warn him of that, she knew there would be a lot of work to do and once she'd filled in all the necessary forms, and it was finally returned to her officially, she would be able to make a start! She knew she would have to scrub every inch of every room, a back breaking task in itself, but she'd do it with gusto. She couldn't wait to bring it back to the way it was, she'd scrub and scrub until her hands were raw, she'd do her damndest to remove every last remaining imprint of all those dirty naval boots.

Suddenly she remembered the Anderson shelter at the bottom of the garden, which she presumed was still in place, right where Frank's beloved greenhouse used to be, she'd have to arrange for that to be taken away! Maybe Bill, Frank's brother, would take it off their hands she thought? And then soon, very soon, come rain or shine, Frank would be back in his garden and she could watch him again from the kitchen window as he nurtured all his beloved vegetables, flora and fauna.

CHAPTER TWO

Ellen arrived at the gate of the small house they were renting
and walked along the short pathway to the front door. Built in
the Victorian era, the little row of terraced houses in London
Road had been thoughtfully constructed, each with a small
covered archway at the front and a pretty bay window
overlooking the small garden. The house contained many
period features inside but it was also in desperate need of
repair.

After turning the key in the lock she swiftly entered the place
they now called home. The welcoming warmth from the
hallway instantly embraced her, reminding her pleasantly of
the fire she'd lit that morning before going out. The house was
empty and quiet as both daughters were out at work and she
hoped they were working hard in their new jobs.

The girls were still in their teens, although Alice was on the
cusp of twenty, but with no qualifications to speak of and no
career aspirations fortunately both girls had been quick to find
work. It seemed that today no one cared about exams or
experience and many business proprietors in the town, still
reeling from the effects of war, were just looking for a
common sense approach and a willingness to learn. Ellen
was proud of the way her girls were growing up into hard
working, sensible young women, although, on reflection, Katy
had perhaps a little more sense than Alice! There was no
doubt that Alice was a hard worker, she was talented in so
many ways and she had a good brain in her head, but Ellen
feared she was far too pretty for her own good. She was
never very long without a besotted young man tagging along
behind her. Vanity was a sin, so the good lord said, and her
daughter's constant preening in front of the mirror had

become a persistent worry for Ellen but she tried not to dwell it and on the whole she was pleased that both girls had managed to find suitable jobs in town, within local retail shops, of those that were still standing of course!

Alice was now a sales assistant at Tuttles, a large department store near the centre of town, and Katy was working at the Co-op nearby. For Ellen it felt that at last the world was beginning to return to normal. Every day on her trips to town she would observe the bomb damaged houses and the rebuilding work going on and her biggest wish was that Frank could find work locally and come back home for good. If that could happen then her happiness would surely be complete.

Keeping her coat on, Ellen walked through the hallway and into the kitchen, collecting up the three bottles of pre-war stout she'd discovered in the outhouse during a recent clear out. Her intention was to return them to Florence Road and hopefully receive a few pennies to help with the family finances. Rationing was still in place, supplies were sparse, and every penny counted.

Just as she turned to leave, a dark shadow blocked the light which normally flowed unhindered from the hallway into the kitchen. Her spine began to tingle with expectation, and a certain amount of inexplicable dread, as she looked up to identify the tall masculine figure now filling her open doorway. Her mood dipped dramatically as soon as she realised who it was and she swiftly returned the bottles to the counter.

'Oh hello Mr Algar,' Ellen managed to force a smile, 'I was just on my way out', she announced as firmly and unambiguously as she could, hoping she might dissuade him from coming further inside the house, but she needn't have bothered because he walked straight into the hallway anyway. She made no move towards him and she did not invite him into the parlour for a cup of tea as she would have done, habitually, for any other visitor.

Ellen spoke swiftly to hide her displeasure, 'I managed to collect the requisition notice from the door this morning' she explained to him breathlessly, 'I've got it right here in my pocket if you want to have a look?'

It was Tom Algar who had informed Ellen of the letter's existence because, as she had come to realise, her landlord always seemed to know everything about her life before she did! Once he had let her know about the notice he had swiftly followed it up by giving her a firm instruction to go round to the house at her earliest opportunity to collect it. At least he had allowed her that pleasure, she thought, for if he'd have taken it upon himself to collect it for her, well, that would have really irked her, that would have been taking the biscuit!

'Well done,' he responded tersely and his low baritone voice echoed throughout the hallway almost as though he were preaching to her from a pulpit. His voice held a low hollow tone which seemed to vibrate from the inner chasms of his rib cage, a talent he used to its fullest extent when singing in the chapel choir next to Frank. In all honesty though, Ellen preferred Frank's singing voice, Frank's voice was a soft tenor, and in her opinion his tone held a much more melodic quality.

'I'll have a look at it later on tonight, if you'd like me to pop round?' he continued, making his offer trivially, but his expression was intense. Ellen's face must have shown her immediate consternation, for indeed the very idea of him coming round that evening sent nervous shivers up and down her spine. She wondered if he might have seen the alarm on her face because he swiftly let the idea drop and thankfully he did not pursue that line of thought again.

After a slight pause he swiftly changed tack and continued with his own matter to hand and apparently the main reason he had called round to see her today.

'Ellen, I'd like you to take a look at these,' he spoke to her in a much more abrupt and business like fashion, 'here are the dilapidation papers for this place.'

He held out several forms which he obviously wanted her to take from him. She moved a couple of steps forward and obliged him with a compliant nod. She took a brief look at the papers, dragging her eyes hurriedly down the list of repairs, and realising they were quite complex. She began to feel more than a little perturbed at the thought of all that work, and she looked up at him again with a slightly confused frown.

Tom Algar continued to look down at Ellen Bedingfield in a supercilious manner and Ellen witnessed again the familiar and strangely inscrutable expression on his austere and, she did concede, darkly handsome face. His moustache began to twitch a little in that slightly odd fashion she'd come to recognise, a frequent forewarning of a strangely discomfiting smile, a smile which seemed rather false to Ellen for it never quite reached his eyes, and his dark penetrating eyes continued to assess her in a rather intimidating way.

Tom Algar couldn't help himself; he always enjoyed Ellen's obvious unease whenever she was in his presence, particularly here, alone in the hallway, as she stood warily before him. There was something about this woman that provoked him, she was an enigma, he realised, and yet at the same time he had a very high regard for her. Ellen Bedingfield was a hard worker; she never stopped for a moment, even to take the smallest break! She was a kind, caring mother to her two daughters, watching over them earnestly, making and mending their clothes, always ensuring they were well turned out. Her pride in the face of adversity was truly remarkable. He had the greatest respect for Ellen's commitment, recognising her as a devout Christian, a loyal wife, and.... but quickly he stopped his train of thought, his rashness must be reigned in, he decided, as sudden feelings of frustration threatened to overcome him, because he realised of course that Ellen was everything his own wife was not!

Ellen quickly turned away from him and placed the papers he'd handed to her onto the kitchen counter. Suddenly she felt claustrophobic! She had to get out of the house and away from him without delay. 'Thank you Mr Algar,' she managed to reply politely, 'I'll have a look at them later on tonight.'

'Ellen!' he instantly reproached her with his haughty tone, 'how long have we known each other? All this time and yet you still insist on calling me Mr Algar, now please I want you to call me Tom, it's Tom from now on, ok!'

Ellen shifted her feet uncomfortably and, turning her flushed face away from his scrutiny, she picked up the three bottles of stout once more. There was absolutely no way she would ever do that she thought to herself!

'I'd really rather not' she replied as firmly as she could, 'I'm sorry Mr Algar but I have to go now. Would you mind shutting the door behind you when you leave?' She spoke to him in a firm and resolute manner but she couldn't help noticing how, rather annoyingly, he made no attempt to move out of her way, or indeed to leave the house before her, and so she had no alternative but to squeeze past him with as much decorum as she could muster, before finally heading through the open doorway and out into the fresh air, which she proceeded to gulp in eagerly and deeply with utter relief.

As the landlord watched her go he followed her out to the doorway and stood for a moment on the small mat at the foot of the step. He noticed her pace quickening as she walked away from him so that the gap between them began to widen rapidly. He watched her with a sense of enjoyment; she was obviously flustered by him and for some reason that made him happy, he liked to fluster women, his masculinity was empowered by it. As she moved hurriedly along the length of

London Road, towards the town centre, Ellen suddenly felt cold, the wind had picked up from the east and an icy blast was heading inland from across the sea. She wished she'd had time to retrieve her hat and gloves but in her mind's eye she saw them sitting, where she'd left them, on top of the kitchen counter, together with her shopping bag and purse, and she determined resolutely not to turn round and go back for them, and so, with both arms clutching the bottles firmly, she continued to walk briskly into town.

As she walked further away from the house she sensed Tom Algar's eyes still fixed upon her, watching her departure. She also imagined the irritating and strangely inscrutable smile still hovering around his pursed lips, his conceit cleverly concealed behind a dark curtain of whiskers.

CHAPTER THREE

Looking back to the relatively peaceful years towards the end of the thirties, Ellen remembered that period of time as the calm before the storm, or perhaps the years of disquiet when many sensed what was coming but preferred to live their lives in blissful ignorance. Those years were dubbed 'the evacuation years' and in December 1938 hundreds of Jewish children descended on Lowestoft via the 'Kinder transport' from Vienna. They had travelled many miles by rail and steamship, after being rescued from Nazi oppression, to arrive safe and sound in the quiet seaside town. After being greeted by the Mayor they were housed at Pakefield Holiday Camp and this place of sanctuary had no doubt saved their lives. The residents of Lowestoft had welcomed them with open arms but unfortunately their stay in the town had turned out to be rather short. When the war with Germany was declared officially in September 1939, the children were evacuated once more, together with many of Lowestoft's own residents and at the end of all of the upheaval, only essential personnel were left in the town.

When Ellen and Frank's house was requisitioned by the navy for the war effort they'd had no choice but to leave Lowestoft as well and so the whole family, Ellen, her mother and father and two daughters had all moved lock stock and barrel to the relative safety of the countryside. From then on Lowestoft could no longer be called home.

Lowestoft, the quintessential English holiday resort, where hundreds of visitors flocked every summer to relax and play on the soft golden sand and swim in the cool, calm sea, was no more! Beaches were now strictly off limits, minefields were hurriedly laid in a desperate attempt to secure the coast. Wire entanglements were constructed, dragon's teeth installed and anti-tank ditches were dug and from that moment on everyone was afraid of an imminent blitzkrieg invasion. By the end of June 1940 Lowestoft was effectively, a ghost town!

Alice and Katy quickly adapted to their new life in the country. They had both attended local schools within the sleepy hamlets of Laxfield and Cratfield. Those sunny peaceful days at Moat House Farm seemed a world away from the worrisome war which was going on at full pelt in other parts of the globe, where so many men were fighting and dying for their country.

Ellen had heard stories during their time in the countryside, about the many German bombs falling along the coast. It seemed that the East of England was considered a prime target for the Luftwaffe as the enemy were desperate to drop any load they still carried before heading back to Europe across the channel. Early on in the war, rumours were rife that the twenty minute flight from Denmark for the Luftwaffe's Dornier bombers was in fact a good test run, and was yet another reason for the town of Lowestoft to become a target, situated as it was at the most easterly point in England, as well as home to a naval base and considerable engineering and ship building facilities.

But now, Ellen thanked the lord, it was 1946, the war was over and the family had returned to Lowestoft. Soon they were settled back into their old routine, their time in the countryside swiftly becoming a dim and distant memory. Ellen knew that her family had been lucky, their country cousins had been a godsend, helping them in that way, but then everyone did what they had to during that terrible time and it was a small sacrifice really. So many people were urged to share their homes in areas of comparative safety and they were blood relatives after all, surely it had been the right thing to do, to offer their extended family a safe haven, away from the horrors of war.

When the family were finally settled back in Lowestoft, they could see for themselves the devastation that had been wrought upon the town. Ellen looked on in horror at the burned out derelict shells of so many shops and houses, particularly the direct hit which had taken out half of the high street, and finding out that among those who'd perished were many people she'd known and grown up with.

CHAPTER FOUR

Alice had just finished serving her third customer of the day and was secretly very satisfied with her performance. So far that day she'd sold two dresses, a smart office suit, and some bridal underwear and it was only just after eleven, not only was she happy with herself, but she'd heard through the grapevine that Mr Tuttle, the owner and manager of the store, had also been extremely pleased with her.

She was right, Mr Tuttle greatly admired the new girl, her youth and beauty were beyond compare and her burnished brown hair, sparkling blue eyes and ruby red lips were a tonic to his old soul. It gladdened his heart to watch her moving around so confidently in her new found environment, she seemed so relaxed and at ease, almost as though she belonged there. Her magnificent window display was in the vein of a vogue magazine and it was definitely enticing additional customers into the store. She seemed to possess that endearing quality of never taking no for an answer but it was always done with an air of civility and charm; her smile could melt a man's heart he thought to himself. There was no doubt she had the customers eating out of her hand and he considered, satisfactorily, that the new girl had definitely earned her wages that day.

With the war now over people were beginning to venture out to parties and dances. Women wanted to wear the latest fashions, at long last they were able to shrug off their boring uniforms and be feminine again, now it was no longer necessary for them to be wartime heroines. They could wear pretty dresses, stockings and heels, their hair could be worn in the latest styles, like the new liberty cut, or they could go casual with the sporty new look from America. According to

Vogue, bare midriffs would be on display in the summer, it seemed girls would definitely be turning a few heads, but as an older man Mr Tuttle considered the new styles to be tastefully discreet!

For men's fashions too, he'd seen a significant change, the American style had also been a big influence on young men who were now actively seeking out those flamboyant Hawaiian and western style shirts, putting them together with high waisted wool flannels and gabardines in the favoured solid colours of green, blue and tan, but always with shirts tucked in! It was definitely a time for new beginnings, and for almost every age, but particularly for the youth of the town, for to be young in 1946 was practically an aphrodisiac!

Alice was really looking forward to the dance that evening at the Palais. She'd decided to wear her pale pastel blue frock, the one her mother had just made for her, together with her new fur coat for warmth. She'd forgotten just how cold it could be on the coast and how persistent that easterly breeze? It could be ferocious in its tenacity, easily penetrating outer clothing to find its way inside and freeze her bones to the very marrow! At the Palais the previous week she'd had such a wonderful time. All the sailors had been there, after gaining some well deserved leave, and that night she'd danced with the most handsome of them all. His name was Keith and he was tall, slim, and well groomed. He had a twinkle in his eye and he'd flattered her the whole night long and what's more he had turned out to be a very good dancer. He'd twirled her round and round until she was giddy and giggling and she really hoped he would be there again tonight. She smiled at the thought and realised how good it was to be back in town at last!

She couldn't help but look back with a begrudging eye over those never ending years in the countryside and she let out a heartfelt sigh. When she thought about that time, away from all the action, she considered those years to be wasted years, so boringly quiet. While she was there, she'd always felt she was missing out on something, that she was being kept away from all the excitement. Of course, there'd been the occasional dance at Huntingfield, which she'd quite enjoyed, and many trips to the pictures with her local friends. She'd seen so many films she'd lost count; 'She Knows all the Answers,' with Joan Bennet, 'Ice Capade' with Dorothy Lumis, and the comedy, 'Gert and Daisy's Weekend' starring Elsie and Doris Waters, which on reflection had turned out to be very funny and made her belly laugh several times throughout the evening. However her spirits had never been lifted for long, as the monotony of everyday life seemed to constantly bring her mood down, and the only indication there was actually a war going on was the occasional glimpse of an army squadron using the local land for their field manoeuvres.

On one occasion a platoon was using her family's farmyard, for cooking purposes. Alice had walked by and she'd caught the eye of a young soldier who'd gawped at her rather obviously from his place behind the stove. She was on her way to the small village shop where she worked most days but as soon as she became aware of him, staring at her, she had turned her face genially towards him, unable to resist sending him an encouraging smile. Flirtation was easy, she'd quickly discovered, words were not really required, it was all about the eye contact! He'd smiled back at her of course, who wouldn't when such a pretty girl walked by, but unfortunately he made the mistake of moving towards her, still holding a metal spatula in his hand, only to be quickly grabbed and hustled back to his station by his jeering comrades. Alice smiled at the commotion she'd caused, watching as they dragged him away from her, and then she sighed yet again, there was never enough time for any of the soldiers to stop and chat, no time for anyone to enjoy life.

As she watched the soldiers return to their duties she'd realised of course that the men had an important job to do but in that moment she hated the wretched war and she couldn't wait for it to be over.

There were odd occasions when she'd heard the sound of bombs dropping way off into the distance along the coast. There was no mistaking the distinct sound of the missiles as they plummeted rapidly to earth. The first indication would be a whistling crescendo, an eerily piercing and doom laden sound, followed not long afterwards by a short silence, and then a final dull explosion. Those distant sounds of war seemed so remote and dreamlike that from her protected paradise it was almost as though she'd imagined them.

However, one particular day there was real tangible excitement in the village when her mother arrived unexpectedly at the small grocery shop with some shocking news. Ellen had come to meet Alice after work and it quickly became rather obvious that something was definitely amiss as her mother proceeded to send furtive glances around the vicinity both outside and then inside the shop. She was clearly very concerned and distressed about something; in fact Alice thought she'd never seen her mother looking so anxious.

Ellen quickly explained about the rumours that were circulating of some German POWs who had escaped and who were now on the run and apparently they'd been sighted in the local area. Her mother had learned that, after having been previously captured and placed inside a prisoner of war camp in Wales, several men had managed to escape and it seemed some of them had headed east across the country. The assumption was that they were heading towards the coast and the channel! This news had truly set Alice's heart racing, but although she was scared, she was excited at the same time. As instructed by her mother, Alice continued to be on the alert, her anxiety persisting for several days as she sent cautious glances around every corner in anticipation of a German officer, who might be very hungry by now, or desperate enough to jump out and capture her at any moment before dragging her off into the woods to have his wicked way with her.

However, after a couple of weeks had passed and there'd been no further sightings, either in the village or anywhere in the nearby vicinity, gradually everything began to calm down. No arrests were made and it was concluded by the police and the home guard that the men had most likely headed off in an entirely different direction, possibly south towards Kent, and so now they were a problem for an entirely different neighbourhood.

Around the same time Alice remembered another bit of excitement when a fighter plane was found ditched and abandoned in a field at Fressingfield. When all was quiet and the plane was standing alone in the meadow, Alice and her friend Violet had climbed all over it but they'd been disappointed to discover nothing much of any interest apart from one small crumpled photograph which Alice had found wedged under the back rest of the pilot's seat. She'd carefully pulled it out and examined it, seeing the face of a pretty young woman smiling up at her happily. Alice felt quite moved by the photograph, feeling it recorded one happy moment from the past, captured on film forever, showing a contented happy face from another time and another place, when all was well with the world. She reckoned the picture had been taken in peace-time, when war was the last thing on that young girl's mind. Alice felt she would like to know the girl in the photo, deciding she looked nice and that in another life they might have been friends, enjoying each other's company without a care in the world. Alice decided to keep the picture and so she stuffed it safely inside her coat pocket. As soon as she arrived home she took it out and placed it carefully inside her small jewellery box, the one she kept in her dressing table drawer.

When Alice returned to Lowestoft, she retrieved the photograph from her jewellery box and moved it into a larger box where it stayed amongst all her other war memorabilia.

Her collection comprised an odd assortment of shrapnel fragments, a few shell parts, plus several war posters she'd found strewn about. One poster she had particularly liked was the 'Waste Not Want Not' poster which had promoted ideas of how to make food go further. It encouraged bottling and preserving of summer produce to make sure it lasted all through the winter in order to keep everyone healthy while rations continued to remain in short supply. This, she acknowledged proudly, was something her mother accomplished prodigiously! Ellen was always in the kitchen, baking or bottling fruit, making preserves of jam and marmalade, shrewdly using the abundance of produce gathered in during the fruitful months.

Alice's shrapnel collection seemed a rather macabre pastime she supposed but she liked the idea of finding the most unusual pieces. She enjoyed looking at them from time to time; studying their exotic shapes, marvelling at how the metal had re-formed itself into twisted, gnarly, but frequently beautiful pieces of sculpture.

Most of her collection had come from the site at Waller's Tea Rooms, the worst raid on the town, which had happened unexpectedly on Tuesday, January 13th 1942 at 6 o'clock, tea time.

She'd listened to the stories told by those who'd witnessed it and apparently all through that particular day it had been snowing and, as dusk had begun to fall, every sound in the High Street became soft and muted. The footsteps of the dwindling shoppers were muffled and quiet as they proceeded slowly and deliberately along the snow covered pavements.

There was no warning of what was to come, the Luftwaffe plane came out of nowhere, although later reports mentioned a sudden shrill whistle that was heard just seconds before the first explosion but there was no time for anyone to escape as the first of the four 500kg bombs were dropped in quick succession. The only survivors inside the tea rooms were a few lucky souls who'd found themselves near to the door of the cellar and who'd managed to dive inside it, remaining hidden under the rubble for many hours, until at last mercifully they were rescued from their silent tomb. Seventy eight people were killed in the raid, civilians and service personnel, most of whom were enjoying a pleasant meal at the tea rooms. There were others that just happened to be walking by the place, and as is often the case, they were just in the wrong place at the wrong time.

Many stories were told about people who'd been killed that day but Alice found the story of the young manageress the most poignant. The newly appointed manageress had been roughly the same age as Alice and in fact on that very day it had been her nineteenth birthday and a party had been organised to celebrate it that very evening. A Naval Lieutenant had approached her in the afternoon explaining there was a shortage of chairs for a function up at the Sparrow's Nest. The Sparrow's Nest had been a former theatre and pleasure gardens, now known as HMS Europa, which had been requisitioned early on in the war by the Royal Naval Patrol Service, who were in charge of minesweepers, armed trawlers and the like. The Lieutenant had asked her politely whether they might borrow some chairs from her tea rooms, which he'd assured her would be returned the very next day, and the young manageress had instantly agreed to his request. However the lieutenant went on to explain that, unfortunately, there was no transport available to collect the chairs to convey them to the theatre. She quickly sought out her father, who also worked at Waller's, and asked him if he would mind taking the chairs up to the naval base in his van. Her father was not happy about this extra chore and told his daughter that he was far too busy. She persisted as he continued to procrastinate until eventually she became extremely agitated insisting, with some urgency, that he must take the chairs straight away. Finally her father gave in to her demands, deciding he didn't want to upset his daughter on her birthday, and so he did as he was told, arriving at the Sparrow's Nest just before 6 pm with the chairs.

As the chairs were being unloaded from his van, the sound of the explosions could be heard in the distance, and within a few minutes a naval officer was running towards him to relate the sad news that Waller's Tea Rooms had received a direct hit!

Although utterly distraught, at the tragic loss of his much-loved daughter, he managed to find solace and immense pride and gratitude in the belief that it had been her insistence and agitation which had persuaded him to leave the place at that critical time and because of that his daughter had indeed saved his life.

Increasingly, Alice heard more detailed descriptions of other raids which had taken place across the town in their absence and she was shocked at the magnitude and ferocity of the attacks. Although a few stories and rumours had managed to permeate through the mire, to reach the sleepy village of Laxfield, at the time they'd meant very little to her. The coastal town of Lowestoft had been so far removed from her everyday life in the country; those stories could have come from another world!

But now Alice had returned home she could see for herself the devastating effects of the raids and her feelings changed, all of a sudden it became real, and now all she could do was thank God and the welcoming charity of her rural relatives, that she and her family were all still alive and well!

Following her successful day at work, she headed home. She walked along, at a leisurely pace, towards the swing bridge and instantly realised that this part of town was extremely busy at that time of day. Everyone was in a hurry to get home after work or school. She stopped half way across the bridge to pull herself away from the bustling masses, allowing the crowds to pass her by, while she held on tightly to the side rail of the bridge. The swarm of pedestrians moved forward, almost as one entity, keeping their heads bowed low against the brisk chilly breeze, always more keenly felt across the open harbour. Everyone walked laboriously, with one hand holding on to their hat, while the other gripped tightly to a satchel or a bag of some sort as they struggled to get across the bridge amid the icy blast, desperate to reach the other side and then get home to enjoy some restful warmth after a busy day.

A heavy convoy of three buses drove past her, one by one, they rumbled and rippled across the shaky improvised street, making her hang on to the side rail for dear life as the bridge trembled beneath her feet. Each bus was packed to the brim with passengers, not a seat was spare, and as they went by, a vision was conjured up of sardines packed tightly in a tin! She decided to wait in her friendless spot for a while longer, taking the time to gaze out over the busy harbour, secure in the knowledge that the bridge was perfectly sound. Built in the 1900s, it had been built to last, and had survived many Zeppelin and Luftwaffe attacks during both world wars.

Once the bridge became a little quieter, Alice continued her journey to the other side, taking a sharp left, as she continued her walk towards the South Pier and head home via the promenade. Again she decided to stop for a while, hoping to soak up the last rays of weak sunshine before the dimly dazzling globe dipped behind the tall town houses along Kirkley Cliff Road. As she walked out on to the pier, she felt the welcome embrace of the sun's warmth, and her upturned face was bathed in its glory, as she stopped and gazed out to sea. A group of fisherman were standing at the end of the pier, casting out their rods in the hope of filling up a large metal bucket at their feet, perhaps with a few mackerel or herring, or if they were really lucky, they might even hook a large cod for their tea.

As she leaned over the rail, she breathed in the salty air and then she looked down, becoming mesmerised by the swell of the sea as it heaved and swirled below the thick wooden planks at her feet. The wrecked Pavilion and bandstand yawned emptily behind her, blackened and splintered, there would be no bands playing there for a while she realised sadly. Apparently it had suffered from a direct hit during a night raid and was severely damaged, but she determined not to look at it, she didn't want to think of all the good times they'd had there, she didn't want to feel maudlin, not today. Now was the time to look forward, she thought, with renewed positivity, not backwards, with sorrow and regret.

As she gazed further out to sea, she watched the white crests of the waves as they rolled and massed, crashing and colliding into each other mercilessly. She revered the sea and respected its punishing power. It was strange, she realised, she'd almost forgotten the effect it had on her spirits, its energy and scale were breathtaking and in that moment she felt that she and the sea were one, she was part of nature and nature was part of her, and suddenly, subliminally, her love for Lowestoft was reignited and she knew then that she would never leave it again. As she watched and heard the waves pounding their way forcefully on to the beach, the strength of the sea was gradually spent, dissipating into effortless ripples as it bubbled and fizzed on the shore like lemonade.

Her attention was diverted by the sight of a steam drifter, slowly puffing its way past her, on its way out to an even bigger sea, hoping to catch a hefty haul and bring it back, ready to spill over Hamilton Dock. She waved to the trawler boy who smiled back at her broadly and then he gave her a brief wave before continuing his task of preparing the vast fishing nets on deck. She hoped they'd bring back a good catch for those who relied upon it, especially those down on 'the grit' beneath the cliffs, and she reflected how good it was to see the fishing fleet up and running again. There were not too many left now. Countless trawlers had been commandeered for the war effort, adapted for use as minesweepers and the like, and so many of them had been lost.

But now she could smell it, she realised, that pre-war nostalgia rising up inside of her, together with a tangible hint of herring, tar and oil, and impulsively, as the boy looked up at her again, she blew him a kiss, with a carefree abandon she hadn't felt for years.

Silently she wished him god speed for his journey, and to all the trawler men who stayed away for days on end, hoping for a successful conclusion to their hazardous mission, ensuring they returned home triumphant.

In a more contemplative mood, she continued her walk along the promenade which was fast becoming clear of society when she spotted two familiar figures cycling towards her. Both her younger sister Katy and best friend, Beryl, quickly dismounted as soon as soon they saw her and almost ran along the prom to greet her. Katy arrived first and instantly began to blurt out a disconcerting story about an annoying policeman who'd just stopped the pair and reprimanded Beryl rather harshly for not having a lamp on her bike!

'There's still danger about' he'd advised them ominously, 'just because the war's over, you must still learn to protect yourselves.'

'Golly, how irritating', Alice sympathised, 'it sounds as though we're all still at war with all the rules and regulations still being forced on us. Don't they know that we're free now, free from oppression? That's what we've been fighting for all these years, our liberty!' she chimed in plaintively with the others.

'Yes, we just want to have some fun' answered Beryl with a big grin on her face, 'but, oh well, never mind, I expect I can get hold of a lamp quite cheaply somewhere, maybe Pryce's will have one!'

'Hey Alice, we're on our way to the pictures', Katy informed her, 'Wings of the Morning' is showing, you know, the one with that gorgeous Henry Fonda! Oh my goodness he's so dreamy', Katy grinned at her sister as she hugged herself with both arms swinging her body from side to side. 'Do you want to come with us,' she asked Alice urgently, with a generosity of spirit and also with an enthusiasm which demonstrated her love and adoration for her older sister.

'Ah no, sorry, I can't,' replied Alice, I'm off to the Palais tonight, I'm just heading home to grab some tea, have a bath and get changed, do you know if mum has heated the copper?'

'Oh yes, she definitely has', answered Katy, with a grin, before she added excitedly, 'oh yes, of course, you haven't heard the news yet have you?'

'No?' Alice answered with immediate interest 'what news is that?'

'Well, mother has received a notice today about our old house in Walmer Road. Apparently the war department is finally releasing it back to us. Can you believe it, after all this time! But unfortunately the bad news is that the naval personnel who've been using it all through the war have left it in a pretty bad state. Mum says the whole place probably needs scrubbing from top to bottom so she's been busy making lists and also she's washing just about everything in sight; sheets, curtains, cushion covers, you name it - she's washing it, getting it all ready to take over there!' Katy and Alice laughed in cheery unison at the antics of the mother they adored, for they couldn't have wished for a better or a kinder one, 'if you get home quickly, you can probably use all that hot water!'

'Ok that's great, it does sound like really good news, I know she's keen to leave our little house in London Road and get back to the old one, but it's funny, I quite like the one we're in now, I think it's adorably cosy, but never mind, it will be nice to get back to Walmer Road too, if a little strange, after all this time and after what we've all been through. Anyway, I'd better go now, I'll see you both later. Have a wonderful time at the pictures with handsome Henry!' she called out to them over her shoulder, with a broad, meaningful grin, and then she walked away from them with a final wave.

When Alice arrived home she was pleased to see that her mother had left plenty of hot water in the copper so she drained it off and had a nice bath and hair wash in front of the warm fireplace.

Later when she was dressed and almost ready to go out, she stood in front of the mirror for a while, gazing at herself admiringly in the dimly lit hallway where there was just enough light to primp and preen her hair into perfect shape whilst seriously contemplating the idea of having a perm. She was earning pretty good money now, she reminded herself proudly, and a visit to the hairdresser was definitely a luxury she could well afford. Alice's dark brown hair was thick and luxuriant, having its own natural wave, and so she didn't have to do very much to it in the way of styling for it to look glossy and perfect, indeed most of the time she looked as though she had just stepped out of a salon.

Her hair had always been her crowning glory, even as a child, but only when she entered her teens had it begun to develop into a significantly striking feature. She was rather proud of it, even when she was young, swinging it from side to side as she walked, but she'd never known who to thank for it, except Mother Nature of course, her own mother's hair was fine and wispy and her father's bald pate was becoming more noticeable every day. She smiled at the thought of her father, ah, poor papa, he was often away nowadays and she really missed him when he wasn't around. She realised how important her father was to her, indeed he was a calm and steadying influence in all their lives, particularly her mother, who always seemed to be much more on edge when he was away. Alice missed his chesty laugh and the twinkle in his eyes. When he was around she felt adored, for it always seemed that in his eyes she could do no wrong, of course he adored her sister as well, but not as much as her, she thought mischievously. She conceded however that now Katy's locks were also growing quite thick and lustrous, with their own gentle wave, but Alice knew she'd been the lucky one in the looks department, with her perfect skin, her stunning blue eyes and her hour glass figure, she knew she always turned heads whenever she stepped out of the door.

'Are you going out again tonight Alice?' Ellen asked her, in a somewhat critical tone, as she stood watching her daughter from the kitchen doorway. She tried to make her enquiry as casual as possible but she realised straight away that she'd failed and that her question sounded more like an accusation. While she continued to watch her daughter, admiring her reflection in the hallway mirror, Ellen's worried expression couldn't help but give away her concern. It was of course obvious that Alice was getting ready to go out, her face was fully made up, her lips were glossy red, *a little too red Ellen thought*, and the blue pastel frock she'd decided to wear that night flowed and rippled gracefully around her daughter's shapely legs. Her blue suede sling backs, together with her elegantly smooth seamed stockings, finished off the look with such a faultless grace that Ellen couldn't help but gawp in awe at her daughter's overall appearance. She acknowledged of course that she had made the dress for her daughter. The simple tea dress with fitted bodice and puff sleeves had been sewn from a 'Style' pattern and had seemed innocent enough, at the time of making, but now her daughter was wearing it Ellen was shocked to realise that it showed off her figure to perfection, the soft cotton material fit where it touched and tonight the gown took on a whole different guise. But Ellen stopped herself from mentioning it.

'Yes, mum, I told you, I'm off to the Palais again tonight, but you don't need to worry, I'm walking there with Babs and Beryl so I'll have company there and back.' As Alice stopped looking at herself in the mirror and turned to face her mother, she caught the anxious look on Ellen's face.

With mild exasperation and a roll of her eyes that couldn't be suppressed, she instantly tried to appease her, 'look Mum, I'm not a baby any more, I'm a grown woman you know, and you don't have to watch over me all the time!'

When no reply was forthcoming, a short weighted silence hung in the air between them, leaving many words unsaid, which in fact was probably a good thing, as both women tried to keep control of their emotions.

Finally Alice sighed, she realised she'd sounded a little harsh, after all her mother only had her best interests at heart. She stopped what she was doing and walked over to her mother, giving her a quick hug, and finally placing a light kiss on her mother's furrowed brow. Ellen closed her eyes, enjoying the strangely affectionate contact, blinking away anxious tears which threatened to overflow. She was being silly, and she knew it!

'Alright, dear', she said finally, 'I'm sorry for being a ninny, you go out and have a nice time, you're working hard now, of course you want to relax and enjoy yourself, but just be careful who you're mixing with, that's all I'll say!'

Alice smiled rather patronizingly at her mother, 'ok mum, I will,' but her humble response held a hollow tone because, if Alice was being totally honest, she knew she would do whatever it took to have a good time and no one, not even her mother, was going to stop her.

As Alice walked away from her mother and made ready to leave, Ellen remained in the doorway of the kitchen and watched her daughter in silence. She bit down hard on her bottom lip for she knew that if she said any more it would probably end up in a spat. Ellen hated rows and confrontation and at that moment all she really wanted was to be able to trust her eldest child. But inside her was a niggling doubt, a strange paranoia which had sprung up and settled in the pit of her stomach, and no matter how hard she tried to vanquish the feeling, it just wouldn't budge. Every maternal instinct was screaming inside her head, warning her that her daughter was too wilful, too beautiful, and most distressing of all; she knew Alice was heading for trouble!

Alice carefully took down her new fur coat from its cotton padded hanger and gazed at it lovingly. It was made of dark brown mink with wide lapels and a deep collar, giving the wearer extra warmth around the neckline, with no real need for a scarf. It was substantially long and lustrous and fell away from the shoulders in an A-line style, with generous sleeves and a glossy lining of light brown silk which spoke of quality whenever its striking sheen was exposed. The coat was certainly beautiful, inside and out.

Alice had discovered it quite by chance, hidden amongst a row of coats at the Tuttles end of season sale. Often she would pore over the style pages in the latest fashion magazines which showed the luxurious garments being worn by film stars and models.

As soon as she'd realised the coat was in her size, she'd whisked it off the hanger to try it on, and after seeing her reflection in the long length mirror, she'd been unable to resist the temptation to own her very own fur coat. Without stopping to mull it over, she'd purchased the sale item hurriedly, before she could think any the wiser of it, spending every last penny of her first pay packet.

But it had been worth it!

In the dimly lit hallway she draped it around her shoulders with a flourish, depicting the same stylish manner she'd seen the actresses use in the latest Vogue magazines, and looking for the entire world as though she belonged with them, on a Hollywood film set, and not standing in a cold uncarpeted hallway of a cramped terraced house in Lowestoft.

As Alice opened the front door to let in the cool, starry night she uttered a final farewell to her anxious mother, 'don't wait up for me will you,' she called out over her shoulder, in a rather glib fashion, before finally shutting the door behind her, and then she was gone.

Ellen sighed deeply and walked back into the kitchen. She picked up the dilapidation papers from the counter and scoured the numerous notes scrawled against many of the items by Mr Algar. Her heart sank as she read through the list of repairs that needed to be done to this small house and in addition she reflected on all the work required at Walmer Road, and suddenly she felt utterly overwhelmed by it all.

She looked around her, in despair, seeing areas of mould on the walls and a desperate need for distemper to be applied everywhere, the windowsills and doors were also rotting in several places. As she read through the list again she noted the total cost of the dilapidations came to around thirty pounds, an amount she could not afford to pay at the present time, and there was no Frank around this weekend to share the worrisome burden of it all. She quickly realised that Frank might also feel obliged to carry out the repairs himself in order to save them money.

Almost instantly she chided herself, she couldn't let him do that! Why would she want to give Frank all that extra effort when he was away, even now, working all the hours god gave him, he deserved better, he needed to have a two day break every now and again! No, she thought, that definitely would not do, she couldn't ask him, the money would just have to come out of the compensation payment for their house at Walmer Road. She would get on to it straight away, she decided, she would go directly to Mr Crawford, the Town Clerk and ask him about the claim forms. She didn't want to be beholden to Tom Algar anymore, his attitude was beginning to rankle, she was tired of his supercilious smile and the way he'd appear unannounced, regularly walking in to the house as bold as brass, as though he owned it, which of course he did, but after all, she shivered at the thought, one day he might walk in when she was washing her smalls!

CHAPTER FIVE

At the end of a deserted garden in Walmer Road, Stefan Schmidt sat, alone and shivering, in the gloomy darkness of a disused air raid shelter.

With just a small candle for light and warmth he held his hands towards it. It had been extremely cold all through the long winter months and he hardly knew how he'd survived for so long, but now he was thankful that the spring days had arrived, bringing with them a few balmy rays of sunshine which had begun to filter through the thin metal roof above his head, affording him a modicum of warmth inside his small prison like cell.

Stefan had been in hiding ever since his arrival in Lowestoft several months earlier. On reflection, and after much soul searching, his decision to escape from the prisoner of war camp had perhaps not been the best idea he'd ever had. The camp huts had at least been relatively warm and comfortable and of course he'd had his German comrades around him for company. When he compared those few years of captivity to these long winter months of loneliness, misery and starvation, he considered that if he could have his time again, he would most likely choose to stay. However, at the start of his journey of course, he'd not been alone, he had Hans with him for company.

It was three long years after his capture and incarceration in the camp, before the escape plan finally came to fruition.

Strangely, no one considered an escape to be remotely possible until one day, in the early morning mist, the sight of a stray deer, standing alone just inside the camp's boundary fence, had triggered those thoughts.

The gentle beast had appeared one morning at dawn, its gentle brown eyes bemused as it fixed upon the few early risers who'd gathered outside their hut for their first smoke of the day. The moist nostrils of the female deer had flared and snorted at the sight of the men and they in turn had been amazed by its presence. The animal stood, shrouded in mist, almost hidden within a small group of trees and remained in position for a while, not far from the hut, quickly becoming a talking point. Strangely, without the men even noticing, the deer vanished as quickly as it had appeared.

Several of the inmates were incredulous that not a single guard had even noticed the animal, but it was Hans, the most daring of the group, some would say the craziest, who had quickly come up with the idea of an escape route. He had railed at them with his theory that if a large animal like that could get in and out of the camp, unseen, then surely they would be able to do the same, the guards must be either half asleep or just plain dopey! After he'd managed to convince them an escape plan was swiftly put together involving, primarily, an underground tunnel.

In order to cover up any noise of digging within the tunnel some of the inmates took to singing loud raucous German songs. This seemed to work very well and the guards didn't suspect a thing, merely delighted that the inmates were happy in their captivity. Every night they managed to gain a few more feet until eventually they were almost there and the perimeter fence was within their reach. The idea was of course to split up once they were all free of the camp for there was no way that a group of ten men wouldn't be spotted if they all stayed together.

As time and the tunnel progressed, Stefan and Hans became quite friendly; both were experienced Luftwaffe pilots and they quickly decided that, once the tunnel was complete, they would stick together and follow their own plan.

Over several months they'd observed British aircraft flying quite low over the camp and they couldn't help but wonder where they were heading? After studying the trajectory of takeoff and landing, they deduced that the airfield must be close by, probably only a mile or so away, and with a plan beginning to formulate, they knew this was the direction they would head after exiting the tunnel. They would have to be quick though, they realised, needing to reach the airfield before dawn, but both were convinced their plan was achievable. They had gone over it and over it, covering every possible scenario, and they were extremely pleased with themselves for coming up with such a daring escape.

But as the time grew nearer, Stefan became a little more reticent. He began to fear for his life and was seriously considering backing out of the whole idea. However, Hans could be very persuasive and, once he'd made his mind up about something, there was nothing that could deter him from it. After a heated dispute between the pair Hans suddenly grabbed Stefan by the throat and shouted loudly in his face *'Ich bein kein feigling!* I am not a coward!' intimating cruelly that perhaps his friend was? Stefan backed down then, he didn't want anyone to think that he was a coward.

Hans swiftly raised the stakes by convincing Stefan that when they reached Germany they would be celebrated as heroes! Their plan to commandeer a small plane from the airfield, to board it secretly and then fly it back over the channel to Germany, although perhaps a little reckless, would surely go down as the greatest wartime escape in history.

After a significant amount of adrenaline fuelled tunnelling, they finally reached the outer fence, plus a few feet beyond, and a date for the escape was set.

The group were lucky because the night they chose was dry and clear, with the added advantage of the weather turning much colder, which helped to ensure their jaded captors were beckoned to their warm beds earlier than usual that night and the number of guards on duty was particularly low. The skies were always at their darkest just after midnight and so this was when they surfaced, one by one, from the tunnel, their journey across the field going unnoticed and enabling them to disperse into the nearby woods without incident. From there, some went north to Liverpool and the docks, a few headed south, but Hans and Stefan stayed true to their word and headed east towards the airfield.

Their escape plan seemed to be going well and, just before dawn, the pair lay together on the brow of a hill, overlooking the quiet air strip. From their viewpoint they spied a small plane at the back of the airfield which seemed to be standing alone and unguarded. There was no one around and so they ran silently across the runway, climbing on board the aircraft swiftly, managing to start the engine without too much trouble.

As the propellers started to rotate, the noise alerted a member of the ground crew, who suddenly appeared from one of the hangars in a state of undress. As soon as the flight rigger realised what was happening he began waving his arms and running towards the aircraft, shouting at them in utter disbelief and confusion. But by then it was too late, the plane was moving fast along the small runway and with Stefan sitting in the front cockpit and Hans at the rear their speed quickly increased and they took off without delay, becoming airborne in a matter of seconds.

Once they were flying high, they became jubilant, hidden amongst the clouds they had made their escape and finally they were able to conduct a proper inspection of the dials and instruments before them. The euphoria they had been feeling up to that point, which had carried them along on a wave of derring do, their excitement and elation at the prospect of possibly arriving home within a couple of hours, suddenly took a positive nosedive as they began to realise that the small aircraft they'd commandeered was only to be used for training purposes and, more importantly, it did not contain a full tank of fuel. Even more disappointing, there was not enough fuel to carry them across the channel to France, let alone Germany. This eventuality had been sadly omitted from their calculations, a small unknown detail they had completely overlooked, but one which turned out to be an extremely important factor. They swiftly came to realise they would not now be welcomed home as heroes, their names would not be going down in history, any time soon, and it transpired, more significantly, that this crucial error would become the catalyst for much blame-laying and disagreement between them from that moment on.

After just over half an hour they were forced to land in a small quiet field just a few miles from the coast. They had actually glimpsed the sea from the cockpit, almost tasting their salty freedom, but the fuel gauge told them otherwise, flashing its warning light ominously.

And so for now their escape was not to be, not this time anyway, but as they ran from the ditched plane to take cover within a small copse, they determined they would do everything in their power to avoid capture by the local police.

As they crouched, hidden amongst undergrowth in nearby woodland, they made a pledge not to give up hope and together they hatched a further plan which was to cross the sea by boat.

They knew they weren't far from the coast and so they began to make their way, on foot, to the nearest port, managing to stay hidden amongst large areas of forest. Each day, as they carefully traversed fields and dirt tracks, they proceeded ever nearer to their goal, their new objective being to stow away on board a ship, any ship, heading for Europe.

On their journey through the countryside they helped themselves to trousers, shirts and jackets taking them from various linen lines whilst discarding their own clothing at the first opportunity, deciding to bury their own heavy woollen Fliegerbluse coats and leather trousers under a pile of soil and leaves. They were sad to lose their coats for they were indeed good quality and very warm but the cut and style were far too conspicuous. However warm and serviceable their uniform had been, their clothing would almost certainly be recognisable as Luftwaffe uniform and knowing they would remain hunted for some time to come, they made the joint decision to dispose of them. They did however decide to keep their sturdy fur lined flight boots, for they would be hard to replace, made of multiple panels of black glossy and suede leather, and with a large zipper running along the shaft, they could be hidden easily under any English trousers.

Because the Luftwaffe had been the first of the German divisions to be captured during the war a decision had been made early on by the British to allow the airmen to keep their uniforms. The government didn't know how long the war was going to last and decided it would be far more prudent for the airmen to keep their own clothing. It would cost a great deal of money to re-clothe the prisoners and more sensible to let them keep their own.

A further decision was made, however, that all German uniforms should be stripped of any Third Reich insignia.

In the early days of the war a strong bond of mutual respect and chivalry had existed between the RAF and Luftwaffe pilots. Inside the camp when Hans had reached the subjugator's desk, at the front of the queue, he'd implored the RAF officer to allow him to keep his eagle badge. He'd used every manner of persuasion open to him whilst holding back from any actual open aggression. The British officer witnessed the look of sheer desperation, verging on harassment, which was plain upon the face of the German prisoner. He felt sorry for the indignant pilot standing before him and tried to imagine himself in the hands of the German Wehrmacht, wondering how he might be treated over there, if the tables were turned. 'Do as you would be done by' his mother had always taught him and so the officer had finally relented, granting Hans his request, covertly returning the Adler Tag motif to the German pilot's side pocket.

Hans was visibly relieved, his sense of duty and pride were still very much intact and although he'd learnt to suppress his unpredictable emotions, in his heart he considered the British still very much the enemy, he remained constantly wary of them, and watched them all through a veil of suspicion and contempt.

Sometime later, sitting on his bunk inside the small hut he shared with the other men, Hans had kissed the badge and tucked it safely inside his front flap pocket. He'd explained to Stefan how much the badge meant to him, how it had been handed to him by the Chancellor himself, and how it swiftly became a symbol of inspiration to him. He knew somehow it would always bring him good luck. After all, as he pointed out to Stefan, he had not died when his plane crashed had he; he was still alive to tell the tale?

Stefan couldn't quite agree with his friend's warped point of view when it came to luck. He considered the circumstances they found themselves in as a 'worst case scenario' and in his own mind he felt extremely doom laden. He often reflected on the catastrophic and destructive raids that had laid waste to so many of Europe's fine buildings, the squandering of so many innocent lives across the globe, and of course his own predicament, this shared futile existence that so many other vibrant young men were being subjected to and who in all probability would remain incarcerated inside similar prison camps across the world for many years to come, and so, no, he could not begin, for the life of him, to share his friend's optimistic view of luck!

During their long walk to the coast the pair managed to forage a few morsels of food along the way. The smell of some freshly baked bread, left cooling on a metal rack under an open kitchen window, enticed them towards the small wooden table where it sat. Stefan would have been happy to take a couple of slices but it had been Hans who'd swiftly grabbed the whole loaf, concealing it under his coat, before they both ran off into the woods without being seen. At the next farm they found a container full of milk sitting on the rough ground, and positioned in front of a large barn door, holding it open. The noise coming from inside the barn told them loudly that it was a cow shed. They cleverly swapped the milk container for a small log which did the job adequately and then they both took off, as quickly and quietly as they could, leaving the barn a long way behind them before arriving at the next small copse. There they sat down in the middle of a group of trees, exhausted, in complete seclusion, appreciatively gobbling down the loaf and drinking the entire container of milk between them, and thankfully quenching their immediate hunger and thirst.

There were several eggs to be had from obliging hens along the route but even so the meagre amount of food they devoured was not sufficient to keep two grown men strong and healthy for those few days on the run. When they finally arrived at the outskirts of the seaside town of Lowestoft both men were exhausted, thirsty and hungry, and not only that, it seemed their patience with each other had run out. They began to enter into heated discussions as to what they should do next and these debates finally escalated into full blown arguments.

Following a serious disagreement about an unattended farmer's rifle which Hans had spotted, jutting out from a wheeled cart, and which he was sure was loaded, they had stood arguing about it behind a tree, and more particularly about whether or not they should steal it? Stefan was adamant that they should not. It would send a direct message to the police that they were in the vicinity. He could justify taking a loaf of bread but this was a different story. The police probably wouldn't bother too much about a loaf of bread, but the theft of a weapon, now that was different matter, they would be hunted down for that! If they stole it they would immediately become armed and dangerous and would most likely be shot on sight. He didn't want to die; he had a lot to live for back home. Stefan had already determined that if he was ever captured again, he would go quietly.

Hans thought the opposite. He would never go quietly, back into captivity? No way, not if he could help it. He judged Stefan's refusal to take the weapon as naive, verging on cowardly, and while Stefan continued to hold him back, he fumed, the act merely fuelling his frustration until finally Hans blew his top and broke free, rounding on his companion with clenched fists. As they squared up to each other, Hans was on the verge of launching a physical attack on Stefan, when a sound behind them made them both dive for cover. It seemed the farmer had come back to collect his rifle and so the pair crawled away wordlessly, remaining in the shadows, until he had gone, whilst Hans made a supreme effort to control his rage.

As they both stared at each other in the gloom of the shaded copse they simultaneously came to the conclusion that their viewpoints were too different, too far apart. Hans was impulsive and fiery, whilst Stefan was cautious and calm, and in the aftermath of the row, when Hans' fiery temper had cooled a little, he realised that he needed to leave Stefan and go it alone.

Stefan had let him go, sad in a way, that their prolonged escapade had finished with such bad feeling, and yet, at the same time, he thought they'd be better off apart, and what's more, he concluded, it might be a lot easier for one person to hide on board a ship than two.

However, now, with the benefit of hindsight, and having lived rough and alone for what seemed like an eternity, Stefan wasn't so sure.

After they'd separated, Stefan had spent his first two weeks sleeping in ditches and watching out at the harbour for a possible ship on which to hide. Disappointingly, it transpired that, for the time being at least, there were no ships leaving for Europe. The only ships heading out from Lowestoft's harbours were small fishing drifters and trawlers preparing to search the vast oceans to the north which were now comparatively safe and free from u-boats and warships. Most trawlers seemed to be on their way to Iceland, to harvest the herring, which could be found in abundance around its southerly shores, and in the end Stefan had no choice but to winter in Lowestoft, making the decision to wait it out until spring.

He'd discovered his ideal hiding place purely by chance as he'd sat within a small thicket of trees adjacent to a quiet tree-lined avenue. He'd been watching patiently as a group of naval personnel appeared to be leaving a house in Walmer Road and it looked as though they were apparently vacating it for good. They were bringing out furniture, desks and chairs, and what looked like radio equipment, some of which they left abandoned at the side of the road whilst the rest was piled into the back of a truck and driven away. Stefan watched as the last uniformed officer locked the front door decisively and then everyone left, carrying with them a multitude of suitcases and bags, as they all marched down the road and away from the premises.

When all around appeared quiet Stefan scampered covertly across the road and over to the pile of items which had been left on the verge. Most of the objects looked old and broken, but after checking the pile, he found there were a few pieces of equipment which might prove useful. Also, although he was no radio expert, he found himself quite excited to see what appeared to be a complete radio set; a power cable, a transmitter unit, a headset and all of it was contained inside a beige haversack. A plan began to form immediately in his mind as he carried the items through the back gate shutting it behind him.

As he walked past the side of the house and entered the back garden, he looked across the muddy patch of land to the end of the grounds, stopping in his tracks at the sight of the old air raid shelter. He recognised the humped hovel sitting snugly at the farthest point away from the house and, knew instantly this would be the perfect cover for him. He'd had a brief thought about breaking in to the house itself but in the end he had decided that if he was to start using the water and gas supplies that might bring attention to his being there and so the shelter was probably the best option for him, for the time being anyway, and it was somewhere he could hopefully remain over the winter undiscovered.

It seemed the war was definitely over! He understood that now! He'd watched the celebrations from afar, unnoticed and alone, and the nation's euphoria was palpable. No-one would have need of that shelter any more, he thought, and if the occupants of the house had truly gone, and he was pretty sure of that, then it was likely he could remain there for some time.

The realisation that all had been lost by his countrymen had been a devastating blow but, as he mulled over the folly of it all, he considered the result unsurprising. He'd always felt the war was unwarranted and now he was just glad it was all over, he'd come to view the outcome in a much more positive light, realising Germany's defeat could actually mean victory, of a kind anyway, for now they were free, free from that oppressive regime which had turned out to be the ruin of his country. He knew it was something his people would have been craving for, when the futility of the war became apparent.

But perhaps he'd just been susceptible to the propaganda he had been fed by the British during his time in the camp. He didn't know any more what was truth and what was lie. But whatever the truth was it became his understanding that the Führer was dead and the force of that egotistical maniac, which had brought Germany to its ruin, was now gone. He clung to the hope that surely his country could rise again from the ashes and now all he really wanted, so desperately, was to go back there and see it happen, to take part in its recovery, and live in its future.

CHAPTER SIX

Ellen finally received the 'release of house' letter from the Town Hall the following Monday. Frank still had not been home but Ellen had written to him with the good news about the house and he'd written straight back to say how glad he was.

A compensation cheque from the War Department had arrived the following day in the amount of £136.

This was the largest cheque Ellen had ever seen and she decided to walk into town that very morning without delay to pay it in to the Trustee Savings Bank. At the same time she would draw out the thirty pounds she owed Mr Algar for repairs to their rented house in London Road. She couldn't wait to be out of his debt as quickly as possible and after a successful visit to the bank she decided to call round to his house with the money.

As she walked tentatively up the smooth marbled steps, she stopped at the top to catch her breath, and then stood for a few moments before the impressive front door. She gazed up at the grand house which towered above her head and noted rather nervously the large old fashioned brass knocker which was positioned in the middle of the old Victorian door. She decided instantly that she didn't like it; she found the lion's head rather repellent, its mouth wide open as though it were snarling at her offensively. But just before she lifted up the heavy knocker, ready to drop it against the matching metal plate, she noticed a brand new modern-looking contraption nearby. It looked as though it had been recently installed and she wondered whether she ought to use that instead. At the centre of the device was a protruding circular button, just begging to be pressed and so Ellen decided to do so, feeling rather rash and impulsive, but also rather interested to see what might happen if she did.   Straight away she was rewarded by the resonant sound of pleasant musical chimes ringing from inside the house.   She assumed they must be announcing her arrival and so she waited patiently for the door to be opened.

After waiting for a good few minutes in the chilly breeze, she began to fear there was no one at home and she gazed up at the house for signs of life.   She concentrated her attention on the many windows above her head, gazing to the right and left, instantly appreciating the value of such a residence positioned in the prized location of Kirkley Cliff Road, a very affluent part of town.   Suddenly she heard a voice calling out from inside the hallway, in a rather piercing, overwrought manner.

'Nancy, Nancy, there's someone at the door! Where are you Nancy?   If it's that beggar from the grit, you must send her away with a flea in her ear! I told her the other day there is nothing here for her.   I'm fed up with that child being sent to my house, asking for hand outs! They all need to stay where they belong, down there in that beach village, why do they keep coming up the scores, wandering around town, begging for money. It's disgraceful! Oh for goodness sake Nancy, where are you?'

Ellen couldn't help but roll her eyes at such an ear-splitting din coming from inside the house.   She felt rather sorry for poor Nancy, presumably a servant of some kind, it sounded like she had her work cut out for her working in this house.   But she had even more sympathy for the sad little child who'd obviously arrived there from the grit, sent into town by her parents, and persuaded to knock on all the upper class doors, hoping to pull on any heart strings for a handout, but the woman inside this house apparently had no heart!

The elucidation behind the furore didn't really surprise her. It had always been her perception that rich people were only rich because they hung on to their money, not because they gave it away, and more often than not it was folk who had very little that were more likely to share it with those less fortunate. She thought of her own experiences when conducting her charitable collections for the hospital, and for the blind, and how very often, it was those living in the smaller houses that were more likely to find a few pennies for the pot.

She began to shiver a little as she continued to wait patiently for someone to come and answer the door, for it was now obvious they were at home and surely it must be opened soon. She was consumed with embarrassment when her stomach made a sudden low growl and she realised of course that she was hungry, she'd forgotten to eat her usual toast and margarine that morning. She'd been in such a rush, after the girls had left for work, to get out of the house herself and head down into town to pay the cheque in to the bank, that she hadn't given a thought to breakfast. Her stomach rumbled once more just as the door slowly opened and she came face to face with the tall willowy figure of Mrs Algar.

The lady of the house stood before her, elegantly dressed and with her face fully made up, making Ellen feel rather dowdy in comparison. Ellen also noted that the lady appeared rather unsteady on her feet. She watched as Mrs Algar swayed from side to side before gripping tightly to the side frame of the large heavy door. It seemed she was doing her best to maintain her balance whilst remaining further back, slightly hidden from view, inside the hallway and peering out rather unenthusiastically into the dazzling daylight.

'Good morning Mrs Algar', Ellen said cheerily, 'is your husband at home?'

Ellen smiled up at the taller woman with as much warmth as she could muster on such a cold day.

After a long pause and a slightly quizzical expression Peggy Algar eventually answered Ellen in a rather haughty condescending manner, 'I'm afraid Tom is out at the moment, I'm assuming it's not urgent, can you call back later?'

Ellen took a small step backwards, uttering a disappointed 'oh I see', and she said it in such a crestfallen manner that Peggy Algar's lips pursed and her eyes began to narrow a little. She found herself rather curious as to why this timid little mouse-like visitor might be calling upon her husband? She knew Ellen and her family from chapel and had always found their meek and mild decorum rather nauseating. Ellen was petite and pretty she supposed, in a rather colourless sort of way, but it would be extremely irritating if Tom was up to his old tricks again.

She didn't think he'd ever been unfaithful but she reckoned it had come pretty close on more than one occasion. He was a flirt, of that there was no doubt, he enjoyed the company of women and always took great pains to achieve his aim which, Peggy knew, was to watch them hanging on his every word, to throw back their heads in unadulterated laughter at one of his brazen jokes, or to maybe go coy at his barefaced flattery, whereas she, his own wife, seemed to only bring out the worst in him!

Peggy leaned nonchalantly against the open doorway, her taut face looking ashen in the pale sunshine, however her equilibrium seemed somewhat restored as she continued to gaze with renewed interest at her unexpected visitor and Ellen realised that the lady was in no hurry to return indoors.

From the side pocket of her embossed satin dressing gown Peggy drew out a packet of Dunhills and a gold Cartier lighter which, Ellen decided, was at least 14 carat gold and with the added embellishment of a large ruby on one side. The ornate lighter was flicked open and a long slim cigarette was lit. After a rather lengthy drag Peggy finally exhaled and blew the smoke only ever so slightly above Ellen's head.

Holding the cigarette aloft, she proceeded to look her visitor up and down curiously as she clawed together the collar on her creamy white gown. Her skinny fingers reminded Ellen of the scrawny talons of a bird of prey although in this case their tips had been dipped in a garish red. Ellen couldn't help but admire the soft delicate material of the gown Mrs Algar was wearing which reminded her of a robe worn by Joan Fontaine in the film 'Suspicion'. Being a skilled seamstress herself, Ellen knew how unattainable satin had been during the war and even today there were many items which had been taken for granted before the war but which, even now, were still out of reach for most people. As she looked down hesitantly, in an effort to avoid Mrs Algar's penetrating stare, she noted the matching satin embossed slippers sitting snugly on Mrs Algar's rather large feet whilst acknowledging enviously that the whole ensemble must have cost her a pretty penny. Ellen wondered how on earth she had obtained it and it crossed her mind fleetingly that it might have been purchased unlawfully on the black market!

Ellen shivered again as she continued to stand on the chilly front doorstep, feeling as though she needed Mrs Algar's permission to leave, which of course she realised was a ridiculous thought. However she couldn't resist the temptation, while she had the opportunity, to glance behind Mrs Algar, and into the beautifully decorated hallway which had suddenly come into view as the door opened up slightly. She saw burnished banisters, lush opulent carpeting, and elegantly embossed wallpaper realising, with a sudden suppressed jealousy, that Mrs Algar probably employed more than just one maid to help her. She would surely need a lot of assistance to run that large imposing dwelling. Ellen deduced that Mrs Algar would have little or nothing to do most days, she was the proverbial lady of leisure, but then she chided herself, for being mean and possibly unfair.

Ellen brought herself up short, she'd come from a different background, every one of her days was filled with chores and today she had plenty to do because from now on, for a while anyway, she would have two houses to keep in order and so she offered a brief 'thank you' before quickly turning on her heels to take the steps back down to the pavement below.

'Now, now, don't be in such a hurry,' Peggy urged, coming forwards quickly to catch hold of Ellen's arm. She'd caught sight of the envelope clutched tightly in Ellen's hand and with a quick change to her inflection she used a kinder tone, 'what is it you've got there dearie?'

Ellen felt flustered, 'Oh, nothing, it's just some money I owe Mr Algar for repairs to our house in London Road,' she answered a little breathlessly, 'but it doesn't matter, I'll call back another time'.

'No, no, don't go sweetie, that's fine, just you give it here to me and I'll make sure Tom gets it later, as soon as he comes home.'

Ellen hesitated for a moment, clutching the envelope tightly to her chest. She was not really sure whether she should hand it over or not. In her own mind, to hand over such a large amount of money to the wrong person, without a receipt, smacked of stupidity and recklessness and it went entirely against her own better judgement.

However like a beacon of light Mrs Algar switched on her most engaging smile, suddenly becoming the personification of kindness and honesty, it seemed to radiate from her every pore until finally Ellen began to reproach herself for her mistrust.

'I'll keep it safe for you dear, now don't you worry,' Mrs Algar persisted, 'Tom should be back for his lunch very soon and after that he's promised to take me out shopping.   Isn't it wonderful! At last we'll be able to buy all the latest fashions from Paris! Have you heard the news about Dior, he's opening a new couture house at Avenue Montaigne, isn't that thrilling?'

Ellen gave the woman a rather noncommittal nod at this rather unrelated news. She was speaking of another world, a world where money was no object, a world in which it was almost certain Ellen would never inhabit.   She could not anticipate in her wildest dreams ever having enough money to own an original design from Paris, the closest she might ever come to it, she supposed, was the purchase of a dress pattern and even for that she would probably have to wait a very long time.

As Ellen looked down at the envelope in her hand, the decision whether to hand it over or not was abruptly taken away from her as Mrs Algar leaned forward and snatched it out of her grasp.

'Well, it is Tom's money after all isn't it!' Mrs Algar snapped in defiance, justifying her action scathingly, and then with the briefest of goodbyes she turned swiftly on her heel and went back inside, shutting the door firmly behind her.

Ellen stood on the doorstep, shocked and bereft, with no chance of a response and fearing instantly that she'd done the wrong thing. However, after a brief moment of hesitation, she shrugged her shoulders, for there was nothing more she could do about it now, and as she walked back down the steps and on to the pavement she determined that the debt, in her mind anyway, had now been paid.

As she walked along the road towards Kirkley Parade she decided she would start working on their old house the very next day. She'd buy scrub, brushes, and bowls from Pryce's and she'd start in the hallway, she thought, she'd make it shine just like Mrs Algar's. After the hallway she'd clean the outside lavatory and then she'd order some new lino for the front room.

She stopped on the way home to see Bill, to ask him if he wanted the air raid shelter from the garden, and was relieved when he said he would gladly come and fetch it and take it off her hands. He told her he would be able to use the wood and corrugated iron in his building work and she realised with joy that soon the whole garden area would be cleared and ready for Frank to start gardening again. He would be able to purchase a new greenhouse and start planting his rows of vegetables for a late summer crop.

Ellen was now looking forward to the following weekend because Frank had written to say he would definitely be home that coming Saturday and her stomach churned with excitement at the thought, not only of seeing him again, but also because she realised they would both be able to go and see the house together.

When Friday came she baked all day, only popping out to Downes stores for some gelatine and to fetch minced beef from the butcher for patties, but this time she'd had to use real eggs for the cakes instead of dried ones because she'd run out. To be honest she didn't care, only the best would do for her Frank, surely they'd all given enough to the war effort over the years and a few eggs wouldn't go amiss.

She knew that Katy had gone to the pictures that evening and that Alice was out again at the Palais and so, after all the baking was done and the containers had been filled with patties, cakes, sausage rolls, choux shortcakes and yeast buns, all piled high on the kitchen surface, Ellen finally flopped into the armchair in front of the fire. She didn't sit for long though, feeling guilty after only a minute or two's rest, her work ethic always kicked in and she sat up and pulled the sewing box towards her.

The sewing box was a small table like affair, effectively a shaped wooden box on legs, with two small sliding drawers at the front. It was made of polished dappled walnut with intricate marquetry on the lid depicting an attractive floral design in various shades of light and dark wood. It stood solidly on four bowed legs with smooth curved handles at each end. It had been presented to Ellen for her eighteenth birthday by her Grandma, who was also a proficient seamstress, and who'd earned her living by making clothes for the local community, although her Grandma's speciality had been wedding dresses!

When Ellen was young she remembered numerous brides coming to her Grandmother's house with excited smiles as they walked eagerly up the garden path to the front door, finally arriving in the small parlour to be measured up for their gowns. They would then choose the pattern and the finest material they could afford. Ellen would watch the glow of excitement shining on their young faces as they returned to the house again and again for regular fittings, eager to see their wedding gowns gradually taking shape, until the day of the final fitting, not long before the wedding, when veil and shoes were worn. Then her grandmother could pin the hem to the correct length for the final full effect and it was always at that moment that the bride's tears of joy would flow.

Ellen looked forward to the day when she might make wedding dresses for her own two daughters, but not yet of course, they were both far too young!

The sewing box sat in pride of place, adjacent to the fireplace, snug against the wall. Inside it was a multitude of sewing implements; hand-made pin-cushions of velvet and lace and packed with pins and needles of every size, ribbons of various widths and colour, material fragments left from past endeavours, skeins of embroidery thread and countless reels of cotton in every colour imaginable. On a small shelf in the corner sat a collection of pretty antique thimbles and a small pair of delicate silver scissors with engraved handles in a pretty floral design, an heirloom passed down through the ages and of such fine quality they had never jammed once.

Tired as she was, Ellen lifted up the wooden lid and pulled out the lightweight taffeta material which had been neatly folded inside. She leaned back in her armchair and continued to sew a neat row of daisy like flowers along the square neckline. Once that row had been completed she commenced a further matching row all around the skirt edge just two inches above the hem. With great speed and dexterity she managed to finish Alice's pink party frock in a couple of hours. As the clock struck ten she held up the gown, admiring the way it dazzled brilliantly in the firelight. She watched with delight as the swirling sheen of the taffeta travelled and transformed with every movement. Ellen gave a smile of satisfaction as she envisioned Alice, dancing in the dress at the Palais, for she would definitely be the belle of the ball and all eyes would be drawn to her beauty.

As soon as she thought of her daughter, a sharp pang of anxiety overcame her and she envisioned her daughter dancing, even now, in the arms of sailor she'd met recently, who most likely had a girl in every port! She had yet to meet this new chap and of course she couldn't help wondering who he might be, who were his family? All she knew was that he was a sailor and that Alice thought he was handsome, but was he kind, she wondered, was he trustworthy? It seemed however that her daughter had become rather smitten with him.

After she'd hung up the dainty dress on its soft hanger, Ellen relaxed again and laid her head back against the comfortable wing of the armchair. She managed to doze off for a while, dreaming contentedly of her dear house in Walmer Road and how wonderful it would be once she'd cleaned and decorated it, from top to bottom, from corner to corner, and she was so happy in her slumber that a smile appeared of its own accord as she slept.

In her exhausted state she didn't hear the key turning in the lock or the footsteps tiptoeing lightly along the hall but slowly she became aware of a stocky male figure leaning over her and when she finally opened her eyes her sleepy smile beamed wider as she reached up to lock both arms around her husband's neck before pulling his smiling face down to meet her own.

CHAPTER SEVEN

As soon as Frank walked in through the front door he smelt the delicious pies and cakes that Ellen had made, God he was a lucky man he thought, pinching himself yet again for his good fortune. Frank had finished work early that Friday and was able to catch the earlier train home but there'd not been enough time to send a wire to Ellen to let her know. It didn't matter he decided for he would just look forward to seeing the surprise on his wife's face when he arrived home unexpectedly and as it turned out he had enjoyed that moment very much!

When he'd raised Ellen up from the chair they'd embraced feverishly and passionately, quickly becoming the young lovers they once were, and confirming the old adage that absence does indeed make the heart grow fonder. The realisation they were alone in the house, with only the crackling of the fire's fading embers for company, was of course an added bonus.

Later, as they lay together in bed with their arms and legs entwined, Frank thought back to the lucky moment that had brought them together.

He recalled both of them sitting on hard wooden pews on opposite sides of a crowded chapel when they'd leaned forward simultaneously to reach for their hymn books. As they'd turned towards each other, their eyes had met across the empty aisle, and that one special moment had been etched into Frank's memory for eternity. Time seemed to stand still and everything going on around him in the chapel became a blur, an insignificant mirage, and only her face was clear and pure. The warmth emanating from her shy smile had instilled in him such an immense amount of pleasure it had struck a chord deep inside, a strong spiritual chord, as though the suitability of their union had been ordained by God himself.

He was indeed a lucky man he thought to himself as he returned to the present and finally drifted off to sleep with Ellen cocooned in his arms where she belonged.

Alice and Katy had walked back together from town quite late that evening, meeting up unexpectedly half way along the road, and they'd chatted with sisterly devotion about their different nights out.

'I met my sailor again', Alice told Katy dreamily, 'we danced all night Katy, the Palais was packed but we stood out from all the others, everyone said we were definitely the best couple!'

Katy did not want to disagree with her sister but quickly described her own night out at the pictures and the excellent couple she'd watched dancing on the screen in a film called, 'You Were Never Lovelier.'

'You may have been good Alice, but I'm sorry, you could never compare to the couple I saw tonight, they were truly magnificent, never in a million years would you be anywhere near as good as Fred Astaire and Rita Hayworth so don't even try and convince me!'

'Ok, I concede' laughed Alice, 'but do you know what, I reckon I am as good as Ginger Rogers' and she quickly poked her tongue out mischievously at her sister and Katy laughed at her in return. In the end Katy agreed, 'ok, maybe, I'll let you have that one!'

They both arrived home, quite exhausted, at around eleven thirty and seeing their mother was already upstairs in bed they decided to head straight for their own rooms, not having the slightest inkling that their mother wasn't alone up there and that she was snuggled up in bed with their father.

After a good night's sleep the girls came down to breakfast the following morning, still completely unaware that their father had arrived home early. Of course, when they found out, the family breakfast quickly became a noisy and excitable affair, both girls vying for their father's attention, anxious to bring him up to date with all their news. In the end Frank felt snowed under by all their chatter, I must be out of practice, he thought to himself with a wry grin, after two comparatively quiet weeks away, but as he sat at the breakfast table with all his family around him, he realised he couldn't be happier and suddenly he found himself surrendering to the girls' charms. After all, it was wonderful to hear their voices at last, after so long apart. And in that moment he decided that the sound of a voice, particularly the voice of someone you love, is indeed a wonderful tonic, it is balm for the soul, and if he were ever pushed to choose, he would exchange every handwritten letter he'd ever received for just a few moments in their company.

After breakfast was over and the girls had gone off to work, Ellen and Frank left their London Road house and walked together, arm in arm, towards their old family home in Walmer Road. As Alice turned the corner and caught sight of the house again, a sudden thrill rushed through her veins and it was as strong as that very first day when she'd come to collect the war department notice. And now she also had the door keys, safe and secure in her coat pocket.

Unfortunately her excitement at receiving them had been tinged with mild annoyance because they'd been handed over to her by none other than Mr Algar. Once again he'd waltzed in to her house in London Road as if he owned it, which of course he did, but that was not the point. There was not a single warning, a knock on the door, or the sound of him calling out from the front porch that he'd arrived, or any such courtesy, no, he'd just walked straight in to her kitchen where she was washing clothes at the sink, luckily it hadn't been her smalls but Frank's overalls, which she was getting ready for him to take back to work the following week. This intrusion into her affairs once more had irritated her greatly because it was totally unwarranted.   She had been the one who'd completed all the forms regarding the requisition!   She'd spoken confidently and deliberately to the Town Clerk, handing over all the necessary paperwork herself at the Town Hall, and all had been perfectly straightforward. The Clerk had informed her helpfully that he would drop the keys round to her himself once the matter had been finally processed, and yet somehow Tom Algar had gotten himself involved again, intervening in her life in a completely unnecessary way, in her view anyway.

But she checked herself again, deciding not to mention any of these unbidden thoughts to Frank, she didn't want to worry him, and she tried to convince herself once more that their landlord was merely being kind and helpful, with no ulterior motive behind it.

As they arrived at their old front door Ellen turned round to her husband with a poignant smile as she ceremoniously pushed the key into the lock and gave it a quick turn. With a sudden sharp push, the sticky and dilapidated door began to open up, ready to welcome the pair back inside again for the first time in over five years. Just as she was about to enter the house, Frank unexpectedly stopped her in her tracks and on a mad impulse he hoisted her from her feet with a flourish and pushing the door wide open with his shoulder, he proceeded to carry her dramatically across the open doorway and into the hallway, thoroughly enjoying her feminine squeals of delight! After he'd replaced her feet onto the hallway's solid hardwood floor and Ellen had recovered from her fit of giggles, they both held hands excitedly and walked together into the front room.

As they stood together in silence, they both tried to take in the deplorable state of their almost unrecognisable sitting room and the smile on Frank's face began to drop away, little by little, until it had completely disappeared and instead he looked rather forlorn. He became distraught at the sight of the peeling wallpaper which was hanging down in strips, remembering how beautiful he'd made the room look when he'd first put it up, the acrid smell of mould now permeating the air was evidently coming from dark damp patches at the lower corners of the room. Finally his eyes looked across the floor and he realised the surface was almost completely compacted with dirt and grime. He let go of Ellen's hand, feeling sick to his stomach, immediately overwhelmed at the prospect of all the work that would be needed to get this place back to the way it was.

Ellen witnessed his distress which she felt probably matched her own and she turned and hugged him to her. As she stood in front of him she placed her hands on each side of his face and looked up at him, consoling him tenderly, 'darling, you don't need to worry about anything, because ... come on now, look at me ..., I will come over every day, I have already bought brushes and scrub from Pryces and by the time you come back in a couple of weeks I promise you it will all look very different. I'm going to order paint and lino for downstairs with the compensation money and Bill said he'd be happy to take away the shelter from the bottom of the garden. And so, soon, very soon my love, we will have our house back and you will have your greenhouse back, it will be up and running again and full of plants, just as it always was, as if that horrible war had never happened.'

Frank blinked several times as tears threatened to flow but he took in a deep breath and finally he looked down at his wife's upturned face and smiled. Ellen always had that knack of soothing him somehow and almost instantly he started to feel better, and a little more positive. He pulled her towards him suddenly and wrapped his arms around her in a big bear hug as he tried to calm himself and then finally he released her with a sigh 'yes I know my darling, and of course, like you, I can't wait for that time, it will be wonderful, I'm more than happy to have our house back again, truly, I'm overjoyed,' he agreed, trying his hardest to join in with her optimism, 'but just look at the state of it!' he continued, 'it's not fair on you my poor love, that you should have to do all this work yourself, I should be here to help you. I hate all of this constant travelling back and forth to Leeds. It's not fair on you and the girls and I've decided it's too far away. As soon as I can I'm going to start looking for something locally.'

'Oh really, oh Frank, that would be wonderful,' Ellen clapped her hands together in delight at the thought.

Frank swiftly brought her back to reality, 'Of course, I'll have to finish my current job first,' he continued, 'but I'm keeping my fingers crossed it will be over quite soon, all the prefabs are more or less complete and some are ready for occupation and so the Leeds project should be over soon, hopefully within a few weeks. It's a good thing Churchill had the sense to set up that housing committee during the war! He must have known how much housing we would lose. Of course the idea of prefabs came from America, as everything does nowadays I suppose. It's a strange thing though? They say they're only temporary structures but I'll tell you something Ellen, they seem pretty solid to me and the layout is so well designed, there's everything you could ever need; three bedrooms, a bathroom, an inside toilet, a fitted kitchen and a living room. Not only that, each one is detached and surrounded by a perfectly ample garden so that families will be able to continue growing their own fruit and vegetables, and there's a coal shed too!

Anyway, that's enough of that, as soon as this job is finished I'll take my card in to the exchange and ask for something local, something that will help our own neighbourhood. I'm missing my family life with you and the girls, they're almost grown up and soon they'll be gone. Now that the war is over I just want us to get back to a normal family routine.' He finished his speech with another hug for his wife.

'I agree darling', answered Ellen, 'I want you to be home with us, just as much as you do, and the girls really need their father!'

Ellen was thoughtful, hesitating for a moment, before continuing, unsure whether she should keep her concerns to herself or let Frank share in the burdens of parenting! She decided, as she had him right there next to her, and with the added advantage of the girls being nowhere around to listen, that maybe she ought to grasp this opportunity to fill him in.

'Frank', she began determinedly in order to gain his attention 'now, I don't want you to fret, but I am rather concerned about Alice, she's always staying out late these days and I don't know where she is or what she's doing half the time and very often I don't even know who she's with, I feel that perhaps some time during this weekend perhaps a little fatherly guidance wouldn't come amiss?'

Frank smiled indulgently at his wife, his mood immediately lifting, 'you worry too much', he answered her calmly, kissing the top of her head tenderly, 'the war's over now and she's still very young, we need to let her have some fun!' he cajoled flippantly, but as he continued to gaze into his wife's worried face, he paused considerately before adding, 'but yes, I suppose you are right, we do need to keep an eye on who she's mixing with, perhaps Katy could find out for us, you know, do a little bit of sisterly spying? I believe they're closer than you think my dear!'

Ellen sighed in agreement, giving him another indulgent hug, 'alright dear, we'll do it your way,' she said, before reaching into her coat pocket and fetching out her measuring tape in order to measure up the front bay window for some pretty new curtains. Frank wandered off on his own, walking along the short corridor, and into the old dining room at the back of the house. This room seemed slightly less dilapidated he observed, with a sense of relief, as he stood at the centre of it, surveying the walls and ceiling, whilst managing to console himself that a little less work might be required in here.

He wandered over to the far end of the room and looked out through the windows, the window frames were starting to rot, he noticed instantly, with areas of wood protruding through the paintwork, but he could feel the warm welcoming rays of mid-morning sunlight doing their best to shine through the grubby glass and light up the shabby room.

As he gazed out half-heartedly into the garden he dared himself to inspect the state of it, having already decided not to venture out there today, because he knew, once he got started, he wouldn't be able to stop.

All in good time, he told himself, noticing the original lawn and flower beds seemed to have merged into one muddy mess and that he'd have to start all over again with the landscaping. He could see small signs of the way it was, the sad-looking Montana clematis still clinging feebly to the fence, and several canes strewn haphazardly nearby which had been bound together many years before, to support his runner beans.

As his eyes alighted at the rear end of the submerged Anderson shelter over in the far corner of the garden he realised it would take an awful lot of work to remove it and he was extremely grateful that his brother Bill had agreed to come and take it off their hands and put it to good use.

It seemed so long ago now, that they were all together in this house, a young growing family, and all so happy back then, it felt like a dream.

He sighed wistfully once more, and the sound not missed by Ellen, who had just walked up behind him, 'what a waste of life' he declared to her despondently, lifting up his arm and placing it snugly around her shoulders, 'but at least we've made it through Ellen, we're still here, all of us together, we've survived where so many others haven't.'

At that moment Ellen didn't care about the past, she thought only about the future and what it might bring, her mind was full of plans for the house and how she would do her utmost to bring it back to life and make it their home again. She knew that very soon they would all be living back in Walmer Road, again, together, as a family, where they belonged.

She placed her head on her husband's shoulder and breathed in the smell of him, a combination of the cologne she'd bought him for Christmas and many months of accumulated tobacco smoke which was embedded in the material of his coat. But she didn't mind, in fact she quite liked it, it was cosy and familiar, it was the smell of safety, and in that moment she couldn't have been happier. Her husband was close, they were standing side by side in their old home, and her heart was full!

CHAPTER EIGHT

Frank announced at breakfast that he wanted to do something exciting with them all that evening, 'let's go on a family outing' he declared, 'we'll go somewhere in town and have some fun, all of us together again! We'll have a meal and then we'll go to the pictures! What about 'The Wizard of Oz,' he suggested, 'I believe it's on at the Odeon this week and I've heard it's very good. When I arrived last night I came out of the station and decided to have a quick walk up to the town centre just to see what they'd done with the place after all the damage it suffered. I was amazed to see how quickly they've rebuilt it and got it all back up and running again after that dreadful raid.'

The girls were immediately excited and offered up an enthusiastic 'oh, yes please Daddy' which warmed his soul. He hugged them both tight, happy to think that they still wanted to go out with their old dad, and had not tried to wriggle out of it with any fabrication of a prior commitment. 'Ok, great', he grinned at them widely, your mother and I will meet you both after work and we'll all have a lovely evening together.'

In fact, the evening turned out to be a truly wonderful occasion; they bought fish and chips from Morton Road and after walking into Kensington Gardens they sat together in a row on the metal bench overlooking the lily pond. This was a good vantage point to watch the numerous fish swimming about happily and also to admire the impressive bronze sculpture of Peter Pan, a copy of the original statue located in Kensington Gardens in London. The new Japanese Pagoda took pride of place and the themed area surrounding it was a flourish of azaleas and rhododendrons, all budding and blossoming, together with a multitude of spring bulbs already in flower. In these beautiful surroundings they sat and gobbled up their meal with relish, straight from the paper, licking their fingers with glee. After they'd eaten, they decided against a boat ride on the lake, on this occasion anyway, and walked straight into town, where Frank treated them to seats in the front row of the circle, at the newly refurbished Odeon. 'The Wizard of Oz' was showing, the first film in Technicolor they'd ever seen, and which they all thoroughly enjoyed.

As they left the cinema, dusk was already falling, but it seemed warmer somehow, suddenly the weather had changed for the better and a tangible sense of summer was in the air. As they headed home, via the promenade, they sauntered along the seafront jauntily, arm in arm, before a rather jubilant Frank suddenly opened his mouth and launched into song! With Judy Garland's superb dulcet tones still ringing vibrantly in his ears Frank could not resist trying out her signature tune for himself. As they walked along, his melodious voice rang out over the gentle swish of the sea as he endeavoured to remember as many words as he could from the title song, 'somewhere over the rainbow', with the odd 'la la la' here and there to fill in the blanks. His gentle voice rose and fell, beautifully accompanied by the continuous rhythm of the rolling waves in the background, until, one by one, each family member joined in and a harmonious chorus was created, gaining many amused glances from passersby.

When they finally arrived home it was almost nine o'clock and night was closing in but as they approached the front gate a shadowy figure could be seen loitering at their doorway.

They quickly realised it was only Cyril, Frank's father, who seemed to be hugging a small furry bundle in his arms. Katy instantly remembered what it might be, swiftly recalling her Grandfather's promise to fetch them a puppy from the next litter at the farm and with a noisy screech of excitement she bounded happily towards him.

'Oh Gramps' she cried out with glee, 'Oh let me hold him, oh please do!'

'Alright now Katy, calm down, let me get him indoors; we don't want to agitate the little feller now do we?' Cyril spoke quietly and calmly as he hugged the small puppy under his warm double breasted wool coat.

Once they were all inside the house, they sat down in front of the fireplace and the little puppy was released carefully and gently from Grandpa's coat. The girls sat cuddling the small furry bundle on the rug whilst Ellen went to put the kettle on the hob for a well deserved cup of tea. Their new pet turned out to be a brown and white cocker spaniel and he was extremely lively and excitable, constantly rolling over and over as if he were performing tricks for them. They all laughed when he stood up on his hind legs jumping up and down, his tongue lolloping to one side of his wide open mouth, whilst his tail continued to wag uncontrollably. The strength in his tiny body was undeniable; he was definitely not the runt of the litter. As he continued to hold himself upright, he was practically dancing before them, his eyes bright and expectant as though he were trying to gain their approval from his performance which of course he did because they loved him instantly, deciding, without hesitation, that a most suitable name for this bundle of joy would have to be 'Trix'!

The very next morning after chapel they took Trix down to the beach. They walked along the prom as far as the newly cleared beach between the South Pier and the Claremont Pier. As they stepped down the shallow steps and on to the sand Frank caught sight of a few of his mates fishing on what was left of the old pier and so he left Ellen and the girls playing with Trix and headed off for a little bit of male company and to see what they'd caught.

Several areas of the beach had been cleared of the anti-tank mines and 'dragon's teeth' which had been laid in haste at the commencement of war. Once the clearance certificates were issued, the beach was designated as safe for public use. Ellen realised that the task was immense. All the beaches, along the south and east coast of Britain, of those declared suitable for an amphibious landing, were fortified with mines, barbed wire and on some beaches even machine guns had been installed within protected pill boxes or trenches.

The obstacles had also been successful in keeping local people off the beaches all through the war years. Even now, Ellen felt anxious, remaining alert, keeping her eyes fixed firmly on the shifting sand, watching it like a hawk for any signs of a rusty metal device 'shaped like a biscuit tin', a description they'd been advised to look out for, which might be seen protruding from beneath the golden sand. It was eminently possible, Ellen determined, that a stray mine could have been missed by the Royal Engineers and she dreaded either of her girls finding one, or worse still, treading on one!

It had been several weeks after the issuing of a clearance certificate at Pakefield beach before she'd dared set foot on it again. But she'd watched as more and more people ventured down there, without incident, and finally she'd relented. But the horror stories still haunted her, lodged in the back of her mind, of a number of men who'd been given the dangerous task of clearing the mines and who'd lost their lives because of it. How unfair, she thought sadly, to have done your duty, to have survived the war and all its horrors, only to lose your life in such a cruel way, when the war was effectively over.

It was a necessary evil, she supposed, but tragic nonetheless, and because that feared blitzkrieg invasion had never materialised not one of those beach fortifications had been necessary after all, in fact every last one of them was surplus to requirements. But as is always the case, hindsight is a wonderful thing and it's far easier to look back on mistakes made than to look forward! If the planned German invasion, nicknamed 'Operation Sea Lion', had taken place, then Ellen and her family would not be playing on the sand today so merrily and the term 'better safe than sorry' sprung instantly to mind.

As Ellen watched Trix running in and out of the water, barking at the waves, his little tail wagging back and forth excitedly, she smiled warmly. He seemed so content in this new wondrous world he'd discovered and finally she gave herself permission to be glad, offering up a silent prayer of thanks that it was all over.

Ellen smiled and waved at the girls, 'we really need to wear him out' she shouted to them in exasperation, trying very hard to make herself heard over the noise of the waves whilst at the same time reaching the conclusion that her father-in-law's good intentions, though well meant, had not really been properly thought through! As if she didn't have enough to do, she considered wryly, and from tomorrow the girls would be back at work and Frank would be leaving on the morning train which left only herself to take on the inevitable extra work that Trix would bring. But as she watched the little puppy dancing and prancing in the sea spray, she relented, he was a darling little thing really, and she smiled resignedly as she watched him bounding in and out of the water, behaving just like a toddler on his first visit to the seaside, one of wonder and exhilaration!

She looked at her watch and realised it was getting near dinner time and although Ellen had already cooked the meat, she still needed to get back indoors to cook the potatoes and the vegetables. She called out to them all, waving her arms and pointing to her watch, so that even Frank looked up instinctively, before offering a brief and cheery farewell to his mates and then he walked back towards his family. They all met up at the top of the steps and began to head back home, along the prom.

There were a number of people out walking that fine Sunday morning, just as they were, everyone taking in the warmer air and all dressed up in their Sunday best as was now the norm after church or chapel. It seemed that a pre-dinner walk along the prom had quickly become a regular pastime for many.

From a distance Ellen could see two familiar figures walking towards them and almost as though a rain cloud had covered the sun her mood dipped a little because, as the couple grew nearer, they became instantly recognisable as Mr and Mrs Algar.

The tall willowy figure of Peggy Algar could certainly not be mistaken and Ellen could see that today she was again dressed rather flamboyantly in the latest fashion. Ellen swiftly noted her attire which consisted of a blue belted short coat over a pale pink chiffon dress, the frilly hem of the dress wafting exquisitely in the soft sea breeze. Ellen observed Peggy clinging on rather dramatically to her husband's right arm whilst teetering along the prom in very pretty pink and silver shoes, possibly designed more for a dance floor than for walking along a windy sea front she thought rather cynically. Trix started to bark crossly at the couple as they drew near and Ellen wondered if he might have picked up on her own mild agitation at the prospect.

As soon as they came within speaking distance Tom's eyes instantly met with Ellen's but she quickly averted her gaze away from his face, looking out towards the horizon and then back to the beach, and in fact anywhere and everywhere, to avoid having eye contact with Tom Algar.

Of course he was the first one to speak, his own lofty importance prevailing over everyone present.

'Good morning Ellen, Tom said, daring her to face him! How nice to see you, and Frank too, great to see you back in town again Frank!' He offered a slight bow and doffed his wide-brimmed panama hat in a rather elaborate fashion before returning it swiftly and snugly to his heavily brylcreemed head. After the briefest of pauses his voiced boomed out once more as he continued his flamboyant attentions to the women, 'and how are we all this fine morning, looking very pretty I see?'

Ellen looked up at him briefly, 'Good morning Mr Algar, we're well, thank you,' she replied in softly guarded tones whilst Frank said nothing and merely gave the man a brief nod. Frank couldn't help admitting that Tom Algar was not one of his favourite people, recalling an odd conversation he'd had with the man once, during choir practice. At the time Algar had made some rather tactless and frankly provocative remarks about how he would be more than happy to look after Ellen while Frank was away. Frank remembered feeling rather irked at the time, noting the suggestive inflection and tone in Algar's voice, which he was convinced he had not imagined.

Aside from the vexation caused by Tom Algar's penetrative gaze, Ellen was quite delighted and relieved to know that her whole family looked very smart that morning, everyone was wearing their Sunday best and she was proud to feel Frank's protective arm positioned around her shoulders for once. Frank was also looking very dapper today, in his new flannels, pullover and sports coat, an ensemble they'd purchased in town only the day before.

After their trip to Walmer Road Ellen had realised how disappointed Frank was with the house, he couldn't get over the state of the place and how much work was going to be required to get it back to the way it was. Ellen had wanted to cheer him up somehow and on impulse she suggested they should both walk straight into town and spend a small portion of the compensation money on some new clothes for Frank. He'd disagreed with her of course but she managed to persuade him.

Tom Algar was continuing to hold court with the small group of listeners while his wife leaned heavily on his arm. Peggy Algar looked as if she was about to fall asleep, Ellen thought, as her eyes remained in a semi-closed state and when she attempted to open them Ellen noticed they looked a little red.

Alice stood waiting with her family a little impatiently, listening half-heartedly to the conversation going on, but quickly realising that she didn't particularly like the Algars. She had a strong feeling that this upper class couple looked down their noses at her parents. More recently she had become aware of a class system existing within the town and the definite 'haves and have-nots' of Lowestoft society.

She was also getting fidgety, continually shifting her weight from one foot to the other, her calves still aching after all the dancing she'd done recently, and on her new high heels too. At that moment all she wanted to do was to get home, have something to eat, and then plonk herself down on a chair and do nothing for the rest of the afternoon.

Katy on the other hand was enjoying the moment. Her easygoing nature meant she was perfectly content to just stand and listen, for as long as it took, constantly yearning to be involved in any grown up conversation, to the point where she'd hang on their every word, hoping for an entry point, where perhaps she could join in and become a part of it. She had quickly learnt that the art of conversation was a two-way affair, a 'to and fro' activity, where long silences should be avoided at all costs but also that lengthy tedious monologues such as this were not the most pleasurable, and obviously this was Mr Algar's failing. In an effort to be more involved, Katy bent down to lift up the puppy in a deliberate attempt to draw everyone's attention away from Mr Algar and on to herself. As she held on tight to the wriggling dog, Trix began to lick her face delightedly, and she in turn began to giggle with pleasure. She hoped that someone might notice and mention it and then she and Trix would be drawn into the conversation. After all, he was a very new and noticeable addition to their family. Sadly her efforts were apparently ignored as Ellen proceeded to shush her into silence while Mr Algar, who was determined not to be distracted, continued to hold fort.

'I must say I did rate the pastor's excellent sermon today, didn't you Frank?' Tom continued in an authoritative tone which required nothing less than complete acquiescence, his words delivered with a condescension borne from education and status, and swiftly followed by his usual twitching moustache and sickly grin. Ellen couldn't help comparing his fake smile to the weak April sunshine which was doing its best to disperse the soft morning mist. It seemed as though, at long last, a warm spring afternoon might be on the cards.

'Yes', Frank agreed, pulling himself up to his full 5 feet 9 inches, suddenly inspired to make his own contribution to the discussion, although he still had to look up at his adversary who was a good six inches taller than he was, 'I found it a very enlightening and thought-provoking speech and I do agree with the pastor's sentiment, I don't think any of us should remain silent if we see wrongdoing of any kind, I fear worryingly that is exactly what the German citizens did, before and during the early stages of the war, sadly they remained silent instead of speaking out, for surely they knew what was going on all around them and yet they just let it happen'.

'Hmm, yes, I agree Frank, but we certainly gave those 'krauts' a beating didn't we? Ha-ha, they won't be so cocky now! I hope they're all hiding in shame and squalor back there, with their tales between their legs', laughed Tom, in a cruel and rather unchristian way, Alice thought, which made her dislike the man even more.

Alice was now becoming quite bored with the whole conversation, it seemed all old men wanted to do these days was talk about the war. They talked about it constantly and about whose fault it was, crowing over the so called victory. The war was over now! Why did everyone want to keep raking over the coals, it was almost as if they were trying to justify the whole sorry mess? Didn't they realise it had been her youth that had been stolen, all those years when she could have been having fun and enjoying life, all that time had been lost to her, and now she was determined to make up for it!

Her mind switched to happier thoughts. She was really looking forward to going out tonight. She'd arranged to meet up with Keith again, her handsome sailor from the Palais, but this time he was going to take her out on his motorcycle.

She dared not let anyone know though, she'd told no one, not even Katy, she couldn't trust Katy, she could be a bit of a goody two shoes and a blabbermouth, and she knew her parents would make a fuss, and so she'd told Keith to meet her down a side road, away from the house, not far from The Trowel and Hammer Pub. She knew there was absolutely no way her mother or her father would allow her to ride pillion on one of those contraptions and she also knew there'd be the devil to pay if they ever found out.

CHAPTER NINE

On Sunday evening Alice bid farewell to her father, 'I'll try and get up in time to see you off on the train tomorrow Daddy,' she promised him half-heartedly, while he continued to puff contentedly on his pipe, cosy and comfortable in his favourite armchair by the fire, 'but if not,' Alice continued, 'I'll say goodbye now, until I see you again next time,' she spoke in an apologetic, slightly ashamed tone, almost pre-empting the event, but she quickly leaned forward to give her father a big hug and a kiss to show her love for him which he returned with warmth and affection.

'Now young lady, before you go, just listen to me a minute will you?' he admonished her gently; 'your mum's been rather worried about you lately, not knowing where you are or who you're with. You're not yet twenty you know....' but then he stopped himself from becoming too stern, it wasn't in his nature and finally he gave her a forgiving smile, 'oh go on with you', he said, standing up and propelling her lightly towards the door 'we don't want to spoil your fun. The war's been very hard on us all, especially on you young people, but just remember, always keep your wits about you, and err on the side of caution, okay? Sadly, not everyone in this world is trustworthy.'

'Ok Daddy, but you don't need to worry about me, I'm always careful,' she responded persuasively, doing her utmost to reassure him, but as the words left her mouth her conscience began to prick and unwittingly a vision was conjured up of her new beau, Keith, who was probably, even now, sitting astride his motorcycle, just around the corner, out of sight, waiting for her!

As Alice left the house, she pulled hard on the front door, closing it noisily behind her. On hearing it clunk securely into place, she had also effectively shut the door on any feelings of guilt or shame because surprisingly and miraculously they seemed to vanish! As she walked away from the house her thoughts immediately switched to much more pleasant things, and above all, the exciting night she had ahead of her.

She admitted to feeling a little anxious, nothing to do with guilt or shame, she was just unsure as to whether she had dressed appropriately for the night ride, although she had decided to take Keith's advice and worn trousers and a warm coat. As she turned the corner into Pakefield Street, she saw her handsome beau in the distance, sitting astride his motorbike and as Keith stood up to wave she noticed he was wearing more or less the same attire which instantly put her mind to rest.

As soon as she was near enough, he got off the bike, and stood back proudly. It was obvious he wanted to show off his vehicle and was waiting expectantly for an enthusiastic expression of her admiration. She smiled at him indulgently and proceeded to look over the impressive and shiny motorcycle, its burnished appearance made her quickly realise that the monstrous machine was almost certainly brand new. Even with her limited knowledge of motorcycles she could see that it was a rather striking model, the paintwork was jet black and its silver chrome trim was reflecting nearby shadows and shapes like a mirror in the twilight. Keith proceeded to explain, animatedly, that his bike was a Vincent HRD Rapide, with a 4 speed 1000cc engine, and that it had come hot off the production line from Stevenage. He was so funny she thought, showing off like that, almost strutting around it like a peacock, but actually she found it quite endearing.

He climbed back on board the bike and indicated that she should sit behind him. In her fevered anticipation for the night ahead she suddenly and impulsively leaned forward to give him a quick peck on the cheek which Keith seemed mightily pleased with. In the back of her mind, Alice couldn't help wondering how on earth he could afford such an expensive looking motorcycle on what she presumed was a lowly sailor's salary but she quickly dismissed her concerns in excitement for the night ahead and eventually she clambered cautiously on board behind him.

As soon as she sat down on the soft padding she felt instantly warm and comfortable. The seating surprised her for it felt quite luxurious. It was made of soft black leather and once she'd discovered the two safe resting places for her feet, which were rubber foot pedals on either side of the bike, she felt instantly secure. However, with Keith seated directly in front of her, their intimacy suddenly became apparent and she was unsure where she should put her hands and so she clutched at the sides of her seat shyly.

Keith grinned wickedly as he started up the engine and without warning he set off, making her squeal with alarm. In her panic she let go of the seat and grabbed hold of his shoulders but even that didn't feel very safe so she let go and wrapped her arms tightly around his waist. This was, of course, exactly what he'd hoped for and whilst thoroughly enjoying her reaction he let out a loud whoop of laughter as they sped off. After a minute or so he had the decency to slow down a little and called out to her over his shoulder, 'keep your arms tight around me Alice and don't let go! I'm gonna give you the ride of your life!'

Alice held on very tight, just as instructed, whilst admitting to herself that she was more than a little scared, it was all so wild and daring, but inside her was the budding of a new emotion, a reckless need for excitement, which was beginning to take hold. Until that moment her life had been boring and mundane. This was what she'd been waiting for, this new feeling of vitality, of living for the moment, and as her adrenaline flowed her fear slowly ebbed until suddenly she was laughing along with Keith, throwing her head back, and even emitting the odd squeal and whoop herself. As their speed increased the cool breeze caressed her blushed cheeks and whipped itself wildly through the lustrous curls of her newly permed hair.

After travelling for some time along the coastal road Keith turned inland along the Beccles Road and began to head out of town. Alice worried fleetingly as to where he might be taking her, realising that she hadn't really thought to ask him about that earlier, but she determined she would just live in the moment and suddenly her doubts disappeared. As they followed several tight bends in the road she had to hang on even tighter but she quickly learned how to follow his movements and to lean into the bend when he did, their bodies acting in unison, and probably the reason he'd decided to go that way she thought to herself rather cynically. However, after only a few miles, he gradually slowed down and pulled off the road into a small pub called The Three Horseshoes at North Cove, Barnby, where he eventually parked up.

After helping Alice to dismount, Keith led her inside the pub for a drink. It was a very old pub, hardly changed over centuries, with oak beams and a large open fireplace, and luckily not very busy on a Sunday night so they had their pick of the best place to sit. She chose a small table in the bay window, adjacent to the fireplace, which warmed her instantly and quickly she took off her coat to enjoy the heat emanating from the burning wood and red hot coals.

Alice decided on a small cider and Keith had a beer and they sat together for a cosy hour or so. Keith talked briefly about his life on board ship and of all the ports and places he'd seen in the navy, his trip to America sounded exciting and also his involvement in Operation Merit, the liberation of the Channel Islands, which impressed her greatly, but it occurred to Alice that he didn't want to go into very much detail and she decided not to pry. She knew he'd probably seen some pretty awful sights.

Keith changed the subject and began telling her enthusiastically about another exploit he was involved in. She noticed pretty quickly that this topic of conversation seemed infinitely preferable to him, and she watched his green eyes light up almost as though a switch had been turned on. The fleeting expressions on his tanned youthful face changed rapidly from seriously intense to laughing and playful in a matter of seconds. She listened attentively while he spoke about it passionately enjoying the way his manicured fingers sometimes pushed back the front quiff of his well groomed hair. He was explaining how the side business he was involved in was a much more lucrative one, topping up his sailor's salary very nicely, and luckily he was able to run it alongside his normal naval duties.

He tapped his finger twice at the end of his perfectly straight nose intimating he was about to let her in on a big secret. As he leaned in closer to her, and she to him, he whispered about the large amounts of money he was able to earn by this method.

It took a while for Alice to understand what he was saying to her, she'd been so absorbed by his handsome face, his unusually green eyes, not to mention his rather animated and sometimes rather endearing expressions, that her thought process had become slightly muddled. But as his words began to sink in and the penny finally dropped she realised that what Keith was up to didn't sound at all savoury. Indeed, he was involved in, what appeared to be, a covert operation for the transportation of black market goods from America to England and then across the channel to Europe and all these goods were carefully hidden on board his ship. The more Alice listened, the more disturbed and anxious she became, for it sounded as though, whatever it was he was doing, it definitely wasn't legal.

By the time he'd finished talking and taken a long swig of his beer, leaning back smug and easy in his seat, she found herself utterly convinced that Keith was in fact a smuggler!

Having grown up within the church community, her roots had been set solidly in the teachings of the bible. With understanding of right and wrong, and the god-fearing Christian she'd become, she suddenly felt very uncomfortable with what she was hearing. Her anxiety was exacerbated by the thought that the mere knowledge of such a crime could get her into a lot of trouble and worse still, it might mean prison!

Her heart began to beat loudly in her chest. She'd been telling herself that she wanted excitement, but not this, not criminal activity, and the words she'd heard earlier that day, spoken by those much older and wiser than herself, suddenly began to ring true; 'not everyone is trustworthy', 'I don't think any of us should remain silent if we see or hear of any wrongdoing'. Anxiously she bit her lip and the thrill she had been feeling all evening began to fade away, she felt bereft and uneasy, wanting nothing more to do with this handsome sailor.

Keith downed the rest of his pint in one gulp, 'shall we head back into town?' he suggested jovially, with a broad smile, completely unaware of Alice's state of mind, not realising in the slightest how his clandestine revelation had affected her. 'We'll go a different way back shall we, a quicker way' he added with a conspicuous wink as he put on his donkey jacket and Alice unwillingly donned her own warm coat once more.

Keith reached for her hand and she instinctively held out her own, still bewildered by his outrageous and tactless remarks; she couldn't believe how stupid he must be to share such information with her? For goodness sake, he didn't know her from Adam?

As he led her eagerly outside, towards his shiny new motorcycle, he commented about the darkness closing in. She watched as he flicked a switch and a bright beam of light lit up the road ahead. However, whereas before she'd have been very excited and impressed by everything he showed her, unfortunately her enthusiasm for the bike and its owner had now been sadly lost.

Silently and timidly she clambered on board behind him and this time, she decided, she would hold on to him very tightly, she didn't need to hear the instruction from him again, realising instantly that his last little hint was a sign of foreboding, and that his obvious intention for the journey home was to drive a whole lot faster.

As they set off back to town, Alice's mindset was in a completely different place, indeed her outlook was quite the opposite and she realised all of her previous enthusiasm and excitement for the night's escapade had entirely disappeared. This time she couldn't wait to get home, she was desperate to plant her feet firmly back onto terra firma, and preferably in a place as close to their house in London Road as reasonably possible, without being seen. But for now all she could feel was the power of the motorcycle beneath her and her heart raced as Keith opened up the throttle once more, raising the speed to yet another level, as he continued to drive crazily through the dark empty streets.

Shockingly, she realised she was grappling to hold on against a force that was pulling her backwards in her seat, she was definitely slipping towards the rear of the bike and her position in the saddle was no longer tucked in behind Keith but moving further away from him. She struggled to pull herself forwards again but the force was so powerful that she began to lose her grip.

'Keith' she shrieked loudly, as abject panic began to set in, and she tried vainly to make herself heard above the noise of the engine, until finally she was virtually screaming at the top of her voice, 'I'm slipping! Keith, please help me', she was crying out in fear, 'I think I'm falling'.

Perhaps he couldn't hear her above the noise of the bike, or maybe he thought she was enjoying herself so much that she was squealing for him to go faster, because for the next few minutes that is exactly what he did, revving up the engine to its top speed, before they finally entered the sleepy town.

Eventually, Keith slowed down, just before turning into a side street and it was in the nick of time because at that very moment Alice lost her grip on Keith's coat and slid from the back of the leather seat finally landing with a hard bump in the middle of the road!

Alice could feel herself rolling over and over, experiencing a strange sensation of looking down at the proceedings from above, watching everything that was happening in slow motion, and having no control over it at all. Eventually she became vaguely aware of a sharp pain at the side of her leg, as her knee scraped against the edge of the kerb, and after that she came to a sudden dramatic halt, as her forehead collided abruptly with a large tree! With her arms and legs akimbo she lay sprawled across the grassy verge.

As Keith felt his bike suddenly become unexpectedly and significantly lighter, he realised instantly what must have happened, and he quickly looked round behind him in abject horror to see Alice lying motionless across the verge. He quickly turned his bike around and parked it securely at the side of the road before rushing over to where Alice was lying, his heart was pounding violently with shock and dismay, utterly aghast at what had just happened whilst also extremely fearful that he might have been the cause of serious injury or even worse, death!

As he bent down to feel her pulse, and to his utter relief, Alice began to move, she moaned and groaned as she rolled over on to her back, eventually manoeuvring herself into a sitting position against the tree. Keith dared not touch her but merely stood close by, watching her nervously, whilst at the same time feeling a deep sense of joy that she had not died. Finally he came closer and Alice peered up into his anxious face. Even in the darkness she could see his pallor was ghostlike, devoid of all colour, and she sensed the understandable fear and dread etched clearly onto his features. Swiftly she lifted the palm of her hand and placed it against his cheek, seeking immediately to put his mind at rest, and then she spoke, as brightly as she could, 'it's alright Keith, I'm pretty sure I'm okay' and then after that she heard him breathe a huge sigh of relief.

Keith bent down on his haunches and offered her his hand which she took gratefully, slowly and cautiously, raising herself up with his help and realising thankfully that nothing appeared to be broken. She flicked away the dirt from her coat and trousers, reassuring him once more that she was fine, apart from a few bumps and grazes.

'It was lucky I wore these thick trousers today' she grinned up at him, despite feeling a distinctly sharp pain above her right knee, and also a slight sensation of nausea, which was probably due to shock, she reasoned, 'I think they probably saved me from the worst of it.'

As she spoke, she knew she was trying to make light of the whole incident, she could definitely feel a heavy throbbing at the site of the sore graze above her knee and acknowledged that she would probably have an almighty bruise there in the morning.

Keith's abject relief was so ridiculously evident that he smiled broadly and then proceeded to talk ten to the dozen in an effort to cover up his own agitation and guilt.

'I'm so sorry Alice, I'll never drive like that again, how stupid of me, I should have realised, you being a novice and all. Do you know, I've learnt something tonight, this has definitely taught me a lesson Alice, they say that don't they, you know that we learn from our mistakes! Gosh we were so lucky you didn't break any bones because that was a nasty fall, wasn't it? Hey Alice, look, you've got a nasty bump on your forehead!' He suddenly stopped talking and pointed earnestly to the graze above her eye before pulling from his trouser pocket a surprisingly clean white handkerchief.

'Wow Keith, I am impressed' she chuckled at the sight of it, attempting to lighten the atmosphere and help him relax. He instantly picked up on this change of mood and joined in.

'Well, you know us sailors, we have a very strict regime, you know, we're up very early in the morning and each item of uniform, including our handkerchiefs, has to be immaculate.'

He leaned forwards, handkerchief in hand, and attempted to apply it rather brusquely to the site of the wound on her forehead. A smear of blood stained the purity of the linen making him wince and curse under his breath at his stupidity, realising a desperate need to make amends in some way for his irresponsible behaviour. Alice swiftly took the handkerchief from him before he could do any more damage and heard his dejected sigh.

Poor guy, she thought magnanimously, I believe he has learnt a lesson here tonight.

'I'd better get you home,' Keith made the suggestion resignedly, fearing the consequence of his actions was about to be felt as he sighed heavily once more, 'Lord, I'm so sorry

Alice, your Dad's gonna kill me! I just didn't realise how fast I was going. I promise I'll go really slowly from now on.'

Surely he didn't expect her to get back on that machine tonight she thought!

'No!' She gave her answer rather abruptly in immediate panic at the thought. The very idea of getting back onto that 'evil' contraption sent shivers down her spine. At that moment she knew she would be perfectly happy if she never sat on a motorbike again for the rest of her life!

However, on seeing the immediate desolation on Keith's face, she managed to soften her response, 'it's ok honestly, I'm fine, I've just got a bruised knee and a slight graze on my forehead, that's all, and I'm sorry Keith but I really don't fancy getting back on that thing again tonight!'

Keith continued to look a little crestfallen at her point blank refusal but she didn't care anymore, there was no way she was getting back on that bike!

It must be getting quite late now she realised, as she felt the darkness of the night closing in on them, and she began to look up and down the street in order to try and get her bearings, wondering where on earth they'd ended up! Negligible light shone down from the night sky as thick clouds obscured the moon and stars and in addition the main street lighting was still dysfunctional since the blackouts. She'd heard rumours that the gas lights were going to be phased out and replaced by electric lighting but only if the new government could find enough money for it, following the heavy costs of war.

As her eyes became accustomed to the darkness and the motorcycle's headlight helped her to see a little better, she suddenly realised where she was! It seemed they were slap bang outside her family's old house in Walmer Road.

'Oh look' she gasped in amazement, 'it's our old house!'

Keith's confused expression and immediate question, 'what do you mean your old house' made her giggle as she explained what she meant, 'it's our old house, Keith, it was requisitioned during the war and it's only just been returned to us by the war department. My mother is so happy to have it back at last. She's hoping to get inside very soon and clean it from top to bottom so it'll be in a fit state for us all to move in.'

She sighed and gave Keith a gentle shove towards his bike. 'Honestly Keith, I'm fine, I want you to go home now, and please you mustn't worry about me anymore, I'm just going to stop here for a while and catch my breath and then I'll head home myself'. And also she thought - *that will give me time to tidy myself up and hide any obvious injuries.*

'Look, I really need to get my story straight Keith' she continued 'I can't tell my parents what I was doing tonight, they'd go off the deep end and I'd be grounded for a month or more, so please don't tell a single soul about tonight ok? I don't live very far from here, just around the corner, so it's not far for me to walk'.

Keith frowned, he still felt bad, and a little uncertain as to whether he should leave her there, alone in the darkness, but he kept looking towards his bike which seemed to beckon him somehow, enticing him to ride away from there and take the easy way out. 'Well, if you're sure', he conceded, noncommittally, but inside he was secretly relieved to think that he might be able to get away from that place, to escape his present predicament completely unscathed, and with his pride still intact.

She nodded vigorously 'honestly, yes, I'll be fine, you go home now.'

'Ok,' he acquiesced at last, 'if you're sure,' and then he continued on a brighter note, 'shall I see you at the Palais again next week may be? Hopefully you'll be dancing on both legs by then,' he joked, a little nervously, before leaning forward impulsively and kissing her softly on her upturned mouth, something he'd been wanting to do all night, and finding himself a little frustrated that his intentions in that department had been seriously stymied. After a heavy pause he eventually turned and walked deliberately back towards his bike, leaving her standing there, alone in the darkness.

He released the kickstand with a sharp jerk and swiftly clambered on board the machine once more and then, with a brief wave, he took off, stopping at the end of the road for a few seconds before finally turning left towards the town centre.

In the silence that followed Alice couldn't help admitting that she was relieved to see him go and instantly she began to hobble over to the familiar wooden gate which led into their old back garden. She stood on tiptoes, as best she could, in view of her painful knee injury and reached her arm up and over the top of the gate, suddenly recalling how difficult the task had been the last time she was there, almost five years ago now. Back then she'd always have to reach for something to stand on, like a log or a brick, and even then she'd have to go on tiptoes to reach the bolt, but now, all these years later, and being a lot taller, she accomplished the task with very little effort.

The bolt seemed to slide to one side effortlessly which surprised her as she thought it might have rusted over the years. She shrugged; perhaps her mother had been over there already and loosened it with a little oil? The gate swung open and she walked in slowly and strangely towards her old back garden.

She'd sketched a plan of sorts which was to head for the outside lavatory where she could wash the blood from her trousers and then use Keith's handkerchief to clean the graze on her forehead and also as a bandage for her knee before heading back home. She felt sure she would have no trouble hiding the bump on her forehead by pulling her hair forward to cover the graze and by wearing a pair of smart trousers to work over the next few days her knee injury would be cleverly concealed. Her parents need never know about her moment of madness and the injuries she'd sustained because of it and this way she would not have to answer any of their awkward questions.

As she walked slowly and silently along the side path she arrived at the back of the house and stopped to gaze across the muddy wasteland which had once been their green grassy lawn. She peered curiously across the length of the garden, into the darkness, until her eyes settled right at the far corner where she could just make out the strange humped shape of the Anderson shelter. The grassy mound rose up eerily from the shadows and she wondered how many times the shelter had been used during the terrifying raids over the town. She realised of course that it would provide no protection at all from a direct hit.

As her eyes swept across the area she was strangely surprised to see a small circular haze of light flickering and fluttering near the entrance to the shelter. That's odd, she thought, as she moved forward cautiously to get a better look. She was several yards away from the shelter, concentrating curiously on the strange orange glow, when all of a sudden she stopped in her tracks. Behind the flame she discerned the indistinct shadowy figure of a man, apparently seated in front of the shelter, but even as her mind tried to register the perplexing image she watched as he slowly rose to his feet. In the darkness all she could see with any clarity were the whites of his eyes which were fixed steadily upon her in a steely gaze.

CHAPTER TEN

Ellen and Frank were sitting together in companionable silence on opposite sides of the crackling fire. Frank was reading from his 'Book of Daily Light' while Ellen was busy mending Frank's clean overalls getting them ready for his return to work the next day. Occasionally they'd look up at each other and smile contentedly. Their last night together was always bitter sweet, knowing that the very next day they would be parted once more. But that thought was always pushed to the back of their minds for as long as possible, they would never allow it to encroach on their last hours together, and in doing so every minute together was cherished.

Ellen let out a long sigh and after putting down her sewing she looked directly at him in an obvious attempt to gain his attention. It was so lovely having this time together, she reflected, with the girls out of the house, socialising, it meant they could talk freely and perhaps solve any problems together.

'I know you had a little word with Alice earlier and I do appreciate that Frank. And I know you think I'm fussing unnecessarily but honestly Frank, I can't stop worrying about her,' Ellen felt instant relief at having shared her thoughts but then she paused, not wanting to say too much, as she waited for his reply.

Frank stopped puffing on his pipe and, taking his eyes off the book, he looked up to gaze lovingly into his wife's troubled eyes. After a moment he returned to the psalm he was reading, deciding to share some of it with Ellen, for he felt the sentiment was appropriate for their discussion and so he quoted a short passage from it.

'Whosoever the Lord loveth, him will he also chasten?'

Ellen understood the message but felt a little frustrated. Frank was a true believer in the power of the lord, his regular visits to chapel whenever he was home told her that, whereas if he wasn't around she didn't bother to go, always making some excuse. Ellen chastised herself for being a doubter and for having sinful thoughts about others. Could she really rely on God to keep watch over her children? She didn't think she could.

Frank's sober reply hung in the air for a moment or two but then he continued with a sigh of his own, 'my dear please stop fretting, it is inevitable that Alice will choose her own path in life and on occasion no doubt she will make mistakes, but it is important that she makes them and that she learns from them,' he smiled at his wife indulgently before continuing, 'I think you worry too much Ellen, she's a grown woman now, you know, nearly twenty, she could be married with children!

I believe it's time to let go, it's time to loosen those apron strings of yours and let them be. As parents we've done all we can, we've given them good advice, kept them safe through that damn war, and now all is well with the world and we are at peace, we need to give them our trust. Perhaps it is a little different for Katy as she is three years younger than Alice and still very much a teenager, perhaps she should be kept under closer supervision for a little while longer, but as for Alice, well she will only end up resenting us for our interference'.

Ellen sighed again, Frank's wisdom invariably helped to calm her spirits, when Frank was with her everything seemed right with the world. However, when he was away and she was alone with only her thoughts for company, her anxiety and overactive imagination always got the better of her.

'Maybe you're right Frank, but you know, to be honest I'm not concerned about Katy at all, she's the sensible one, she worries about everything and she will always check with me before she takes on anything new. But Alice is different, she's headstrong, I might even say she's a little wild and impulsive Frank, and I worry for her. I fear that one day she'll get herself into serious trouble and we won't be there to protect her. While she's living under our roof I think she should be respectful to us, don't you agree? We're her parents after all, we gave her life, she owes us that much, at least. And there's another thing', she carried on, 'which I know makes me sound mean and puritanical, but Frank, I've noticed her becoming rather vain and self-centred!   I'm sorry to say it but I think we might have been too soft on her?'

'Now now, my dear, you are getting yourself all worked up unnecessarily, Alice is a charming young woman and she cares about her appearance that's all. I know it's hard but you can't watch over them every minute of every day. You've got to be reasonable about it. Now, please let it be! Come now, this is our last night together, for a week at least. Let's not spoil it by arguing about the children. I promise you they'll both be fine as long as they keep their wits about them and don't put themselves in any unnecessary danger!'

CHAPTER ELEVEN

Alice's head felt oddly fuzzy, as she stood within the strange but familiar environment of her old back garden, while a feeling of confusion and bewilderment reigned. She continued to stare at the stranger who stood before her, quiet and motionless in front of the old dugout, staring back at her!

She decided to be friendly. 'Hello', she called out, 'can I help you? What are you doing here?'

Stefan clamped his mouth together, tight shut. He'd recently been aware of some movement inside the house and had come to realise that now might be the time to move on. Why on earth had he waited? He should have just upped sticks and gone.

If he spoke to her now she would almost certainly recognise his accent. He knew it would frighten the girl and she would immediately be suspicious. He decided to play dumb, even though he did know a little English his German accent would be hard to conceal, and so for now he decided it would be best to remain silent and passive. He crouched back down again, sitting once more on his makeshift chair, one he'd fashioned himself from fragments of old wooden crates, strapping them on top of a stone slab and placing a blanket inside for warmth. Within the air raid shelter he'd found only one set of bunk beds to lie on but no chair, not that he was complaining, those beds had served him well, keeping him warm all through the winter.

Alice decided the stranger seemed harmless enough as she watched him return to his seat and after a minute or two she walked a few steps more across the scruffy lawn to reach the shelter.

She sat down in front of him, stretching out her bad leg cautiously and finding that the grassy bank beneath her was cold but it was actually quite dry. She smiled up at the stranger in an open and friendly manner. At first glance he seemed quite young, even though she couldn't see him particularly well. His longish hair hung down limply over much of his face, just touching the collar of his thick black coat and he had no fringe, just a rough parting. As she studied him, he lifted up his hand and tucked a section of the floppy mane behind his ear, thus preventing it from flopping forwards over his face, like a curtain, and allowing her to see his countenance. Close up, in the candle light, she could see his eyes were a pale liquid blue and within them, as they continued to stare at each other across the pathway, she discerned a mixture of emotions. Fear seemed uppermost but there was also an underlying melancholy which made her feel sad for him.

On closer inspection, she decided that he wasn't much older than herself, maybe twenty-one or twenty-two, but she didn't recognize him, she'd not seen him about, and his grubby, unkempt appearance made her believe he might be a vagrant, or an orphan, or perhaps just a homeless feller come up from the grit, merely using the shelter for a while before moving on.

With that possibility firmly fixed in her head she decided that she didn't mind him using the shelter, in fact she thought 'good on him' for being so resourceful at a time of need, it wasn't as though the shelter was being used for anything else now that the war was over. She supposed that all air raid shelters had become obsolete and would soon be dismantled.

He must be very hungry, she realised thoughtfully, deciding there and then that she wanted to help this poor young man in any way she could.

'Can I get you something to eat or drink' she asked him in a compassionate, affable manner.

Alice considered herself to be a good Christian, always wanting to do the right thing. She knew the difference between good and evil, observing that many people who thought they were good Christians often behaved in a rather unchristian way, in her eyes anyway. She had been taught by the church and her parents to always lend the hand of friendship wherever necessary and she felt that this poor vagrant surely qualified as someone in dire need. She recalled a quote from the pastor, when he had been espousing from the chapel pulpit, and it was a message which had resonated with her; *'kindness gives hope to those who think they are alone in this world.'*

She always wanted to be thought of as kind and considerate, and then she checked herself, for she sincerely hoped she was kind to everyone she met, even if it did result in more sales for Tuttles!

Stefan had been studying the pretty girl before him. He knew enough English to understand that she was being kind to him. It definitely didn't seem as though she was about to run off to the local authorities. He couldn't believe his luck! His relief was so great that he feared it might be palpable. He'd been surviving alone and living hand to mouth for so long now, managing to steal the odd fish or two every now and again from the harbour, herring or mackerel mostly. There were still a few fishing vessels returning to port with a catch and he knew they wouldn't miss a couple here and there. When the trawlers arrived and offloaded their catch on to Hamilton Dock he'd hide and wait for the right time to nip out and grab any that fell from the baskets, unnoticed. At other times when the trawlers weren't sailing he'd resort to pilfering, managing to forage a few meagre morsels of food from people's bins. He'd actually become quite proficient at living rough, even fashioning a larder of sorts for food which could last a few days through the cold winter. He'd also found a resource of water in a static tank which he presumed was for use if the mains ever needed to be switched off for any reason during the war. Stefan had become weak though, his girth had dwindled, but so far he'd managed to survive pretty well and he didn't want to give up now.

This new situation, with the girl's arrival, could so easily have gone the wrong way, and he drew in a deep breath to gain control over his feelings. Indeed he managed to suppress a strange sob which was threatening to emerge. Recently though, he'd felt himself overwhelmed at his predicament, almost as though he was on the verge of losing control, that if something good didn't happen soon he would resort to an act of foolishness in his desperate need to return home, across the sea. But for now he clamped down hard on his emotions. He needed to stay calm and assess this new situation logically! He didn't want to harm the girl. He'd managed to get this far without hurting anyone.

Of course it had been very different when he'd been looking down at the enemy from the cockpit of his Dornier aircraft, then he'd felt nothing for them, he'd dropped his bombs indiscriminately, without compassion. The enemy below him was just a sea of nameless faces, their lives of little consequence, his only duty was to drop the bombs and get home, to return to his motherland and his loved ones as quickly as possible.

However after many months of living in England, amongst the 'enemy', and learning of the reasons behind the war and the crazy idea that one race could be considered superior to another, that word 'enemy' had somehow lost its meaning. He had come to realise that as a human race we are in fact all the same, just fathers, mothers, brothers, sisters, children, each and every one of us doing their best to protect their own kith and kin.

After he was captured, the tables of course were turned and he knew then that *he* had become the 'enemy'.

When he looked back to the night of the escape he couldn't believe how long he'd managed to stay hidden in this seaside town of Lowestoft. But now he was running out of patience and his desperate need to get back to his homeland would be in jeopardy if this girl decided to call the authorities.

He nodded vigorously in answer to her question about food, and did his best to return her smile, even though salty tears were beginning to swim unbidden in the depths of his sad eyes. He realised it had been a long time since he'd smiled, and more to the point he couldn't remember a time when he'd even felt like smiling, acknowledging that the sight of it might look odd, for it felt pretty odd to him!

Alice smiled back at him encouragingly. She was sensitive enough to recognize his emotions were very near the surface, she could see his watery eyes, and it moved her. Helping this poor man had stirred up her own altruistic feelings even though, in a sudden rush of self interest, it also made her feel extremely virtuous.

As she stood up, she announced graciously, 'I'll just go and ask my mother if there are any spare pies you can have. She always bakes far too many, she loves to bake, you'd think she was feeding an army,' she laughed, 'I'm sure she won't mind'.

At the word 'army', Stefan instinctively reached up and grabbed her wrist. 'No, no! You tell no-one!' he urged her forcefully, looking up at her in fear but when he saw the flicker of alarm flash across her face he instantly let go and bowed his head submissively, before adding a heartfelt 'pleez' to his request.

Alice was a little stunned and shocked at his violent reaction. With a frown she began to rub her wrist where he'd grabbed her but she understood he must be frightened, the poor man was probably terrified at the thought of being arrested. But surely, she thought, he wasn't committing any crime was he? Apart from trespassing, she supposed, but it didn't seem fair to throw him in jail for such a minor misdemeanour, he wasn't really harming anyone, was he?

She thought of what her mother might do if she told her about him. Would she want to inform the police? Yes, she probably would. Would her mother stop her coming back to him with food? Yes definitely!

Alice stopped rubbing her wrist. 'It's ok,' she placated him, and she reached down to squeeze his shoulder gently. 'I promise I won't tell anyone, I'm sure my mum won't miss a pie or two. I'll try and come back later on tonight with some food, and maybe a bottle of stout, if I can manage it, ok?'

Stefan understood most of what she was saying and nodded his head several times before replying in brief monotones 'thank you lady,' in as meek and mild a manner as possible which he hoped demonstrated his contrition whilst at the same time trying very hard to conceal his strong German accent. If she suspected he was an escaped prisoner of war he would surely be done for, but it seemed he had struck lucky tonight.

He'd been so worried about being discovered in his secret hiding place, constantly preparing himself for that eventuality, ready for all the shouting and the guns, but always prepared to hold up his hands and surrender immediately, without any fuss, willing to go back into servitude submissively if he was ever found out. But what he hadn't considered was who that person might be? The prospect that it might be a kind young girl like this, someone who wished to help him, well, that idea had never entered his head, and now it had happened, he was utterly surprised and confused. He sensed the girl was inherently kind-hearted, if perhaps a little stupid and naive, but he was optimistic that she would keep her word and that she would return to help him.

'I'm Alice,' Alice said warmly, holding out her hand to him, 'glad to make your acquaintance.' Stefan stood slowly and stared at her sheepishly, 'I, Stefan,' he said, reaching forward to take her hand, noticing straight away how soft it felt to the touch, how the creamy purity of her delicate skin made him ashamed of his own, which were dirty and calloused. The girl didn't appear to notice though, and she left her hand in his firm grasp for quite some time, not snatching it away in disgust as she might well have done. For the first time they looked at each other properly and he noticed her pretty flushed face which had been lit up by the luminous glow of the flickering candlelight. Her gentle blue eyes gazed back at him warmly, reigniting a sudden yearning, a memory which stirred of someone by his side, of his home, and the girl he'd left behind.

With a sudden smile of encouragement, Alice let go of his hand and walked away from him. After only a few steps she turned round to give him a final wave before she headed back towards the side gate.

CHAPTER TWELVE

Ellen heard Alice coming in very late that night. It must have been after midnight when she heard the front door open and close, and the telltale creak from the middle step of the staircase confirming to her that Alice was safely home. The rest of the household were already in bed, including Katy, who had also been out that night but who'd arrived home from the pictures at around ten thirty. Ellen and Frank had finally gone up to bed at eleven but Ellen couldn't sleep. She'd lain wide awake as Frank snored softly beside her, her eyes refusing to close, as she lay there watching his chest rise and fall, while she waited and listened for Alice's key in the latch. When she heard her daughter's quiet footsteps padding around on the landing outside her door Ellen could relax at last so that sleep came to her almost immediately, like a warm blanket of oblivion.

Alice moved around her bedroom for a while as though she were getting ready for bed. She knew her mother often laid awake listening out for her to come home, but after a few minutes had passed with nothing and nobody stirring, Alice carefully opened her bedroom door once again and, as quiet as a church mouse, she went back downstairs and into the kitchen.

She quickly found several patties in sealed containers, perched on the middle shelf of the larder and taking out one medium and one small patty she wrapped them in tin foil and placed them carefully inside her bag. She hunted around for a bottle of stout and spied two bottles on the floor just inside the cupboard, she dared not take them both for that would be far too obvious, and so she popped just one inside her bag with the pies. She took several biscuits from a large tin, a small stale loaf, and a jar of homemade marmalade, before heading quietly through the front door once more, and out into the midnight air.

CHAPTER THIRTEEN

Alice woke in her bed to the warm April sunshine which glittered brightly through the thin cotton curtains. She felt the comforting tendrils of warmth creeping across the bedcovers helping to ease her various aches and pains which seemed to become more evident as the night progressed.

As she lay there stretching out her aching limbs she thought back to the events of the previous night, the frightening motorcycle ride, her lucky escape without serious injury, and finally, her strange encounter with Stefan in the back garden at Walmer Road.

She remembered the sheer joy upon Stefan's face when she'd eventually returned to give him the food, how she'd sat down before him, emptying out the contents of her bag, and then watched him devour every last morsel with gusto. She couldn't remember seeing anyone so hungry and she closed her eyes to relive the evening again, enjoying the warm fuzzy feeling she had inside, knowing she'd helped to make that poor young man's life a little better. She reckoned he'd probably slept very well that night, with all her mother's food inside his belly.

A small flicker of guilt flashed across her mind at the secrets she was now going to have to keep from her family, but all in all she was very satisfied with her actions, deciding it had been worthwhile, if only to see the pleasure on Stefan's face.

She could hear the sounds of breakfast from downstairs, the laughter and chatter in the dining room was beckoning her and in order to prevent her mother from coming up those stairs and rousing her out of bed, which she often did, she knew she must act quickly.

With supreme mental and physical effort, endeavouring to hold back any outward moans of agony, she pulled back the covers and slowly lifted her legs out of bed one by one. She touched her head where it had collided with the tree and realised how lucky she'd been as it seemed to be healing up already and was now turning into a slightly bumpy graze which should harden off nicely. She planted both her feet firmly down onto the rug and felt a sharp pain just above her knee. As she pulled up her cotton nightie to check the area, she saw that a darkening bruise had appeared overnight, reddish purple and lumpy in the middle, which she touched tentatively. The pain from that bruise had not seemed nearly so bad last night when she'd hobbled across the empty roads with her food parcel. But now, in the morning light, it was very evident. She winced every time she touched it and the throbbing seemed to grow worse as she stood up to put her whole weight upon it. Luckily, after a quick examination, the rest of her body seemed to have escaped injury, and she could only find a couple of bruises here and there, one on her shoulder and another on her elbow. But there was one other noticeable bruise around her wrist, a distinct circular imprint where Stefan had grabbed her in fear, worried about her exposing him to the authorities. However she decided with hindsight that his reaction had been quite understandable, and so she forgave him.

After a while, as she padded slowly and carefully around the bedroom, the pain above her knee eased off a little and she felt rather relieved that she was able to walk on it quite well. If she could suppress any noticeable limp, she was sure her family would be none the wiser.

Alice rifled through her wardrobe and quickly pulled on her high waist cream flares, fastening them neatly and smoothly at the waist, thinking to herself, 'these will definitely do the trick', before matching them with her dark green blouse.

After a quick wash and a splash of perfume she stood admiring herself in the mirror deciding in fact that it was a perfectly stylish ensemble for work. As a final touch, she pulled out her cream woollen beret from the dressing table drawer. It had been crocheted for her by her mother and after shifting its position around on her head for a while she eventually managed to find the correct jaunty angle to cover up the graze above her eye. She had concealed the slight bruising around the graze with a little make-up and, as she fixed the beret neatly into place using a pretty pearl hat pin, she decided she was very happy with her overall appearance. No-one need ever know about her antics of the previous night!

Her knee remained sore throughout their farewell family breakfast but she was quite hungry and managed to eat a slice of toast and margarine with a little homemade strawberry jam. After the rest of the family had left the table Alice stayed in her seat watching them all assemble in the small hallway just inside the front door. Everyone was hustling and bustling and getting in each other's way while they struggled to put on their coats and shoes. Katy was trying to hold on to Trix, giggling and scolding him at the same time, as she tried to untangle herself from the lead which he'd managed to wind several times around her legs. Alice watched them with a mixture of amusement and regret but when Katy finally untangled herself from Trix and had a tight hold of him she called out to her sister that they were ready to leave for the station.

'Come on Alice, what are you doing, aren't you coming with us?'

Alice stayed put in her chair and called out to them from the dining room, 'sorry not today, I'll just stay here a bit longer. I might have another cup of tea,' she said, excusing herself from the usual family jaunt in as light-hearted a fashion as she could muster, 'I have a slight headache today, but I'll see you next weekend Daddy!'

Ellen left the others waiting at the doorway and started to walk towards Alice with a confused and quizzical expression on her face, and looking for all the world as though she was about to interrogate her daughter some more. Alice always came with them to the station, why not today? However she stopped herself short, just as she reached the bottom of the stairs, remembering her promise to Frank about loosening her apron strings and in the end she just smiled at her eldest daughter through the doorway, 'ok darling, see you later' she said calmly and then she turned and walked back to the doorway, not missing a look of attentive indulgence that was shrewdly displayed on Frank's face.

Alice was relieved she'd not had to explain further. She knew there was no way she would be able to walk all that way down to the station on her bad leg and her complaint of a mild headache was actually quite true. She struggled up from the table anyway and walked as smoothly as she could towards the group in order to bid her father a proper farewell.

After she'd seen them off at the front door she was entirely satisfied that they didn't suspect a thing. She stood under the covered porch and watched them walking away from the house, along London Road, as they headed into town. She waved to her father once more as he turned and blew her a final kiss before linking arms again with Ellen and Katy. Alice smiled as she watched Katy desperately trying to hang on to Trix as he bounded off in front of them, yapping in excitement and pulling heavily on his lead. With his tongue hanging to one side of his open mouth and his tail wagging wildly he sprinted briskly along the empty path, displaying a great deal of strength in his tiny body, plus an immense amount of enthusiasm for being outside in the fresh morning air. As the group disappeared into the distance, Alice suddenly felt alone, as though she had effectively excluded herself from her family. At that moment she held secrets inside her that she could share with no-one.

She sighed and shrugged her shoulders, deciding that maybe these new complications were all part of growing up. She was an adult now and must make her own decisions in life.

After going back inside the house to find her coat and bag, she contemplated how she might get to work that day, finally coming to the conclusion that a bus ride into town would probably make the most sense today.

After Ellen had bid a tearful farewell to Frank at the station and then parted ways with Katy who was about to start her shift at the Co-op, she finally arrived back at the empty house with Trix in tow. She settled the dog in his small wicker basket in the kitchen and smiled at the thought of what she was intending to do that day. She had worked out a budget for the house and her plan was to head over to Walmer Road and measure up for a nice new stair carpet. It would probably have to be lino everywhere else, she sighed, for they couldn't afford to carpet the whole house, but the wooden staircase would have that ultimate luxury and she was instantly excited at the thought.

Suddenly there was a knock at the front door and after a few moments' hesitation Ellen finally opened it to see the smiling face of her mother-in-law, Joan, standing before her on the doorstep. Ellen's buoyant mood dipped a little as she took in Joan's smile which always seemed a little strained. Joan carried the world around on her slight, bony shoulders, she would whine rather than converse, complain rather than compliment, however, deep down Ellen realised that Joan was a kindly soul and there was no harm in her. Today Ellen perceived a relative cheerfulness about her visitor and so she smiled expectantly in return.

'Good morning my dear, I was wondering whether you fancied a walk into town this morning, I really do need to go to Woolworth's to get a few bits and pieces.'

Ellen felt her heart sink. She was immediately torn, she had really wanted to get started on the house at Walmer Road today, and she was already fatigued after her long walk to the station and back. The thought of another long walk did not exactly fill her with glee but Ellen suppressed her ill will, never one to be churlish, her natural instinct was always to say yes rather than no, particularly if someone was asking her a favour then the word 'no' would become an anathema to her. The look of sheer anticipated pleasure on her mother in law's face was something rarely seen and Ellen felt herself automatically nodding in agreement. Smiling warmly at her visitor, she reflected there was no rush to get over to the house, she could always go the following day, and in any case she'd waited all this time, surely one more day couldn't hurt!

'I'll just get my coat and bag' she said to Joan, spinning on her heel, 'oh and I'll have a quick look in the larder to see if we need anything,' she called out again as she headed into the kitchen, 'come in for a minute, I won't be long.'

Ellen's mindset soon became more positive and she decided that in fact she wouldn't mind a trip to Woolworths. It was still the store that had 'everything'.

Before the war it had been advertised as the 'Threepenny and Sixpenny store' and the company prided itself on keeping its prices low. That model had worked extremely well with stores opening up and down the country in many towns and cities. Even when war broke out the firm continued stoically to provide for the community, with shops staying open for as many hours as possible, even though many stores had been bombed and staff members had been killed whilst still serving at their counters. Thousands of sixpences were collected by staff to pay for a spitfire for the RAF and the directors of the company had matched the amount penny for penny and plane for plane.

But now the war was over and prices were increasing rapidly, a shortage of supplies meant that even Woolworths could no longer keep to their famous motto, their ethos of low profit margins and low prices could not be maintained and the famous signs had to be removed.

'I've got a coupon for some socks,' Joan informed Ellen, I hope they've got some in stock. When I came in last week they had nothing at all! There's a hole in the toe end of my bed sock and it's really fidgeting me at night. My feet get so cold in bed Ellen, even though we're already into April, oh I do hope we get some warm weather soon,' she lamented, continuing to complain about her feet and other ailments all the way along London Road and into town, whilst hanging heavily on to Ellen's arm as they walked. Ellen had decided to leave Trix at home, he'd already had his walk and to be honest she didn't think she could cope with the two of them. Ellen tried her best to console Joan, assuring her that if they couldn't find any socks, she would gladly buy some wool and knit her a pair!

After searching through the store, Ellen's spirit, together with many others shoppers, was mercifully restored when they finally managed to locate and purchase some warm woollen socks for Joan. Ellen finally left Joan sitting on a chair for a few moments to go off in search of her own shopping requirements. She needed biscuits apparently, surprised to see that her stock had diminished so rapidly, and she purchased two more bottles of stout, astonished that Frank had drunk more than his usual quantity that weekend. He must be feeling very stressed she reflected and once again she prayed that he would soon be able to change his job to a more local one and then return home for good.

CHAPTER FOURTEEN

After Hans had parted ways with Stefan, he eventually managed to find his own place to hide, staying there all through the winter months, only venturing out at night to forage for food and supplies. But, at last, the spring had arrived and his taste for freedom had become much more acute. His provisions were becoming depleted and he found himself growing increasingly desperate and much more daring in his search for decent food.

One particular night he found himself ensconced within the grounds of a tall town house, situated in an affluent part of town, not far from the seafront. He'd watched the bedtime activity from his hiding place and as the lights in the house went out, one by one, he stood silently in the shadows and surveyed the exterior of the building. He noticed, with excitement and delight, that a window had been left open in the downstairs kitchen. It was his lucky night, he thought to himself, as he crept forwards, slowly and silently, along the outside wall to get a closer look and see what might be inside.

As he crouched in the darkness beneath the kitchen window he slowly raised his head to peer inside. Hans saw that the room was dark and empty and so, carefully and quietly, he pushed upwards on the lower sash window realising he could raise it high enough above his head to be able to crawl inside. Placing both hands on the window ledge, he hauled himself upwards, and once in a good position he leaned forwards and dragged himself across the ledge. When his body was inside, he crawled on all fours along the wooden draining board, finally manoeuvring his dirty boots over the edge of the sink to jump down as quietly as he could onto the flagstone floor.

All seemed quiet in the rest of the house, there were no sounds coming from above, and it appeared to Hans that the homeowners had already gone to bed. Gradually Hans relaxed as he peered around the room searching in the darkness for any signs of food or drink.

As he looked around, he instantly spied a white envelope perched just above his head, propped between two large jars, on the shelf over the sink. He took it down and opened it. He couldn't believe his luck for inside the envelope was money! Cold hard cash, he thought to himself, as he rifled through the contents, maybe even enough to buy himself a passage across the channel, for it looked as though there were several notes of five and ten pound denominations. Although he wasn't particularly knowledgeable about English currency, or what that amount might buy him, he could add up the numbers and it looked as though, if his maths was correct, the envelope contained around thirty pounds. If he'd held thirty German marks in his hands it wouldn't have got him very far, but thirty English pounds, now that was worth having! He was sure the funds would come in very useful, perhaps enough for a bribe!

He quickly rolled up the notes and stuffed them inside his pocket replacing the white envelope between the jars on the shelf where he'd found it. With a bit of luck, he thought to himself, no one would notice the money was missing for a few days maybe. He didn't like to think of himself as a thief, food and drink was one thing but money was something else, but desperate times called for desperate measures. He quickly consoled himself when he saw how rich these people were as he looked beyond the kitchen doorway to survey the opulence of the place, the ornate furniture on display, the exotic lighting, and the plush carpeting covering the floor from corner to corner. It stretched before him as far as his eyes could see, all the way from the kitchen step, across the hallway to the front door and then continuing over the wide stairwell and onwards up the stairs. He looked around at the immediate vicinity, taking in the modern kitchen equipment on display. He knew that whoever lived here would not miss a few scraps of food, they were obviously very wealthy, he could see they had plenty and surely they could share some of it. He decided selfishly that his need was greater than theirs. After all, wasn't this the reason they'd gone to war, his country was being suppressed, their destiny held back, stifled! It wasn't fair that other countries were enjoying an existence that was so much better!

A long white cupboard door in the corner of the kitchen looked inviting and without a sound he crossed the room to take a look inside. As he turned the handle slowly and quietly he opened the door. His eyes suddenly popped out on stalks when he took in the vast array of food that was piled up inside that cool larder. He gauged the kitchen had been built as a deliberate outhouse, keeping it separate from the rest of the building and designed specifically to keep the food as fresh as possible. As he meticulously examined the items contained within the larder he realised they were all nicely cold to the touch. He couldn't remember seeing that much fresh food inside any other larder in his entire life! Sitting upon the marble shelving were several bottles of milk, a large portion of cheese, rashers of bacon, a pile of sausages and several cartons of eggs. Hans calculated that he might have a little trouble transporting the eggs via his exit through the window; however, as he pushed the eggs to one side, he began to cram as much of the meat and cheese into his large coat pockets.

Luckily the old fisherman's oilskin he wore had many huge pockets sewn into it, not only in the outside layer but the inside layer too, all stitched strategically into the towelling lining. As he walked away from the larder he noticed a small tin of biscuits on top of the counter and so he scooped them up and dropped them inside a separate pocket. Once his outer pockets were bulging he gingerly carried across two bottles of milk and placed them carefully into the bottom of the large square sink just under the window ledge. He reckoned he would be able to climb out through the window and then reach back inside for the bottles. His plan set, he quickly realised that he could probably do that with the eggs as well, and so he went back to the larder picked up one of the egg cartons and placed it beside the milk in the sink.

Just as he was getting ready to leave he heard a muffled sound coming from above, on the first floor of the house. He heard a door being opened which he supposed was a bedroom door and soon afterwards he heard voices, quite loud, verging on shouting, of a man and a woman who he assumed were husband and wife. Suddenly a light was turned on at the top of the stairs and the voices became louder. Hans deduced the couple were arguing and they were on their way down the stairs? There was still time though, he thought, touching his Adler badge for good luck, there was still time to get out of there and escape!

The noise of footsteps stirred him into action and he clambered urgently up onto the draining board, quickly manoeuvring his body in a one hundred and eighty degree turn, so that he was facing backwards with his feet sticking out through the window, and then, with a final push, he landed with just a slight scrape to his wrist, on to the soft grass below. Quickly he reached back inside the window for the milk and eggs and after shoving them roughly into two empty pockets on the inside of his coat, he sprinted away from the house as lightly and speedily as he could, heading back across the garden and towards the hole in the fence he'd come through earlier that evening.

Tom Algar approached the kitchen cautiously, finally arriving in the semi darkness at the same time as a few slanted rays of moonlight suddenly materialised from behind a dark cloud to shine helpfully through the window. With the shallow silver beams of light being Tom's only guide he walked briskly across the room and looked out anxiously through the open window into the dark gloom of the garden. As he peered across the lawn he spotted the dark shape of an intruder moving stealthily across the grass and heading towards the far corner of the grounds. He shouted into the darkness, 'Oi you, you lousy bugger, I'll have you, I will,' and then he reached behind him, quickly grabbing the shotgun he always kept hidden under the bench, propped and loaded, ready for action, as it had been all through the war in anticipation of a dreaded German invasion. Thankfully, the invasion never came, for Tom had always been determined to go out fighting, he would never surrender, not willingly anyway.

He aimed the gun through the open window, pointing it towards the dark shadowy target. Unfortunately, due to his inexperience and ineptitude, his aim was rather wild, mainly because he'd never actually had the opportunity to wield the weapon in earnest. The shot he fired was clumsy, missing its mark by a mile. This blunder enabled Hans to duck and weave and continue his unhindered flight to the end of the garden, eventually managing to scramble through the hole at the back fence and then run for his life along the sea front.

Hans knew he'd taken a chance back there, it was the closest he'd come to getting caught, and yet he'd escaped once more. He couldn't help but be gleeful, his heart was pounding in his chest as he ran, pumping the flow of adrenaline coursing through his body. The exhilaration of his achievement was irresistible and that feeling overcame any fear he should have felt, as he continued to run onwards, clutching at his prizes covetously. Now he had food, he gloated, and good food at that, not rubbish out of a bin. He almost yelped with delight at the very thought of it and his hungry belly growled loudly in response.

CHAPTER FIFTEEN

Tom shut the kitchen window angrily and did a quick inspection of the room to see if anything was broken or missing. He walked over to the larder, seeing instantly that the door had been left ajar. He grabbed the handle and swung the door wide open noticing straight away that a substantial amount of food had been taken from the shelves. He swore loudly.

After completing a quick survey of the entire kitchen he realised thankfully that nothing else had been taken and no actual damage had been done to the property. Whoever the trespasser was, it looked as though they were merely after food. It soon became obvious to Tom that the scoundrel hadn't broken in, for there was no broken glass anywhere, it seemed he had simply entered the property by climbing in through the kitchen window, and helping himself, quite effortlessly, to most of the rations in their larder.

Tom concluded that someone must have left the kitchen window open and his thoughts immediately turned to his wife! How stupid of Peggy to do that, after all his repeated warnings! Time and again he'd told her to check last thing at night that all the doors and windows were shut securely. For goodness sake, all through the war, he'd bleated on about it, and now he cursed her under his breath for her foolishness.

A sudden sound made him swivel round in panic! Still in a state of alert, he held his gun tightly in his hand, instinctively raising the weapon and pointing it warily at whoever had crept up behind him. Of course he quickly discovered it was not an intruder but merely his wife who had suddenly appeared from the murky shadows at the entrance to the kitchen. In the dim light he watched as his wife swayed strangely from side to side. Dressed as she was, in a white silken gown and with a white lace shawl wrapped lazily around her shoulders, she appeared as an apparition, a phantom, and it was an image Tom found sickening and disturbing.

Pulling himself together he relaxed and lowered the gun.

'God Peggy, why on earth would you creep up behind me like that, you could have been shot!'

Peggy didn't say a word but her eyes spoke volumes as she continued to stare at her husband unblinkingly. It was then that he recognised that familiar glazed look about her eyes, the vacant gawp, together with her distinct unsteadiness, and it was all the evidence he needed to realise that she'd been drinking. Peggy continued to smile at him inanely, not even registering the weapon he still held in his hands, cocooned in her drunken haze, until suddenly she stirred herself and in a trancelike state she began to waft dreamily into the kitchen, tiptoeing down the shallow step silently in her soft satin slippers and virtually dancing across the cold flagstone floor. As she swivelled round to face him, her attempt at an awkward balletic manoeuvre failed disastrously so that she managed to trip over her own feet and, with arms flailing wildly she reached out for the kitchen counter, gripping it frantically, somehow managing to steady herself, before finally resuming her grinning status, utterly oblivious to the close shave they'd just had and also the disapproving frown on her husband's face.

'You see, I told you; you were just imagining it!' she scoffed at Tom's angry face, slurring her words drunkenly, but doing her best to enunciate each and every word with deliberation and care, before smiling up at him stupidly.

Tom let out an exasperated sigh and pointed to the open window above the sink as though that might clarify the situation for her but Peggy just continued to smile up at him stupidly until eventually he grabbed her arm and dragged her roughly over to the empty larder!

'Look my dear,' he ground out gruffly. 'Can you see what has happened here? I wasn't imagining it at all! Someone has been in here and helped themselves to most of our food rations. We could have been murdered in our beds, Peggy! I knew I'd heard something. How many times have I told you to make sure all the windows are locked tight before we go to bed at night? Luckily for us it seems the thief was only interested in our food and so he was probably just a scavenger or a traveller chancing his luck!'

Peggy frowned, rubbing her arm where Tom had grabbed her, but eventually, through her drunken haze the content of what he was telling her began to sink in.

'Oh my goodness Tom, I'm so sorry', she replied, in feigned consternation, still slurring her words as she leaned forwards to stroke his arm in her feeble attempt at appeasement, her intoxicated breath caressed his face as she continued, 'I bet it was Nancy, she's so forgetful these days you know? Ever since her brother was killed in that raid she's stopped being so reliable, I think I'm going to have to get rid of her, she's becoming utterly useless!'

Tom gasped in dismay at his wife's total lack of compassion and suddenly he felt he could no longer be in her presence.

'I'm going outside to check the grounds,' he told her in clipped tones, 'You'd better go back to bed and sleep it off. I'll let the police know what's happened here.'

'Ok dear,' she answered him dreamily, before adding as an afterthought, 'be careful,' but he didn't hear her.

Peggy opened the larder door and tutted when she saw how much food was missing. As the empty shelves stared back at her, she became rather irritated to think that she'd have to fork out again on the black market for groceries. She glanced sideways to the shelf above the sink where she'd stashed the envelope from Ellen Bedingfield, gasping with relief when she saw it was still perched there. She'd really been hoping to treat herself to a new hairdo or perhaps buy a few trinkets from her 'friend' Keith. Now he was a handy person to know, she thought, the handsome sailor who kept her supplied with silk stockings and numerous bottles of scotch, the one who'd told her she was beautiful! Surely every woman needs to be told she's beautiful at least once... or perhaps twice in her life, she reminisced, in a melancholy moment.

She placed her hands over her eyes, her head was still feeling remarkably fuzzy and she proceeded to rub her temples with her fingers in a soothing motion. Why was life so irritating, what had she ever done to deserve all this bad luck and stress? Tom seemed to be constantly moaning at her these days, berating her for every little thing, and more particularly for every penny she was spending, 'prices are going up, you know', he'd informed her brusquely, 'the war might be over Peggy, but it's going to take us a long time to get back to normal!' and then, as a final blow, he'd told her rather unkindly that he was going to have to reduce her allowance! She'd rankled at the thought! She'd get him back for that, she decided, who did he think he was? He was becoming far too domineering, too controlling, and if he carried on like this she'd go to her father and tell him how she was being treated, and then Tom would be sorry! He wouldn't want to upset her father!

CHAPTER SIXTEEN

Alice couldn't wait to return to the garden at Walmer Road and so she did so at her earliest opportunity, entering stealthily through the gate at the side of the house. She closed the high wooden gate behind her, carefully and quietly, not wanting to alert any passers-by, and then she smiled secretly at the thought of all the lovely food she was bringing to her new friend.

Their little terraced house was empty when she'd arrived home after work and Alice was able to help herself easily to the generous supplies in their larder. She couldn't wait to see Stefan's face as he opened up the parcel before her. She'd managed to get hold of another two bottles of stout, some leftover chicken, and she'd added to the feast a large slice of her mother's mouth watering Victoria sponge cake.

Worryingly, that morning she'd overheard her mother explaining to Katy how desperate she was to get over to the house and start cleaning it from top to bottom. As Alice listened further it seemed her mother was intending to take steps, scrub and bowls to the house at the first opportunity, ready to begin her maniacal sprucing up session. As soon as Alice heard this, she began to fear for Stefan, certain that his hiding place would soon undoubtedly be discovered. In her mother's excited anticipation she also explained to Katy that Uncle Bill would be dismantling the old Anderson shelter. He'd told her he would load it piece by piece on to his truck and take it away explaining he would be able to make good use of the corrugated steel panels, the bolts, and all of the wood and metal from the bunk beds, for his engineering works.

Alice caught sight of a note her mother had left on the kitchen counter to say she had gone to the pictures with Grandad. She breathed a sigh of relief when she saw it but realised she could prevaricate no longer, it seemed there was no option but for Stefan to move out of the dugout as quickly as possible, in fact that very day if possible. However she'd promised herself she would not tell him until after he had eaten his meal and then, and only then, when his stomach was full, would she give him the bad news!

Alice approached the entrance to the shelter slowly and quietly, not wishing to frighten Stefan in case he was asleep.

As she got nearer to the dugout she became confused when she heard a strange crackling sound coming from inside. It sounded like a radio, she thought with a frown, stopping to listen for a while to the strange voice which was echoing from within the shelter. It was not an English voice, she realised in panic, as the harsh tones of an alien voice began to strike fear to her very core. The dialect used was one of the most recognised in the entire world and to her ears the voice sounded cold and cruel, because suddenly she knew without doubt that it was German! Instantly her heart began to thump wildly in her chest as she tried to understand what this meant and more importantly was being said.

'Hallo, Hallo, Mein Name ist Stefan Schmidt, ich bin ein entflohener Kriegsgefangener'

Alice froze as she listened to the response coming towards her from the transmitter.

'This is Germany calling, Germany calling, woe sind sie? Where are you?'

'Ich bin Lowestoft in England'

As she heard Stefan's reply, Alice immediately started to back away from the shelter. She needed to get away from there at once, but as quietly and carefully as she could, hoping and praying that her approach had not been heard by Stefan, but in her anxiety her foot caught on one of the sandbags which had become dislodged from the shelter's entrance. In a flash she tripped and lost her grip on one of the bottles of stout which instantly fell from her hand and smashed loudly on the path in front of the shelter.

As she turned to run, Stefan suddenly appeared at the entrance, his eyes wide open in shock, as he took in the scene before him, instantly realising what must have happened. Alice had heard the radio transmission!

Stefan immediately lurched forwards to grab her leg, pulling her down to the ground, before dragging her roughly back inside the shelter. As Alice opened her mouth to scream, he clamped his hand down hard over her mouth and pulled her back towards him in a tight embrace. His face was so close to hers that even in the dark interior of the dugout she was able to witness his own fear and panic. Their eyes locked together in consternation but as she continued to struggle for freedom his grip tightened, holding her fast, and preventing her escape. She could hardly breathe and yet she was fully aware of Stefan's heart beating inside his chest, harmonizing bizarrely with her own, while his warm breath caressed her face heightening her senses as he tried to catch his own breath, panting in and out in short sharp bursts. Until eventually he managed to speak to her gruffly.

'I'm sorry *das Fräulein*' he gasped breathlessly, 'you must stay here now. I will not hurt you, but you must stay here? Ok?'

Alice's mind was in a whirl. She tried to think straight but her head just would not function. She wondered how on earth she'd got herself into this predicament. Why hadn't she recognised his German accent before?   What a fool she'd been. And now here she was, in huge, huge trouble, more trouble than she could ever have imagined.   There was no one around who could help her, no one outside of this garden who knew of her situation, because of course she'd made sure of that hadn't she? So much for her silly secrets, stupid, stupid girl! Her heart continued to beat loudly in her chest and her breathing was hindered and heavy but as the seconds ticked by, somehow, gradually, she grew calmer.

She thought back to the rumours of the escaped prisoners in Laxfield and her fears that a German soldier might be hiding around any corner, ready and waiting to drag her away into the woods. And now, here she was, in the exact same scenario as her imaginings.

But was it?

As she continued to stare into the fathomless depths of Stefan's watery blue eyes she saw only regret and sadness within and suddenly she was convinced that he didn't want to hurt her. If he'd meant her any harm he would have done it by now, she reasoned, and he certainly wouldn't have let her leave the last time and so, impulsively, she decided to believe him, she knew somehow in her heart that he meant her no harm.

She nodded her head slowly, pleading for mercy with her eyes, until gradually he released his hold over her mouth and at long last she was able to draw in a few deep juddering breaths. As he released his arms from their strong grip around her slim, quivering body, she began to recover her composure. Finally, she was able to relinquish the last remaining bottle of stout which she'd held on to so faithfully throughout their struggle. She placed it on the ground next to him, almost as a kind of peace offering.

Stefan looked at the bottle as though it were a flask of poison. He couldn't bear to touch it and immediately moved himself right away from her, shuffling back on his rear end to the opposite side of the shelter, sitting as far away from her as he could, allowing them both space and time to recover. Alice brushed herself down, straightening her clothes, and wiping the back of her hand across her mouth which still tingled from his grasp.

Stefan sat in the shadows, shamefaced, watching her movements intently. They both remained very still for a long time, neither of them speaking, as they tried to recover their senses, maintaining their opposing positions steadfastly, whilst staring at each other warily across the dark gloom of the shelter.

'Sorry if I hurt you,' he offered at last, apologetically.

Alice didn't reply but she felt herself relax a little. On hearing those few words she felt sure she'd been right to trust him. As she continued to look across the divide at his dirt-stained face she was struck again by his youthfulness. He could surely only be in his early twenties, she thought, just a year or so older than herself, and yet here he was in a strange country, miles away from home. How long had he been away she thought, had he been here all through the war? Suddenly her heart went out to him. Of course he would be hiding out, he must be terrified of being caught, and naturally he would be trying to contact his own people, why wouldn't he? Wouldn't she do the same if the tables were turned?

She slowly pulled out the wrapped chicken and cake from the pocket of her tweed jacket, slightly squashed but still intact, and she offered the small parcel to him. He leaned forwards and took the package from her, sheepishly. Then Alice picked up the bottle of stout which remained largely unharmed, even if a little shaken up, and after quickly dusting it off with her sleeve, she handed that over to him also.

He pondered his luck at finding someone as benevolent as Alice, completely overawed by her continual gestures of supreme kindness to him, particularly after he'd manhandled her so cruelly. He finally came to realise that the girl before him was probably his only chance of returning home, she was his true ally, his saviour, his angel of mercy!

As he opened up the food parcel and saw what was inside, he realised he was starving and he began to gobble down the contents with relish, washing it all down with a few large swigs of stout. But whilst continuing to nibble on the bone for the last few remnants of chicken he also began to agonize over his options? What on earth was he going to do with her?

CHAPTER SEVENTEEN

Ellen couldn't believe that she had not yet had the opportunity to get round to the house in Walmer Road. There always seemed to be someone on her doorstep, either asking for help or wanting her to go somewhere and of course being the good-natured person she was she never had the heart to turn them away. Margaret Tilley had arrived early that morning to explain that her mother was poorly, in bed, and that her father needed to get to work without delay and so would Ellen be able to pop round to help her mother with any chores that needed doing.

With little Margaret's freckled five year old face staring up at her plaintively, and her ginger ringlets all askew, of course Ellen consented wholeheartedly to her sweetly worded request, coming virtually straight out of her own front door to follow little Margaret along the pathway and round to her neighbour's front door, which had been left slightly ajar. After checking on Mrs Tilley and fetching her ailing neighbour a cup of weak tea she immediately sorted out a bag of washing to do later and then she gave young Margaret her breakfast and got her dressed and ready for school. Finally, she took her there herself, ensuring she arrived just in time for the school bell which always rang punctually at nine! Margaret was such a sweet girl, so polite and good tempered, Ellen didn't mind looking after her at all.

Indeed the hour she'd spent with Margaret that morning had taken her back to a much happier time in her own life, a time before the war, when she'd enjoyed looking after her own two girls at that young age. She recalled the innocence of their chatter and the ease of being a mother back then, when all one had to worry about was how to feed and clothe them, plus the satisfaction of teaching them some of the joys of the world. She recalled her own pleasure at seeing their young faces light up whenever she read them a story. How they'd all sing along together to light hearted songs and nursery rhymes, and how she'd teach them to count, using only shiny pebbles from the garden. Life had been so much simpler then, she thought to herself dispiritedly, for when girls became women, and strong minded women at that, who begin to voice opinions that are different to your own, when their vanity and carnal urges appear to be somewhat unrestrained, then the responsibility becomes so much trickier! Oh how she longed for the good old days, the happier times before that wicked war had become even a small hint on the horizon.

Later, that same morning, just as she'd hung Mrs Tilley's washing out to dry, Cyril, her father in law, had popped round to see her, his eyes sparkling, with a verbal invitation to take her out to lunch and then afterwards to the pictures. He told her excitedly how keen he was to see the new Deanna Durbin film 'Because of Him'.

Ellen loved musicals almost as much as her father-in-law and she could see the enthusiasm on his face, coupled with his obvious delight at the thought of taking his only 'daughter' out for a treat. Frank had been one of three sons, two of whom were unmarried still, and so Ellen had provided Frank's father with two delightful granddaughters who'd quickly become his pride and joy. Unbeknown to Ellen, Cyril had come to the conclusion that the three females residing in this house were the people he most enjoyed spending time with, and this meant he was often calling round without much need of an excuse.

'I've already asked Joan if she wants to come,' he explained 'but of course she's far too ill, and so I've left her at home nursing her poor aching back,' he grinned slyly at Ellen, and then he winked at her cheekily, showing a distinct lack of sympathy for his wife who, as Ellen was quite aware, was always moaning about something or other and who milked any ailment for all it was worth.

Cyril, on the other hand, was the very contradiction of that! He was always full of positivity, regularly quoting old sayings such as; 'the future is bright,' or 'don't look back, only look forward!' He was a complete contrast to his wife, never complaining, always saying he was 'fit as a fiddle,' if anyone ever asked how he was. She supposed Cyril might be considered quite elderly now, but he didn't seem it, and as he often reminded her 'age is just a number.' Ellen knew her father-in-law as a man who was determined to enjoy every minute of life he had left.

'I'll pop round to Walmer Road with you some time if you like, I can put in some shallots at the front,' he offered, 'the weather's warming up nicely now. To be honest they probably should have gone in already but if the weather stays good I reckon they'll be shooting by early summer! Of course I'll leave Frank to sort out the back, I don't want to interfere there, I know how much he loves planting out his own rows of veg, especially his runner beans and potatoes', he continued. 'I remember his Ulster Chieftains being rather delicious before the war. No doubt he's excited at the thought of getting back into his own garden. It's grand isn't it m'darling, I'm so happy for you all. At last you've got your old home back again. I just hope Frank can get some work around here soon because it's not good for you two to be apart like this'.

'I know Gramps, it does get me down sometimes,' Ellen stood on the doorstep agreeing with him wholeheartedly. 'We've just had such a lovely weekend together and you're right, soon it will be just like old times, but to be honest I was thinking of going to see Mrs Fuller about all the time we spend apart, you know, see if she has any advice for me?' she smiled at him lackadaisically, 'they should write a book for us women called 'how to cope while husbands are away,' she laughed at the very idea, but even to her it sounded false because this was something she was really struggling with.

'Mrs Fuller had to deal with absences for months on end, didn't she?' she continued, 'when her husband was away in the Far East. At least Frank and I are only apart for a week or so at a time I suppose. I'm so glad you and mother are nearby. With my parents staying in Laxfield, the girls have definitely benefitted from your company and your wonderful fatherly input!' Ella finished on a sigh.

After she'd got that concern off her chest she leaned forwards, smiling at him now, before patting his cheek generously. She watched as the playful glint in his pale blue eyes lit up at the gratifying gesture. He grinned back at her with obvious delight but then quickly cleared his throat before any tears came, saying to her brusquely, 'Come on then, let's get going lass, before it rains. It looks like there's a storm brewing!'

Ellen went back indoors to fetch her coat but she hoped Cyril was wrong about the weather as she'd just hung out a line of washing for Mrs Tilley, but she shrugged her shoulders, there was nothing much she could do about it now, if it did decide to rain. What will be will be, she thought as she quickly grabbed her coat and slipped it on, glancing reluctantly at the bowl, scrub and brushes all lined up on the kitchen counter, ready for use. Once more she sighed, her plans would have to wait yet another day, she thought to herself resignedly, before padding down the hallway towards the door.

She placed her small stockinged feet into her comfortable green shoes which were newly polished and sitting neatly to one side of the front door mat. They did look very smart, she acknowledged, after having been recently 'toed and heeled' and now they felt as secure and solid as if they'd been brand new and with that positive thought in her mind she strode out through the front door and closed it firmly behind her.

After looping her arm through Cyril's, they sauntered along London Road towards town, chatting together effortlessly about anything and everything, as they headed towards the Marina Theatre which was indeed a fair walk.

CHAPTER EIGHTEEN

Alice sat very still in the darkness of the dugout and watched Stefan who, it seemed, was determined to remove every last morsel of meat from the chicken leg she'd brought him. Stefan himself had not realised the extent to which starvation could drive a man's taste buds into overload and how every greasy mouthful was pure ecstasy. Alice waited silently, biding her time, before delivering the bad news, but suddenly she could wait no longer.

'Stefan, you do realise that you have to leave here, don't you!' she told him bluntly, 'my family will be moving back into this house very soon and there'll be the devil to pay if they find you here. And there's something else; my mother has arranged for my uncle to come and dismantle the shelter and take it away, very soon, maybe as early as tomorrow. You will definitely be discovered if you stay here any longer. We have to find you somewhere else to hide.'

Stefan heard the words coming out of Alice's mouth and did his best to reassemble them inside his brain with limited understanding of the language so that they made some sort of sense to him. He didn't feel able to reply straight away and so he quietly wrapped the remains of the ransacked chicken bone in the tin foil before sitting back against the wall of the dugout in melancholy contemplation as the repercussions of her news were realised. It seemed that he must leave but where was he to go?

Alice racked her brains as she tried desperately to think of somewhere else Stefan could hide. She realised of course that she was now entering dangerous territory. In the eyes of the law she shouldn't be helping him, but her Christian values were strong and she wanted to prove to him that she could be trusted, in fact she realised now that it was probably the only way he would ever let her go and return to her family.

Stefan's hangdog expression deepened as he began to fear the worst, all this time he'd hidden from the world successfully, all that effort would be wasted if he were to be discovered now. He'd learned from the radio transmission that Germany was now under the control of four nations Russia, America, France and Britain but his plan to go back there remained unchanged, he still wanted to return and somehow reunite with his family.

Alice's mind was whirring at fever pitch, thinking of various options as to where he might hide, until finally a plan began to hatch. She'd been mulling over a risky possibility involving Keith and his black market trade! Surely if Keith was able to hide illegal goods on board his ship without discovery, there was a chance he might be able to hide a person? She remembered Keith explaining to her that his black market goods were transported easily across the channel from America to Britain and then on to Europe. During the war they'd been hidden in the cargo hold but when the war came to an end many war ships had returned to mercantile use and illegal goods were often hidden inside the lifeboats. Keith owed her a favour didn't he? She would promise to keep her mouth shut about his undercover operations and also the fact that he'd nearly killed her on his motorbike if he would agree to help her friend Stefan. It was a long shot but it was definitely worth a try.

She reigned herself in though, she must stop jumping ahead she realised, instantly coming back to Stefan's immediate predicament which, for the time being, was to find somewhere else to hide. That would hopefully give them a bit of respite and the time she needed to work out the rest of her plan with Keith. Somewhere not far from the harbour would be the best idea she thought, racking her brains.

As her mind conjured up that stretch of coastline she had a sudden inspirational moment, 'of course, why didn't I think of it before', she declared, as a vision of the old abandoned trawler came to mind! 'Stefan, you could hide in the old wreck', she exclaimed suddenly, breaking the silence. Stefan looked up at her in puzzlement as she explained further, 'there's an old vessel, it was originally a trawler which they converted into a minesweeper, but it was wrecked at sea and eventually it washed up on shore sometime at the beginning of the war and it's been stuck there ever since, not doing much, and presumably it's just been left there to rot.'

She recalled the difficulties surrounding her idea and sighed with exasperation, 'unfortunately that part of the beach is still cordoned off with barbed wire, masses of it, impenetrable really, but still, maybe....' she tried again to think positively, 'perhaps there is a way through it? There are still plenty of warning signs about the mines; apparently they're hidden under the sand, planted there ready for the German invasion that never came. But I'm not sure whether that is completely true, I think it might have been just a ruse to keep people off the beaches!' she told him cynically.

Stefan tried hard to understand what Alice was saying though his English was not fluent. However, over the past few months he'd managed to gather together many more words and he understood well enough that she was trying to help him. The words 'mine' and 'wreck' were similar in the German language, translating to *'die mine'* and *'wrack'*. He admitted he had been aware of a wreck at the far north of town, he'd caught sight of the masts once or twice in the distance, but it had been obscured behind a forest of barbed wire. He sat up suddenly, with renewed vigour. He was feeling distinctly better now, after having eaten something substantial and the knowledge that someone was on his side, that Alice seemed to actually care about him, had unexpectedly instilled within him a much more optimistic outlook. For the first time in several months he didn't feel so alone and to be honest he was willing to try anything.

'*Das ist gut*....', sorry I mean, that is good, thank you, we go now,' he answered her stiltedly, but his frown had vanished and there was a renewed light in his eyes. He stood up as well as he could, bearing in mind the low roof above his head, stooping uncomfortably as he moved diligently around the dug-out to collect up his few meagre possessions, his radio apparatus and some clothing, and anything else that he thought might prove useful from the bags of various items he'd accumulated over the months.

'It's getting dark' Alice noticed, as she looked outside, 'I think maybe now is as safe a time as any to get going. Hopefully most folk will be indoors having their tea and I'll put my scarf up over my head so I won't be recognised by anyone,' she whispered to him conspiratorially, adding 'just in case!'

In a strangely morbid way she was starting to enjoy the escapade, the constant rush of adrenaline was becoming increasingly intoxicating and now that her trust in Stefan had been somewhat restored she felt she was the only person he could rely on. She'd observed from his countenance a distinct aura of vulnerability and suffering which had ignited a protective instinct in her. He was not a bad person, she reassured herself; his eyes were gentle and kind, and yet he'd been through so much. You could tell a lot from a person's eyes, she decided, they are 'windows to the soul' or so she'd heard? However a small but persistent doubt still niggled concerning his need to keep her with him and how desperate he might become in order to remain free. But whenever his eyes met hers she saw only faith and hope gazing back at her and all those other worrying thoughts were banished. He'd put his trust in her and she'd gone too far now to let him down. She was doing was the right thing, she was convinced of it.

There was just one small warning voice she couldn't dispel which kept ringing in her ears as her father's prophetic words kept coming back to her, over and over again, she heard him say, 'keep your wits about you at all times and always err on the side of caution.'

Alice knew, without a shadow of doubt, that neither her mother nor her father would approve of what she was doing.

At the very thought of her father's comforting voice and the sanctuary of their warm, secure home, Alice's stomach did a sudden nervous somersault. If only she could turn the clock back, she thought, if only she had taken more heed of her parents' warning and wisdom, she wouldn't be in this position now. But it was all too late for that, she realised, and for the time being she was in this up to her neck!

As she hoisted up one of Stefan's bags and slung it over her shoulder, she left the comparative safety of the shelter to head off into the unknown, with Stefan following on behind her. They both moved stealthily across the garden towards the back gate. Stefan kept his distance, allowing Alice to take charge, watching her somewhat admiringly as she searched along the road for any sign of movement. When all appeared quiet she beckoned him to follow her and they headed out, along London Road, towards the seafront.

CHAPTER NINETEEN

Ellen and Katy were alone in the house, keeping each other company that night, as they sat in the front room enjoying the warmth of the fire after tea. Alice was out again, goodness knows where, thought Ellen, but she quickly clamped down on that train of thought. Her fears were becoming entirely irrational she told herself and Frank's encouraging words advising her to take a step back had finally rung true. She was being silly, she knew that, what harm could come to Alice in a sleepy town like Lowestoft. Now the war was over, the place had quickly returned to the way it always was, a pleasant seaside town and fishing port, and she must stop fussing over the girls so much. She made a supreme effort to suppress all thoughts of Alice, concerning where she might be tonight, and who she was with.

Ellen felt warm and comfortable in her cosy armchair by the fire, the lid of her sewing box was open once more, and that evening she was busy sewing a grey frock for Katy for work. Katy herself was giggling pleasantly as she played with Trix, making Ellen smile as she worked. Her younger daughter was bouncing around a small ball at the back of the room, keeping it away from the fireplace, for the small puppy to run after and capture, rather frenziedly Ellen thought, but she said nothing, just allowing them to play. Trix was definitely becoming quite lairy as he jumped around the rug chasing the ball. Every time he got near to it, he struggled to get a proper hold, neither his paws nor his mouth seemed to have any coordination at all, and so the ball was continually slipping out of his grasp, lurching off in all directions, bouncing away into a corner or sometimes rolling steadily under a chair or a cabinet. It was then that Trix's attempts to reach it became quite comical. He'd flatten himself down on his tummy and stretch out his front paw in his desperation to reach it, panting, squealing and squirming, with his tail wagging ten to the dozen, and then he would just stand back and bark at the stationary ball in frustration. Katy and Ellen were both smiling and laughing at him and so absorbed in his crazy antics that they were completely taken aback when out of the blue they heard a loud almost thunderous knocking at the front door.

Mystified, Ellen frowned at Katy who in turn gazed up at her mother, holding up her hands in confusion, before suddenly jumping up from the floor in a sprightly manner, eager, as young minds often are, in their innocent curiosity, to see who might be coming to visit them at such a late hour. However Ellen reached out and caught her daughter's arm, stopping her from going anywhere, and then she held a finger up to her lips while she shook her head. She did not feel it was fitting for her youngest daughter to be answering the door at this time of night. But when the banging started up again, Ellen decided that the door had better be answered.

She replaced her work carefully inside the sewing box and begrudgingly hoisted herself out of her comfortable armchair wondering who on earth it could be, making that sort of racket, at this time of night. Katy quickly grabbed hold of Trix who had suddenly started bounding around the room in abject excitement, forgetting all the fun of his ball and hopeful, no doubt, that a late night walk might be on the cards.

When Ellen finally opened the door, a rush of cold air hurtled into the hallway towards her and she found herself clutching at her woollen cardigan, pulling it tightly across her chest, whilst at the same time being confronted by the tall manly figure of Tom Algar who only just managed to stop himself from lurching into the hallway after it. He pulled himself back from her, with dignified aplomb, while Ellen looked up into his face to see a deep frown of deliberation etched severely across her landlord's brow.

It seemed he was on the verge of delivering some bad news and so she stood silently, waiting for him to speak. His penetrating stare continued to deliver a deep sense of foreboding and she worried that he might be searching for the right words to tell her what had happened, as it was perfectly obvious to her that he was agitated about something.

Tom immediately picked up on her alarmed expression and hoped fervently that he was not the cause of it. He didn't want to believe that the mere sight of him at her door had somehow raised her hackles into a fevered turmoil. However, solicitously he backed away and stood a good yard away from her, blowing warm breath on his hands in the cold night air whilst also stamping his feet in a dramatic fashion on the front door mat.

Ellen could see he was cold but she resisted the temptation to invite him in, which of course normally she would have done, under any other circumstances, she realised, if it had been earlier in the day perhaps, or indeed if it had been anyone else standing there at the door, but him! Tonight she determined that the hour was far too late for visitors and it was her excuse and her reasoning behind any apparent unfriendliness. She held on to the door tightly, pushing it towards him a little, closing it on him in fact, so that it became a virtual barrier between them whilst also having the additional benefit of keeping in at least some of the heat.

As he stood in the doorway Tom could feel the warmth coming from inside the house, he could smell the freshly baked meat pies that Ellen had obviously cooked earlier which were now cooling on the kitchen counter. He desperately wanted to be invited in, to feel cocooned in that warm welcoming space even for a short while. This small house, he decided, was what a real home was like, a proper home full of comfort and calm, and nothing like the cold, uninviting place he'd just left behind him.

In that moment he began to feel extremely sorry for himself and an emotion rose up inside him of abject regret swiftly followed by a fervent wish that he could turn the clock back on his life, and start all over again.

'Hello Alice' he ventured at last, 'I'm sorry to disturb you at this late hour but I didn't know if you'd heard the news? I wanted to warn you that you need to be on your guard. My own house was burgled a few nights ago.'

Ellen put up her hand to her throat in dismay 'Oh my goodness, Mr Algar, I'm so sorry, how dreadful', she offered instinctively, but then fell silent, unsure what else she should say.

Tom continued, unabated, 'and the police have informed me that they've received several similar reports of burglaries and pilfering in the area. They reckon it is some sort of vagabond who's been raiding people's rubbish bins, and the like, apparently it's been going on for many months now, but it seems that recently he's become much more daring and is now entering people's homes and raiding their larders and so I thought I must let you know Ellen. Make sure you lock up all your windows and doors tightly before you go to bed tonight, and I mean tight Ellen, with you being here on your own and Frank away, you are especially vulnerable,' he paused emotively for a good few seconds, and then he continued, 'I wouldn't want any harm to come to you.' He almost whispered the last few words, staring deeply into her eyes, before adding, as an afterthought, 'or your family, of course'.

Ellen was immediately taken aback by his tidings, remembering the stout and other food items which had gone missing from her own larder and she worried to think that someone might have come inside her house to help themselves. However, she found it all very confusing as she always made a point of locking up securely at night or whenever she went out. With Frank being away, she had taken it upon herself to carry out all the security checks around the house, but she was glad of Mr Algar's warning nonetheless.

She felt churlish for not inviting him in on such a cold night but she couldn't help noticing the very personal way he spoke to her. She knew it was definitely not the way a landlord should speak to his tenant, his voice was far too intimate, it held an element of tenderness, as though he had real feelings for her, she sensed it, and also the ever-increasing notion that he seemed to want much more from her than she was prepared to give.

She began to back away from him, retreating further into the safety of the house, 'well thank you Mr Algar' she replied a little breathlessly, 'thank you very much for letting me know'.

It was now time for him to leave. There was no way she could reveal to him how flustered she was by his unwanted attentions, how uncomfortable he made her feel, somehow she needed to return their relationship, if that's what it must be called, on to a much more business like footing!

As she started to close the door on him, she watched as he took a rather reluctant step back before he quickly doffed his hat, but then, just as he turned to leave, she suddenly remembered the money.

Opening the door wide again she called out to him, 'oh, by the way, Mr Algar, did you get my thirty pounds from your wife?' her question seemed to register just as he reached the gate.

He stopped in his tracks and turned to face her with a slightly puzzled expression and then he walked back the few steps to the front door before finally answering her question with a bewildered frown, 'No, I'm sorry Ellen, I didn't'.

'Oh,' Ellen faltered, rather confused and not quite sure what she should say next, but then suddenly feeling that on this occasion only the truth would suffice, 'well it's just that, you see, I gave the money to Mrs Algar, last week,' she explained, feeling a little panicky and hoping fervently she hadn't put her foot in it. She really didn't want to be the cause of a row between husband and wife. She watched as his expression changed, turning from a confused frown to what she thought was a small flicker of suppressed rage, as he began to back away from her.

After releasing the gate at the far end of the path, he walked through it, with his head bowed, but as he shut the gate behind him to rejoin the empty roadside he looked up at her once more and called out across the short pathway, 'I'm sure it's just a misunderstanding Ellen, I'll check with Peggy as soon as I get home.'

With a final short wave he walked slowly and solemnly away from the house and down the road, but as Ellen stood watching him from her covered doorway, he quickly gained speed, until finally he was sprinting away from her as if the very devil was right behind him, snapping at his heels.

CHAPTER TWENTY

As the pair of outcasts trudged through the deserted streets and slums of the beach village, Alice tried to explain to Stefan, in simple English, the story of 'the grit'. She told him that the dilapidated area had once been an extremely vibrant and affluent part of Lowestoft, in itself a small flourishing town, which had grown up beneath the cliffs, a prime position adjacent to the sea.

'People moved here because of the vibrant fishing industry', she told him 'it was a very industrious neighbourhood with net, rope and sail makers, lamp makers for the ships, and repairers too. New houses were built, a chapel, and thirteen pubs, the little town even had its own brewery,' she advised him with a smile, hoping he understood what she was saying as she emphasised the words 'brewery' and 'pub' with crazy pump pulling antics and pretending to glug down a glass of beer so that he smiled and nodded along with her.

She recalled stories she'd been told about the town beneath the cliffs and how for centuries people had believed that because the sun always rose first on 'the grit', before any other town in England, the sea would always offer its first and best catch of the day, bringing good fortune to the town and its inhabitants.

Sadly, this so called good fortune had been short lived. After several bad years of flooding together with the devastation of two world wars, fate had finally put paid to that idea and now it seemed the area had been designated a slum.

'I believe this whole area is due to be demolished' she told him, waving her free arm to encapsulate their surroundings.

While she spoke she watched Stefan's sombre expression as he surveyed the boarded up houses around them. As they walked slowly through the village, they were themselves observed by a solitary female resident. She sat shabbily on broken steps at the bottom of her dingy doorway, dragging succour from the tiniest cigarette fragment Alice had ever seen, as though her very life depended on it, whilst at the same time keeping a sluggish eye on her dirty errant children who scampered up and down the street, happy-go-lucky, with no shoes on their feet!

Stefan nodded his head in doleful understanding, he knew what she meant, and how this place, as well as many others like it across the world, would suffer and die from the effects of war.

When the pair finally arrived at the north beach, they could see the whole of the Denes, north of the ravine, was closed, the entire area still criss-crossed with wire obstacles. They peered hopefully through the mesh of barbed wire, immediately encountering several large red notices on display. The skull and crossbones sign, with its menacing black lettering, sent out a stark warning, 'Danger Mines – Keep Out.' But as they looked to their left, across the length of the beach, they could make out the telltale woodbine funnel and masts vaguely visible above the rusty metal forest and belonging to the old wreck, almost entirely hidden from view a few hundred yards away.

As they moved along the sea wall to get a closer look they registered the rolling impenetrable mountain of thick barbed wire spread before them, in coiled layers across the entire length of the beach. The task ahead of them seemed daunting, to say the least, and as Alice gazed across the impenetrable landscape, it reminded her, in some bizarre way, of a fairytale castle, hidden behind a dense thicket of thorns, and a handsome prince on his mission to rescue a sleeping princess, trapped within the castle walls.

They would surely need special wire cutters to get through that prickly maze, or perhaps a crazy alternative was to dig shallow tunnels beneath and crawl through. The fear of unexploded mines still hidden beneath the soft golden sand turned their mission into a hopelessly dangerous prospect and even the thought of trying to climb through the spiky monstrosity seemed foolhardy as it could lead to their permanent entanglement.

Alice's thought processes suddenly switched to another tactic. She could see that the stern of the wrecked ship was jutting out to sea and she quickly realised the very real option of approaching the problem from an entirely different angle.

Her grandfather's rowing boat sprung swiftly to mind and she remembered regular outings in the small craft with her grandfather during those serene days before the outbreak of war. She knew he kept it nestled within a row of fishing boats, all bobbing together along the harbour wall, jostling for position.

She tugged gently onto Stefan's shoulder, to gain his attention, and then she pointed back towards the South Pier. 'We have to go back,' she explained, quickly picking up one of the larger bags, and starting to walk with it back to the harbour.

Stefan had no choice but to follow her lead and so he collected up the other bags and walked behind her, though he was not really sure where she was heading this time. With his head bowed low, he followed her like a little lamb, concluding that her original plan to access the wreck must have now been abandoned as a rather bleak prospect.

After another tiring walk, back through the beach village and over the swing bridge, they finally arrived at the harbour once more.

Alice quickly located the metal ladder attached to the harbour wall which led down to the narrow wooden platform at the water's edge. Removing the heavy bag from her shoulder, she carefully lifted it over the top of the wall and dropped it down, as quietly as she could, on to the wooden planks below, before climbing down after it. Once she was standing at the bottom of the ladder she looked up and quickly motioned for Stefan to pass down the other bags. Stefan did as she requested and then followed her down the metal rungs himself. Luckily there was hardly anyone about, only a couple of odd stragglers in the distance, two men in overalls loitering outside a pub, probably stopping off for a pint on their way home from work and so engrossed in their own chatter they were not taking a blind bit of notice of anything else that was going on around them.

It seemed to Alice, now the war was over, everyone had dropped their guard. No one had even the slightest inclination or concern that there might be an escaped prisoner in their midst!

After collecting up the bundle of bags they headed along the narrow wooden planks to a row of small boats, bobbing about jauntily at the water's edge. As the waves licked and splashed at their sides, knocking them into one another, they emitted a strange hollow wooden sound, like a lilting tune played on a makeshift xylophone! Alice located her grandfather's boat very easily; it was the smallest one there, probably only fifteen foot long, but instantly recognisable by its bright blue colour. Inside the boat was a red metal Tilley lamp wedged tightly beneath the seating but also tied with a matching red chain and bolted securely to the side of the boat for safekeeping. It meant that the boat was always ready for the occasional night fishing expedition.

A sudden thought crossed Alice's mind that her grandfather might go out tonight and come looking for his boat, but on gazing around and across the sea at the weather conditions she quickly dismissed the idea. She knew that her grandfather would never venture out on a murky night like this; he would only ever go fishing on a perfectly clear night and on a calm sea.

It was true the sea wasn't particularly choppy that night but once she realised that the visibility was quite poor, she began to relax. There was a distinctly misty atmosphere swirling around and as she looked further out to sea she could see a wall of dense fog hanging in the air, just off the coast. Strangely this sight came as a bit of a reprieve because she felt sure that her grandfather would never venture out on such a night and so there was a good chance their escapade would not be discovered. She was a little concerned about being lost in the fog though, if it should thicken or move inland that would worry her, but she tried to shrug off her fears. They weren't going far after all, only a short way along the coast to the north beach.

Once they were both seated inside the small craft and Stefan's bags had been stowed away at the centre Alice retrieved the oars from under the thwarts and pulled them out as quietly as she could before settling them into the rowlocks at each side of the boat. Stefan leaned over to untie the boat from the shiny black bollard at the water's edge and then he pushed it away from the wooden boardwalk.

From his seat opposite Stefan watched Alice with awe as she skilfully manoeuvred the boat away from the wooden sidewalk dipping the oars into the water smoothly and quietly. The few possessions he had brought with him were contained in the pile of bags nestled at the centre of the boat.

Alice was thankful her grandfather had taught her how to row. He had taken her out in the boat a number of times and he'd always insisted that she should take her turn. She had learned there was a definite knack to it and now she expertly manoeuvred the small craft through the mouth of the harbour and out into the open sea. As they exited the harbour Stefan gazed out longingly over the English Channel wondering if there was any way he could attempt the crossing to Holland or France in the small boat. He quickly realised what a crazy idea that would be and common sense told him he would have to wait and bide his time in England a little while longer.

They didn't have far to go as the wreck was beached just north of the harbour not even a mile away. Alice turned on the Tilley lamp which shone out rather murkily across the semi darkness but there was just enough light for them to see along the coast line. Luckily a row of houses perched high on Gunton Cliffs were lit up like a beacon. Alice suddenly realised how strange it was to see them like that, with their bright lamps on, no longer the enforced darkness they'd all been subjected to. During those early black outs, before the family had left for Laxfield, the smallest chink of light would cause the warden to knock on their door, the tiniest speck would become a beacon for the enemy to hone in on. It could give the game away and reveal to a German pilot exactly where you were and where he should drop his bombs. Now, thank goodness, there were no more Messerschmitts or Dornier bombers flying overhead and gradually the nation's fear had subsided. There was no need to hide from the enemy any more.

Alice suddenly looked across at Stefan and chewed her lip in confusion.

He would have been the enemy back then, dropping his bombs indiscriminately on poor innocent families. Who was he now she asked herself, friend or foe? She found that she didn't want to know the answer to that question.

Stefan watched the expressions passing swiftly across Alice's face and wondered what she was thinking. He could see anxiety there and apprehension but there was something else too, he saw the shadow of doubt, and he considered she might be regretting her decision to help him. He knew how lucky he was that it had been Alice who'd found him. She was a beautiful person inside and out, with an undeniable strength of character, but she had physical vigour too. He was impressed by the way she moved the oars backwards and forwards with great ease, smoothly and tirelessly, keeping up the momentum as the boat moved slowly towards their goal.

He would have gladly taken over the oars to give Alice a rest but it seemed the young woman before him was perfectly capable. His own bodily strength had drained away from him after their walk. He had noticed over the past few months that his physical prowess was definitely dipping and he was weaker and less able than he should have been for a young man of twenty two. The near starvation rations he'd been surviving on had reduced him to a mere shadow of his former self, the strong and brave fighter pilot he'd once been had now gone, and for the moment he was content to just sit and rest, gazing out to sea in companionable silence. As the small boat skimmed smoothly across the surface of the water he listened to the rushing of the oars as they dipped and pulled, dipped and pulled, their repeated sloshing sound becoming hypnotic as they sped onwards towards their destination.

Feeling calmed by the constant lapping of the waves and the soothing sensation of being rocked by the swell of the sea, he recalled, unexpectedly, the arms of his mother, wrapped tightly around him when he was young, of being rocked and cocooned in the warm pillow of her bosom. He'd almost forgotten that sublime feeling of security, it seemed to reach out to him from a distant past, something vague and intangible, from so many years ago, but slowly he sensed her coming back to him. In his mind he could see her, his adoring mother, standing at the front gate of their home in Dresden, a strong breeze blowing her long flaxen hair across her face and the tall brown grasses of their wild garden waving to and fro behind her. He knew she was calling out his name but he struggled to hear her voice, it came to him like an indistinct whisper on the wind, '*herkommen, Stefan, herkommen.*' He knew what she was saying; she was calling him to come home. The constant rocking of the boat simulated a blissful feeling of comfort and he yearned to be in her arms again.

Tears welled and pooled in his eyes causing him to wipe them away roughly with his ragged sleeve in utter consternation. There was no way he wanted Alice to see his vulnerability, if she knew how emotional he was feeling, she would think him weak, and so he drew in deep ragged breaths. He must remain strong not only for himself but for her too, he realised, as he rested his weary bones, concentrating on the horizon and the continuous movement of the boat, allowing the silent void around him to calm his inner turmoil.

Suddenly the silence was broken by a strange and eerie sound, a hollow yawn that echoed and resonated around the boat. In the darkness, it sounded ethereal, like the strange ghostly moaning of a large animal in pain calling out to them across the wide expanse of the sea.

'*Was ist das*?' Stefan had to mouth the words as his voice could not be heard over the bizarre monotonous reverberation.

'Don't worry', Alice smiled and chuckled in enjoyment at his consternation, 'it's only the fog horn!' she told him, adding worryingly, 'it looks as though the sea mist is rolling in! Can you see the lighthouse above us?' she asked pointing upwards over her shoulder. 'The light', she said again, before pointing to the Tilley lamp on the floor of the boat so that he knew what she was talking about and then she put down the oars and made a grand gesture with her hands 'big light' she said again, can you see it?' As Stefan followed her pointed finger he saw the large white light shining out from the top of the cliffs, an intermittent beam of radiance which continually changed direction as it shimmered across the waves, clear and pure one minute but suddenly becoming more indistinct as it collided with the mist. It also enabled Stefan to focus on a disturbing blanket of fog which was rolling in, hovering over the sea and coming ever closer to the coastline, like an ominous deathly veil.

As they began to approach the shore line, the wreck suddenly materialised, rising up ahead of them, stark and frozen in time, like a ghost ship, appearing and disappearing in the ever thickening mist, so that Alice had to steer the small boat in a slightly frenzied fashion to avoid a collision. She finally managed to manoeuvre it successfully and landed the small vessel with a scrape and a crunch on to the sand-pebbled shore.

Alice was highly delighted that they'd made it to the beach without too much difficulty and also without incident, but her arms were aching terribly, she realised, as she began to massage them with her fingers, kneading and probing her upper arm muscles, first one side and then the other, before finally lifting her hands to reach the back of her neck and shoulders, realising that this was the part of her body that seemed to have taken most of the strain. She would be glad of a rest before heading back she thought.

Observing her distress and without a sound Stefan immediately reached forwards and placed his hands gently on to her shoulders. He motioned for her to turn around in her seat so that she had her back to him. She complied with his request cagily and they sat together silently except for the sound of the sea lapping against the shore while Stefan proceeded to gently massage her neck and shoulders.

His touch was sublime, so gentle and soothing, it sent shivers down her spine and as she began to lean back into him she realised she was enjoying it so much that she really didn't want him to stop. Whatever he was doing it was definitely reducing her stress levels and swiftly she began to relax, not realising just how taut and anxious she'd become. As she turned around to thank him she caught him looking at her strangely, in that timeless old fashioned way which caused the world around them to melt away, so that it was just the two of them, sitting alone, together in the darkness.

Had they been sent somewhere, Alice pondered, to a world of dreams, a life detached from reality? The thought crossed her mind that she'd like Stefan to kiss her but in his eyes was a faraway look, a wistful look of longing for another time and another place, and she began to wonder about his life in Germany and who he'd left behind.

As the cold clammy air began to permeate her trance-like state she was swiftly brought back to the present. She offered him a friendly smile, 'thank you Stefan that's really helped' at which point he instantly stopped what he was doing and drew away from her. This was all becoming far too complicated, Stefan realised, this poor girl had been dragged into his crazy world and he was sorry for that, it just wasn't fair, he should have let her go back to her family, she didn't deserve to be going through this ordeal with him.

Utterly oblivious to Stefan's thought processes Alice stood up, stretched her arms a little and, feeling a whole lot better, she jumped out of the boat. Stefan drew in a deep breath and followed her lead by stepping out of the boat himself, his legs were a lot longer than hers and there was no need for him to do much jumping. Alice grabbed hold of the tow rope and attempted to pull the craft further up on to the beach while Stefan, seeing her struggle, used the small amount of strength he had left to run back into the water and push from the other end. Eventually Alice moored the small craft by tying it securely to the wreck's slightly rotten rudder, deciding it was robust enough for the purpose, and by doing so, it was also hidden from view beneath the wreck's shadowy hulk.

Alice took out the bags one by one and dumped them on to the sand before she went to unhook the Tilley lamp. She thought the lamp would come in useful inside the dark interior of the ship's cabin.

The old fishing trawler towered above them, creaking and groaning, even in the moderately gentle breeze. Alice beckoned Stefan to follow her as she made her way round to the other side of the wreck and they stood for a moment to admire the tall woodbine funnel, still pointing upwards, even though it was at a strange angle and inside they could see its blackened smoky interior from fumes which had been spent long ago, on its final mission. The stranded wreck lay tilted towards them almost as though it was beckoning them to climb on board. As they gazed across the empty deck they observed a few gaping holes where the wood had splintered in some places, however, for the most part, the ship seemed solid and sturdy.

Alice grabbed hold of the steel rail and hauled herself upwards with the aid of her good knee perched on the rim and soon she was able to manoeuvre herself through the gap so that eventually she was standing upright on the slippery deck. She quickly leaned over the rail to help Stefan and he gratefully took the hand she offered. With Alice's help he managed to climb aloft and then he too scrambled through the rail just as she had done and eventually they stood together side by side.

As they looked around the deserted trawler they saw rusty discarded equipment, ropes coiled and uncoiled, all lying abandoned and unused across the deck, they could hear creaking and groaning in the rigging which seemed to grow louder somehow as if the ship was a cranky old sea captain who'd seen better days and who was now complaining he'd been put out to pasture. The clanking and chiming of the chains and supports seemed to call out to them in continuous discord as the sea breeze suddenly whipped itself up around the mast, creating an ominous environment well suited to their situation, as though the ship was trying to communicate with them, desperate to share its secrets.

Alice had heard a few stories about the wreck, HMT Rowan Tree, the old trawler which had been requisitioned for minesweeping duties as part of the war effort. It had been decided in the early stages of the war that local fishermen would know the waters around English harbours far better than any seaworthy sailors. They were also familiar with their own trawlers and rather than retrain these men on naval ships the Government decided merely to requisition their own vessels, to use them in the hunt for enemy submarines and mines along the coast line, and so the ship's trawl was quickly and easily switched to a mine sweep.

Soon after the Rowan Tree had set sail on the 21st November, 1941, the mission had gone horribly wrong. Not far from harbour the ship had run aground on a newly formed sandbank. The team had radioed for help and the Lowestoft Lifeboat crew had quickly come to their aid but once the men had been rescued there was nothing more that could be done for the trawler and so it was just left where it was, stuck on the sandbank. However, time and tide eventually set it free and although it was quite badly damaged it began to drift with the current, finally washing up on the shores of the north beach, where it had been left to rust and rot ever since, neglected and abandoned on the pebbled-sand. The navy had managed to recover the large guns which had already been reused from World War One. It was felt they could still serve a purpose and so they'd been dismantled and removed to another ship. However, the minesweeping gear, the ropes, the kites and the oropesa sweep were all still on board, lying in a heap at the back of the deck.

The pair walked gingerly across the deck's slippery surface, towards the hatch which led to the lower deck, the windows of the bridge above them were gaping and broken and they realised there would be no warmth up there. Both of them were hoping and praying that the area below deck might at least be dry and comfortable and they continued down the wooden steps, into the dark, gaping abyss. After they'd stepped off the bottom step Alice lit the Tilley lamp once more and held it up before her. As the beam of light shone around the cabin, Stefan's eyes were instantly drawn to Alice's face which had been suddenly illuminated by the lamp's orange glow. He found himself staring at her delicate beauty, her striking features, each one perfectly positioned. Her eyes, an unusual violet blue, were shielded by dark sweeping lashes which fluttered coyly as she became aware of his penetrating gaze. Even the misty sheen, which glistened in silver droplets and peppered her dark wavy hair, was delicately enhanced by the light's soft focus.

As she walked away from him, she shone the light around the trawler's shabby interior and Stefan's attention was instantly diverted as they both became struck by all that lay before them.

As they surveyed the kitchen area, they took in the array of fresh food which appeared to have been deposited rather haphazardly on the counter; they also saw and smelt a pot of what looked like soup sitting on top of the stove. As Alice swung the lamp over to the other side of the room, it lit up a shabby unmade bed, an open newspaper lying on top of it, and upon the newspaper sat a plate of half-eaten cheese and biscuits. All of it revealed to the onlookers, without a shadow of a doubt, that someone was already living there.

CHAPTER TWENTY ONE

Tom Algar turned the key in his own front door with great difficulty as his hand was shaking so much!

The reason for his tremor was a seething potent rage that he dared not unleash. Once inside the hallway he kicked the door shut behind him noisily, releasing some of his pent up anger, and then he walked determinedly into the empty parlour. He began breathing in slowly and deeply in order to resume some semblance of calm and leaning both hands heavily against the mantelpiece he stared down ignominiously at the unlit fireplace. The grate below him was cold and uninviting, he noticed at once with a grimace, and it always would be unless he could be bothered to go and fetch in the coal himself and light it. He glanced up at his reflection in the silver antique mirror, hanging by a chain against the blue floral wallpaper and a wedding present from his own dear mother. His mother had always known how to make a house a home, he thought, remembering his strict but happy childhood and then he sighed at the thought of his loving mother, now gone to meet her maker. He considered his countenance, he wasn't old or unattractive his dark brooding eyes informed him wistfully, he was only forty five after all, but it was time to face facts, Ellen Bedingfield was not interested in him and it was time to let go of that silly daydream.

He thought about his own wife and of this, the home they shared. But he didn't really consider it a home and surely it never would be. It was just an empty shell with no children to fill it, but he'd given up on that idea long ago. The house around him seemed cold and quiet. Where was Peggy, he thought to himself angrily, annoyed that she must have taken Ellen's money without telling him about it and that she'd obviously decided to keep it for herself. What silly frivolity had she thought to spend it on, he pondered? A few more bottles of Scotch seemed to be the most likely scenario, he concluded unhappily.

He remembered what had happened earlier that evening. How he'd left his wife lounging in their bedroom, virtually incomprehensible after only a few glasses of the stuff, the toxic liquor she'd come to prefer more than his own company. It was because of her indisposition that night, her irritatingly nonsensical language, the provocative way her gown kept slipping from her shoulder, that he'd finally decided to leave the house and head up to see Ellen, his pretext being to warn her about the news he'd just learned from the police.

Eventually he stood back from the cold fireplace, at a loss what to do. He expected Peggy would be sound asleep by now, out cold probably, and suddenly he felt bereft, the quiet solitude of the room pressing down on him. However one familiar sound kept him company, it was the 'tick tock' of the wooden wall clock which seemed to resonate with him as a persistent echo of his own death knell. He turned to study the pendulum as it swung continually from side to side, interminably, eroding every second of his life with Peggy, while she, his companion of almost fifteen years, seemed to grow ever more distant with each passing day. They'd loved each other madly once, what on earth had happened?

He gazed at the clock's face, registering that the time was only nine thirty, much too early to go to bed but probably too late to do anything meaningful. He considered his options; he could go out and get drunk he supposed. Why not, if you can't beat them join them! That's what folk always said. But he knew that the news of his falling from grace would be all around town in no time. Tom still held a respectable position within Lowestoft society, and it was one he would do his damnedest to protect.

He thought about waking Peggy and having it out with her, but did he really want to have a blazing row with her at that time of night, and with her in that state, what would be the point, no, it would be far better to wait until morning and deal with her antics then, in the cool light of day? What on earth had she spent that money on though, he wondered? A new hairdo, some jewellery, or perhaps it was food? His mind whirled with the possibilities. What had made her so desperate that she felt the need to steal that money? Perhaps he'd been too hard on her lately, with the latest reduction in her allowance, was it that which had finally pushed her into skulduggery, but as he looked forward rather bleakly to his future life, he felt that any hope of happiness with Peggy seemed incredibly slim. Where had he gone wrong, surely he'd given her everything she desired?

When he'd first met Peggy his prospective father-in-law had been mayor of the town and by the time they were married he'd been chairman of the district council, travelling on an upward trajectory towards Parliament. An arrogant man, John Woodall had effectively spoiled his only daughter to the point where she'd already become vain, self-obsessed, and extremely hard work for any suitor to cope with. But Tom had been somewhat smitten, drawn in by her elegance and grace, her beauty was beyond compare, and also, at the time, he'd thought, selfishly, that her fine breeding and aristocratic background would help him to improve his own good fortune. In addition, of course, she would look very good on his arm. He frequently overlooked her petulance, fussing over her, buying her nice things to please her, in fact he realised now he'd spent his whole married life trying to make her happy. Her father had given his blessing to the pair wholeheartedly, he'd been very impressed with Tom who was a wealthy up-and-coming property owner and had swiftly concluded that this young man might be the only suitor who could give his daughter the life she craved.

Tom remembered Peggy, as she was then, young, impetuous, full of life, coquettish even, and he imagined her as she was now, probably sprawled across their huge luxurious bed in a drunken stupor. Even if he tried to waken her now she would most likely be incoherent, and so no, it would be best to let her sleep he thought, and he sighed heavily once more.

Suddenly, he heard a noise from upstairs, the sound of something falling perhaps, and he realised that Peggy must still be awake. His mind instantly switched to another gear and towards an impending altercation, the one he'd been putting off until the morning, but with his anger still simmering just below the surface, he decided that perhaps now might be the opportune moment after all and so he decided he would indeed go and have it out with her.

He bounded up the stairs, two at a time, walking briskly across the large landing and into their bedroom. But as he reached the open doorway he stopped dead.

The stark image that met his eyes turned him cold.

Staring back at him from the bed were the wide frightened eyes of his wife. Like huge beacons of dread they implored him silently for help as she sat slumped against the pillows, bound and gagged, her wrists red raw and dangling from each side of the headboard. Before Tom could make any sense of what he was seeing, or indeed make any move to help Peggy and release her from her appalling predicament, something solid and heavy landed on the back of his head and with a sickening thud everything went black.

CHAPTER TWENTY TWO

Alice grabbed hold of Stefan's hand and pulled him away from the dark interior of the cabin towards the steps once more. She picked up the bag she'd brought with her whilst at the same time motioning to him silently that they should get out of there fast and retrace their steps. He understood immediately what she meant and likewise he picked up the rest of the bags and followed her up the steps again, arriving at the top, and back on to the cold slippery deck. Alice looked around furtively, wondering who on earth could be living there and worried now that whoever it was may already be on their way back. But how on earth could anyone gain access to this place without a boat? When she looked at the landscape surrounding the wreck and across the beaches to either side all she could see was a mass of tangled barbed wire. How on earth had anyone found their way through all of that?

They started to slither once more across the damp deck and eventually clambered down through the rails to land on the sand-pebbled beach once more and ominously at exactly the same moment as the clamouring mist finally reached shore and enveloped them. The freezing fog's icy fingers encircled them, clawing them into its cold embrace, making them shiver uncontrollably as they headed blindly towards the small rowing boat once more. Alice's teeth were chattering ten to the dozen, but somehow she managed to untie the small boat from the wreck and quickly re-attach the Tilley lamp to the red chain once more. At least it would give them a small amount of light for the journey back. They quickly stowed away their bags once more and as they grasped the boat on either side they shoved it swiftly back into the sea, running along beside it, into the water. As soon as it began to bob about on the grey, murky waves they quickly jumped back inside, positioning themselves securely on to the cold wooden seating and Alice began the job of rowing once more. But this time it proved more difficult. The fog had become extremely dense and it was also suffocatingly cold, nevertheless she could just make out the lights of Hamilton Dock and a little further along the coast the small flickering lights of the north and south pier, way off into the distance. It was comforting to see the main lighthouse above them on the cliff, still sending out its reassuring beam of light, helping to guide her in the right direction. However, this time her hands were becoming useless, they were virtually frozen stiff and she struggled to get a good grip on the oars which were constantly slipping from her fingers. Her arms were excessively tired and weak from before and she continued to struggle fruitlessly.

Stefan quickly realised her distress and delved into one of his bags. After rummaging around for a while, he eventually drew out a pair of remarkably dry woollen gloves which he motioned for her to put on. The warm gloves did the trick and instantly she was able to grip the oars more successfully. He delved into the bag once more and quickly found a second pair for himself. He was delighted that he had been able to afford some assistance to aid their mission, even in this small way, and immediately he felt less of a burden to her, but as he watched the strain and fatigue becoming more evident on Alice's face, her tired arms wrestling uselessly with the oars, he had another persistent thought.

'Pleez, Alice, you will let me,' he pointed to the oars and it was obvious he was offering to take over.

She was profoundly grateful for his offer but she didn't believe he would be able to manage it.

'No, Stefan, don't worry, I'm fine.'

She watched as he leant back in resignation, his face drawn and his pallid skin stretched tightly across his cheekbones.

His face seemed almost luminous in the swirling mist as he closed his eyes and she looked down at his arms and hands, seeing how thin and wasted they were.

She remembered the feel of his hands. The care and attention he'd given her when he'd massaged her neck and shoulders, and how strong and deft they'd felt at the time. She also recalled his arms wrapped tightly around her body, the taut strength of his firm embrace, when he'd wrestled her down to the ground inside the shelter.

Suddenly he sat up again, almost begging with her, 'pleez' he reiterated once more 'you must have rest now'.

Finally Alice gave in, to be honest she was glad he'd asked her again, because she knew she couldn't go on, and this time she didn't argue. She was so physically drained, her strength had all but left her, and at that moment she could barely raise her arms in the air.

As he moved forwards, to take the oars from her, Alice slid backwards off her seat, out of his way, moving herself clumsily into the bow. The weight at the front of the boat shifted so that the bow dipped dramatically however, in the nick of time, Stefan managed to grab a couple of bags and move them to a new spot behind him which instantly levelled off the boat, ensuring no water came in.

Stefan struggled at first to get his momentum going, but he'd been watching Alice's rowing expertise and eventually he got into his stride. With Alice giving him instructions, they eventually entered the quiet foggy harbour once more, tucking the boat snugly between the same two rowing boats, exactly where they'd found it.

Alice slowly exited the craft, utterly exhausted, physically and mentally, and not really knowing what they should do next. After retrieving the bags and depositing them on the harbour side she helped Stefan out of the boat swiftly realising they had achieved nothing! They had merely gone full circle and ended up back at square one. Her plans had gone completely awry and she looked around dismally for some kind of inspiration.

As she peered through the mist, looking beyond the bridge, and along the estuary, towards the inner harbour of Lake Lothing, she was amazed and astonished to see the tall masts of a naval frigate which must have recently docked there on some sort of layover.

She swiftly remembered the second part of her plan and the information Keith had shared with her about how he was able to hide black market goods on his ship. She immediately wondered if there might be some way she could sneak Stefan on board so that he could hide somewhere on the ship. It would only be a temporary solution for now, she realised, she didn't know how long the ship was going to be there, or where it might be heading, but it would give her some time to think.

She beckoned Stefan to follow her, giving him a brief outline of her plan, and they made their way across the bridge, moving stealthily behind the industrial buildings, and towards the large vessel.

The area was very quiet. The usual hive of activity had been shut down for the night and the heavy lifting gear and loop line tracks were silent. The fog helped to conceal their approach as they progressed along the edge of Lake Lothing. As they advanced and grew nearer to the ship Alice was excited to see that the gangplank was down. She looked around furtively for any signs of life but as far as she could tell there were no guards on duty. Before she took another step, she became aware of male voices up ahead and she quickly turned around and grabbing Stefan by his lapels she pulled him roughly behind a pile of wooden crates.

Breathing together heavily in their small hiding place, they peered through a rectangular aperture and watched the two men, dressed in smart naval uniform, appear through the double doors of a large industrial unit. As the sailors walked out into the goods yard Alice and Stefan remained hidden and quiet behind the crates.

The sailors stopped for a while to light a couple of cigarettes, after which they continued smoking and chatting as they walked further away from the buildings, stepping over the railway lines, and looking as though they might be heading for the ship's gangplank.

As they drew nearer to the crates where Alice and Stefan were hiding she could hear the men's voices quite clearly. She could hardly believe it but she immediately recognised one of them! It was Keith, her supposed new beau, the chap that only a few days ago she was madly in love with, until the fiasco of Sunday night!

What a stroke of luck, she thought, as an idea suddenly sprouted! In the small tight space that was available she turned herself round to face Stefan, swiftly placing her finger against her lips for silence and then she gently pushed him down to the ground, ensuring he was tucked away safely behind the crates and out of sight. She stepped over him and out into the open, and then she grabbed the bags, positioning them all around him and in front of him for additional cover.

'You stay here,' she whispered, and he nodded at her in silent acquiescence while pulling the bags closer to him and trying to make himself as small as possible behind the crates.

Alice stood away from him, brushed herself down, and then sauntered over to the two sailors with as much sassy confidence as she could muster. She knew she wasn't looking her best, her hair was probably damp and frizzy from the sea mist and it was more than likely any make-up she'd put on earlier had been well and truly washed away by now, but she held her shoulders back, pushed out her chest, and then she called out to the men in assured tones, 'Hi Keith, fancy seeing you here!'

Keith looked up in amazement! He couldn't believe who was walking towards them out of the mist! In fact he wiped his eyes because he thought he must be seeing things. Her sudden appearance was so totally unexpected!

As Alice continued to walk towards them, she watched Keith whisper something covertly into the ear of the other sailor and she couldn't help wondering what he might have said. After hearing Keith's tall tales from the other night, she quickly deduced that he and his mate suddenly looked a little shifty at her appearance tonight, almost as though they might have been up to something. Putting two and two together she reckoned they were probably in cahoots. It was highly unlikely that Keith could run his black market trade alone. He would definitely need help from others, probably paying them a little extra for their cooperation and silence.

As Keith started to walk towards her, his mate disappeared dutifully into the shadows.

'Why Alice, hello!' he answered. 'What on earth are you doing around here? I'd have thought you'd have been tucked up in bed at this time of night. It's a pretty nasty one too isn't it,' he said, gabbling away a little nervously, remembering warily that the last time he'd seen Alice she was standing injured at the roadside and he'd been riding away from her, after her nasty fall from his bike. He was convinced she would let the cat out of the bag and report him, and that by now her parents probably knew all about her injury and his being the cause of it. It had given him just one more thing to worry about. In fact he was waiting for the day when the law caught up with him about something or other. He consoled himself that he was only involved in petty crimes and misdemeanours, that no one was getting hurt, indeed he'd convinced himself at one time that he was actually helping people, providing a service in hard times, but just recently he'd decided to pull out of the game. He was fed up with constantly looking over his shoulder.

'Is this your ship?' Alice enquired as calmly and politely as she could.

'Yes', he nodded with obvious pride, 'there she is, HMS Lowestoft, isn't she grand! What a ship! She was almost sunk in the Battle of the Atlantic,' he informed her proudly, 'all through the war she did her duty, escort to numerous convoys, protecting them, shielding them from enemy strikes. She suffered a bit of damage of course, but that's hardly surprising, after all the u-boat attacks she had to endure, but every time they patched her up and sent her back out again. She's definitely done her bit for King and country, but now her life as a war ship has come to an end, and she's been sold, sold off as a mercantile. She's been properly kitted out with all the latest equipment, new radio, new masts, lifeboats, and below deck there's every home comfort you could possibly imagine! They've even renamed her; 'Milaflores' which means 'look at the flowers,' it's a bit pansy if you ask me, considering her history, but there you go, I have no say in it, and tomorrow she's bound for Zeebrugge and then on to Hamburg. We're just a small crew now, delivering her to the new owners. We're scheduled to leave here in the morning and after that I'll be heading back to the USA to join my old crew mates on HMS Holmes!'

Keith stopped talking and studied Alice's face for a while. She seemed thoughtful and quiet and not cross or angry at all. He imagined she must have forgiven him for being the cause of her nasty fall the other night and in an effort to fill the silence, he added impulsively, 'listen sweetheart, after this trip, I'll have a few days back here in Lowestoft and, well, I was wondering if maybe you'd like us to get together again?'

After finishing his short speech and with a smile and a wink, he slid his arm craftily around her shoulders, pulling her towards him for a quick kiss. Alice was utterly oblivious to Keith's crassly optimistic overtures but her heart was beating loudly in her chest for an entirely different reason. Alice had registered two important details from Keith's diatribe; the first was that there were lifeboats on board his ship and secondly, although her geography wasn't that great, she was pretty sure Hamburg was in Germany!

'Look Keith', she said, pulling out of his arms easily, 'I really need a favour and I think you owe me one too, don't you? After all, I could have been killed the other night!

'Sure honey', he replied with more than a little relief, 'anything you want, you just say the word!'

CHAPTER TWENTY THREE

Another opportunity had arisen, quite by chance, for Hans to secretly enter Tom Algar's affluent abode and requiring very little effort on his part. He had found himself in the right place at the right time yet again and if providence had decided to smile on him at that moment then who was he to turn his back on that advantage.

He had returned to the house several times to carry out reconnoitre missions after his previous straightforward entry and lucky escape. He guessed, wisely as it turned out, that there were other riches inside that house apart from food, all just sitting there, asking to be taken, and he knew if he bided his time and kept watch he might get lucky again. He'd spotted the ideal opportunity when he'd seen the tall man leaving the house at around nine. Hans was particularly wary of the man because on the last occasion he had tried to shoot him, but this time the man with the moustache appeared to be distracted, apparently in a great hurry to leave the house. In fact, he looked visibly upset, obviously on a mission to get away from the place, pronto, with the presumed intention of being somewhere else as quickly as possible. His lack of attention and foresight proved useful because, as he left the house, Hans observed him pulling the door shut behind him rather carelessly. The action turned out to be futile, and intriguingly Hans watched as the door bounced open once more and remained slightly ajar. He'd already witnessed the maid leaving the house a little earlier, at around eight, and he wondered if perchance the house might now be empty. The temptation was far too great for him to resist and so he crossed the road deftly, looking to his right and left, in case of any traffic. Luckily the deserted road offered no potential witness to his crime and, completely unobserved, he reached the top of the stone steps in a matter of seconds.

He pushed open the door and quickly stepped inside the opulent hallway.

Standing silently on the sumptuous carpet he turned and then, slowly and carefully, he shut the door behind him. All seemed quiet in the house and carefully he inched his way forwards, initially heading for the kitchen once more, when suddenly he heard a strange noise coming from upstairs. It sounded like a woman's voice and she was either singing or possibly crying, he wasn't quite sure!

He swore softly to himself, '*mein gott!*' This was not the way he had intended it to go.

He turned back to the foot of the stairs and as he moved silently upwards, the opulent carpet cushioned his footsteps, keeping his intrusion a secret. He had intended to go upstairs anyway. He knew this was where all the money and jewellery would be kept, but he'd hoped to wander around the rooms unseen and at his leisure but obviously that was not to be. Stealthily he stopped at the top of the stairs and looked around. Instantly he spied the strange singing woman sitting on the side of her large magnificent bed and cradling what looked like a large glass of scotch in her hands. He saw that she was caressing it, stroking it, talking to it as though it were a baby.

He must have moved ever so slightly because she turned her head towards him.

Peggy gasped at the sight of the stranger standing in her doorway but she retained enough presence of mind to return the glass of scotch carefully to the bedside table.

As he approached her, their eyes locked, and she started to make strange whimpering sounds as he began to speak sharply to her.

'Wo ist das geld?' 'Where is the money fraulein?'

Peggy couldn't speak, she snivelled at first but then a sudden violent wailing emerged from somewhere deep inside her and Hans realised he had no choice but to deal with her harshly. He stood before her, watching her distress with frustration, before he finally slapped her face hard, which had the immediate result of stopping her noise for a few seconds but then, as he bent down to grab her wrists, she began to scream. He looked around quickly for something, anything he could use to shut her up. He spied a bundle of silken scarves piled in an untidy heap across the back of a nearby chaise longue and they gave him an idea. He quickly grabbed a couple of the scarves and whilst holding her wrists together with one hand, he used his other hand to stuff one of the scarves roughly inside her mouth. He had trouble holding on to her as she began to struggle and gasp for breath and as her hands became free she clawed at him wildly. He quickly grabbed a second scarf winding it tightly around her head to hold the first scarf in place inside her mouth. Once the outer scarf was secured with a double knot at the back of her head he grabbed hold of her hands again. Blood was trickling down from the corners of her mouth but he was annoyed rather than sympathetic. Why had she made so much noise, it was her fault, she'd made him do it!

He clamped down hard on his remorse. He didn't care about her, she was the enemy. He'd waited too long to escape from this *'drecksloch'*, this English shithole he'd found himself in all these months and now it was time to take action. He was sure that somewhere in this house there was fine jewellery and cash, that all important commodity, to pay for his passage out of there.

He stood back and looked at the woman again thoughtfully, she was silent and sombre, but could he trust her to remain that way? He bent forward to touch her but instantly she recoiled, attempting to break free from him once more and make her escape. Like a caged animal her instinct for survival was intense, but instantly he stopped her in her tracks and grabbed hold of her flailing arms. Cupping both of his hands around her elbows he hoisted her backwards on to the bed, lodging her there with his own body forcing her into a sitting position against the wooden headboard. He needed to make sure she couldn't move again and so he tugged at the silken belt around her dressing gown. When it became loose he tied one end of it tightly around her wrist attaching the other end to the beautifully carved finial post at the corner of the elaborate headboard. Grabbing another thin scarf from the chaise longue, he tied it tightly round her other wrist, before moving swiftly round to the opposite side of the bed and attaching the end of it to the other finial.

As Hans stood away from the bed, he admired his handy work, congratulating himself on a job well done. The woman was now sitting upright, gagged, and with both arms held aloft by the bed posts. Her chest was heaving and she continued to stare at him with a terrified, wary expression. But at least, he was relieved to see, she had become passive and submissive. Hans continued to watch her through hooded eyes. She was a fine looking woman and he smiled as he walked up to her, snatching at the half empty bottle of scotch, before topping up her glass. He held the glass up to her as if in salute and then he took a large swig before replacing both the bottle and the glass back on to the bedside cupboard.

Perhaps a peace offering was needed he thought and he quickly found a soft pillow to insert gently into the small of her back for comfort. He wasn't completely callous, he consoled himself, as he turned his back on her again and began his search.

Peggy sat on the bed in abject fear, her mind spiralling with dreadful thoughts of imminent foreboding, every one of her senses was now fully alert, almost as though she'd been doused in a vat of ice cold water and become suddenly, inexplicably sober.

The scruffy vagrant had appeared in her bedroom at a timely moment just before she'd lifted the glass of scotch to her mouth ready to commence her second bender of the night. Or perhaps it would have been better for her if she had managed to consume more scotch, it might have numbed her senses and made the ordeal less terrifying.

After replacing the scotch to the bedside table she'd been sober enough to offer up a silent prayer that her worst nightmare was not about to materialise, but it had all been in vain. As the intruder towered over her and she'd looked up into his dirty desperate face she had let out a sudden fearful sob. An unfamiliar guttural sound had swiftly followed, coming from a region so deep inside of her that she didn't even know she possessed it, it was a wailing sound, like an animal in pain, and all the while her gaze was fixed on those menacing black eyes, coming ever closer to her, and informing her that this man was definitely not her friend.

As she watched him, from her inhibited and uncomfortable position on the bed, moving steadfastly around her bedroom, plundering and ransacking every drawer and cupboard, her tears had flowed freely with self-pity and a sense of hopeless vulnerability.

Where was Tom, she thought in anguish, please Tom, come back home and help me. But as she wept for her wellbeing, she came to realise that truly she didn't care what the reprobate took, as long as he left her alone now, and she stayed alive

As far as she was concerned he could take anything he wanted. Her fear in that moment had brought home to her how shallow her existence had been and how material possessions come to mean nothing when your life is in danger. She thought back over just how much of her life she'd wasted. She didn't want to die, she realised, she wanted to live, and now she prayed fervently for this man's mercy. After all her pretentious worshipping at chapel, for once, this night, she really meant it, and she made a promise to the almighty that she would give up her drinking and her bad ways if only she might be allowed to live.

Hans continued his search, going from room to room, moving along the corridor systematically, collecting treasures as he went, gold chains, necklaces, rings and bracelets, he took them all!

On returning to the bedroom Peggy recognised her black velvet bag in his hands, it was bulging and presumably full of all her fine jewellery, she hoped he was happy with his findings and that now he might be on his way out, but her ordeal was apparently not over as he stood in the doorway of her bedroom and began to shout at her, angry words, which had no meaning. She couldn't understand his dialect, not that she could answer him anyway, her mouth was sore from the chafing, and so she just watched him as he continued to search her room. What on earth was he looking for, she wondered?

Suddenly at the back of the large wardrobe, behind a row of her husband's expensive suits, Hans found it. Tucked in the corner of the wardrobe was a small safe-like cupboard and as he looked round at her he pointed to it smugly. Peggy frowned in confusion, while Hans was instantly gleeful. He couldn't believe his luck! He knew there would be a safe hidden somewhere in this impressive house. After manoeuvring a jagged knife, plundered from the kitchen, inside the padlock, he eventually sprung the locking mechanism, and as Peggy watched in confusion from her position on the bed, she became dumbfounded as the intruder helped himself to what looked like hundreds of pounds, all rolled up and bound together, on the shelves of the safe which he took and placed enthusiastically inside the bag with the jewellery. When the bag was full he carried on filling his coat pockets with the remaining bundles. All Peggy could do was sit and watch, her eyes wide, staring and incredulous, never having known that all that money had been stored in their house, right under her nose!

A sudden noise from downstairs made them both start! It was the front door! *Verdammt,* thought Hans, the husband!

Hans quickly left the main bedroom and went to hide in the smaller adjacent room, the one he'd discovered earlier which overlooked the road. As he waited, just behind the door, he looked around and took in the contents of the room once more. It was more or less empty, but he noticed that it had been decorated as a nursery, the only furniture was a small abandoned crib in one corner and a box of dusty toys tucked neatly beneath it.

Hans assumed correctly that it was the husband who'd returned and so he waited patiently for him to arrive upstairs. He waited and waited, for some considerable time, wondering what on earth the man was doing down there, not coming up at once to see his wife. When there was no sign of him Hans became unsure as to what he should do next? All seemed quiet but if he tried to use the stairs to escape he might meet the man half way up. The shotgun he'd discovered on his search of the house was held snug in his hands. He'd found it propped up in the kitchen and had quickly slung it over his shoulder in delight. At last he had a weapon, he thought, and one which might come in useful if he ever found himself in a tight spot, like now, he grinned, grasping hold of it possessively! He recalled the argument he'd had with Stefan over the farmer's rifle they'd seen sitting in the cart, and he was pleased he didn't have to justify his actions to anyone anymore. As he looked out over the road, he realised the windows were very high, far too high for him to jump to the ground, well, not without injury, he concluded prudently!

While he was considering his options he heard a loud noise from the main bedroom. Damn, he thought, she must have been able to reach something, probably that glass of scotch he'd been meaning to finish off, but it had slipped his mind. She must have somehow knocked it to the floor as a warning to her husband downstairs. Damn, he cursed himself, he should have moved everything out of her reach, too late now though he realised!

In a matter of seconds Tom Algar arrived at the top of the stairs. Hans watched him covertly as he walked across the landing to stand, shocked and speechless, at the doorway of the main bedroom. Moving swiftly out of his hiding place Hans raised the butt of the shotgun and brought it down heavily on to the back of the man's head.

For a few seconds Tom swayed on the spot, one arm rising up in front of him, as though he were reaching out to Peggy, and then he dropped abruptly to the ground.

Hans gazed at his victim, lying motionless on the bedroom floor, watching as a small pool of blood escaped from his wound. As the crimson puddle seeped into the wooden floorboards beneath the man's head, Hans bent down to feel for a pulse, strangely relieved to know that the man with the moustache was still alive, for murder had not been his intention that day.

As he looked across at the woman on the bed, he could see she was visibly shaking, still fighting against her ties, staring at him wildly from her place on the bed, but all he could manage to say to her was, 'sorry Miss Frau,' and with that, he turned away from her and left.

After reaching the front door, Hans wrenched it open, leaping from top to bottom of the marbled stone steps outside in one bound, gleeful that he had successfully completed yet another mission at the affluent address in Kirkley Cliff Road. Clutching his reward tightly, he ran hell for leather, down the street and on towards the seafront.

There was just one dark cloud of shame hanging over his head which threatened to tarnish his accomplishment that night. But as he held on tight to the black velvet bag, full to the brim with fine jewellery, plus the large amount of cash he'd found in the safe, he couldn't help grinning to himself, and all of a sudden the cloud and his conscience cleared.

CHAPTER TWENTY FOUR

Ellen paced up and down in her warm sitting room, glancing now and again at the fading embers of the fire, which revealed to her just how long she'd been waiting for Alice to return home. Her eldest daughter was still out, and it was very late indeed realised Ellen, as she looked for the umpteenth time at the clock on the mantelpiece. It was now chiming half past midnight and all she could think of was Tom Algar and his stark warning earlier that evening.

If only Frank were here she thought to herself. He would know what to do. He would surely go out in search of Alice but where would he even begin? She had absolutely no idea where Alice might be!

Another concern was the missing food. She'd noticed that rations had been disappearing recently but Tom Algar's caution hadn't really helped. When Frank was away, she felt particularly vulnerable, always locking up securely at night, taking her responsibility for the girls' safety very seriously. The only possible conclusion was that one of the girls was taking the food.

She'd mentioned it to Katy who'd answered straight away that it wasn't her and Ellen believed her, her younger daughter could always be trusted to tell the truth, and so this left only Alice as the culprit. But why would Alice take food from the cupboard and if it wasn't for herself then who was it for? Ellen began to pace up and down the room again. Her thoughts were becoming more frantic, whirling around her head in an erratic, uncontrolled manner, her anxiety increasing until in the end she decided that 'action' was the only way forward. She couldn't stand this waiting any longer and so she made a sudden decision to go out in search of Alice herself. Her imagination was spiralling, beginning to run riot, Alice could be lying in a ditch, stabbed in the back by some criminal who'd taken advantage of her, who'd left her bleeding to death, and even now she was calling out for her mother, a sob rose in Ellen's throat, she couldn't bear to think of it!

Ellen went upstairs and tiptoed in to Katy's bedroom but as she moved closer to the bed a small furry mound at the foot of the bedcovers began to stir. Trix's soft brown ears pricked up at the sound of Ellen's stockinged feet stepping quietly over the rug and he began to whimper as though he knew something was wrong. Ellen stroked his head and whispered to him 'all is well my little Trix; just you stay here and look after Katy for me.'

She rubbed the shape of her daughter's shoulder buried deep beneath the covers, 'I'm just popping out Katy' she whispered, 'I'll lock up before I go, but while I'm out, please don't let anyone into the house, ok?'

Katy grunted sleepily from under her blankets and eiderdown but as the portent of her mother's instructions began to permeate her slumber she slowly surfaced from the bedcovers and turned to face her mother. Katy squinted up at Ellen in the darkness, confused at being woken up so strangely in the middle of the night. She immediately remembered the last time it had happened, right at the beginning of the war, during that first raid, the noise had been dreadful, the sirens wailing eerily, and the sound of aircraft buzzing overhead which meant they all had to leave their beds and rush across the lawn to that horrible shelter at the bottom of the garden, damp, dingy and smelly! She began to panic, worried that the war had started all over again, and that they needed to take cover once more!

In her bewilderment, she complained to her mother in confusion, 'what's going on mum, what's all the fuss about?'

but Ellen was already standing at the bedroom door 'please don't worry my dear, it's nothing, I just need to go out, I won't be long' and then she blew her younger daughter a kiss before pulling the bedroom door shut firmly behind her.

CHAPTER TWENTY FIVE

After what seemed like an eternity to Peggy, but was in fact only ten minutes or so, Tom Algar finally began to emerge from the dark void of oblivion his mind had sent him to, as he struggled to regain consciousness. With great difficulty he opened his eyes to see only vague blurry shapes and shadows around him. But as his world of darkness gradually receded he became aware of a searing pain which began to throb intermittently at the back of his head. He lifted up his hand with great difficulty and touched the wound gingerly. As he brought his fingers round and held them in front of his face, he forced his eyes to focus on the dark scarlet blood that was smeared there. That's not good, he thought to himself, but realised with relief that he was able to move his limbs and gradually he sat himself up and began to take in his surroundings.

As he looked across the room, towards the bed, he saw Peggy, still bound and strapped heartlessly to the dark wooden headboard, and he swore at the sight, but peculiarly he found himself rejoicing that she was alive! He stood, slowly and cautiously, but, as he rose to his feet, the room began to rotate and swim around him, so that he thought he might be sick, but gradually the sensation eased and when he finally brought himself up to his full height, the dizziness seemed to diminish and his equilibrium was restored.

He walked slowly over to the bed in a strange, sickly stupor. He felt as though he was drunk and his legs were like heavy wooden logs that he was dragging with him at each and every step, until finally he reached the bed and sat down heavily next to his wife. As she looked over to him for reassurance he lifted up his hand to touch her cheek, immediately cursing his thoughtlessness when he saw his own blood smeared across her pale skin. He quickly rubbed it away with his thumb in an attempt to remove it from her tear stained face. As they studied each other, in the silent aftermath, tears were flowing freely again from Peggy's eyes and he saw within them an emotion that he hadn't seen in a long time. Finally he tried to shrug off his stupor and began to deliberate on the job in hand which was to release her from her torture. Slowly he reached up and with unsteady hands he began to loosen the ties from the back of her head. Once he'd pulled the silk scarf from her mouth Peggy began to cough and then to whimper and finally she lamented passionately, 'oh Tom, Tom, my darling, thank god you're alive' she cried 'you were lying there for the longest time, I thought he'd killed you, I thought you were dead!'

Tom looked at her but he felt unable to speak, he opened his mouth, but nothing would come out. He felt fuzzy as though his mouth and his brain were not coordinated and so he remained silent and turned slightly, before reaching up laboriously to the bed post finial, trying to untie the satin belt which had been attached there so securely. He struggled! He couldn't do it and so instead he grappled with the bindings around her wrists which had also been tied extremely tightly. Finally he was successful and, as the bindings became loose, Peggy sighed and moaned with relief as her hands came down into her lap and she could examine the damage. Both of her wrists were badly grazed and bruised and her mouth was also slightly swollen and sore but other than that she seemed unharmed.

All of a sudden Peggy wrapped her arms around her husband, 'oh Tom, Tom, thank god you're alive, we're both alive!'

She continued to kiss every part of his face, weeping uncontrollably, but Tom found he could not respond. He sat in silence, enveloped in his wife's arms, his whole body felt heavy as lead and after a matter of seconds his brain shut down once more and he passed out cold.

CHAPTER TWENTY SIX

Keith looked at Alice in horror, 'are you mad!' he replied to her question, 'you're crazy, there is no way I could do that, what are you asking me, you want me to help the enemy?'

'He's not the enemy,' Alice reasoned with him calmly, 'not anymore! The war is over isn't it? The Germans have surrendered and I just want to help him get home to his family. He didn't want to fight in the war any more than we did, Keith. When you meet him you'll understand. He's not much older than us! Try and imagine what it would be like if the boot was on the other foot. If it was you trying to get back to England from another country, if you'd been captured and managed to escape, you'd want someone to help you get home, wouldn't you?

'Well, yes, I suppose so, but....'

'Look, you told me that you could hide goods on board your ship, in the cargo hold, or maybe in the lifeboat, surely you could hide a person in there too?'

'Yes, but if I got found out Alice, it would be a court martial for me, you know that don't you?'

'Yes, I know, but it won't come to that, if your goods can remain hidden on board ship then so can he. I really believe this is the right thing to do Keith, it's the Christian thing to do, I know you're not a bad person, we've all done things we're not proud of, at some time or another, but this is your opportunity to do something good, this poor young man just wants to get home and we're his only chance.

Keith sighed, a long sigh, and then afterwards he was silent for a while, scratching his head and pacing around in random circles thinking about her crazy plan and its possible implications. It was very risky, he concluded, but he liked Alice, he really did, and he didn't want her to think badly of him. If the worst happened and the guy was discovered, he supposed that all he would have to do was just to pretend he knew nothing about it! As he weighed up the odds he reckoned there was a good chance they could get away with it. He turned to face her again.

'Do you promise this is just between you and me then? If it gets out we're both done for, you know that, don't you?'

'I promise, cross my heart,' she reassured him, making an elaborate physical sign across her wet woollen coat.

'Ok, where is he then?' asked Keith, sweeping his eyes around the deserted docks looking for her friend warily but also making sure no one was watching them.

'I'll just go and get him' she answered, with an impish smile, 'oh and Keith.... thank you,' she added in a whisper, suddenly appreciating the risk he was taking for her, perhaps he wasn't so bad after all, she thought to herself, and on impulse she reached up to kiss him on the cheek, before walking away and heading over to the pile of crates where she'd left Stefan.

After walking around the crates, so many times she lost count, calling out Stefan's name feverishly and earnestly into the foggy darkness, she finally gave up, coming to the disappointing and undeniable conclusion that Stefan had obviously scarpered!

CHAPTER TWENTY SEVEN

As Ellen walked dismally towards town, the freezing mist enveloped her, its icy fingers penetrating her outer garments mercilessly, but she didn't seem to notice the cold, her mind was still whirling with possibilities, and she had absolutely no idea which direction she should be heading. This was probably a daft idea she concluded as she began to fret about Katy whom she'd now left alone and vulnerable at home. '*Who'd be a mother*', she asked herself compassionately.

At Kirkley Parade she decided to turn right towards the Army Training Centre at Claremont Pier. The pier seemed very quiet now, ruined and desolate, and not at all how it used to be before the war. She recalled those carefree times when the pier was full of people, dressed in their finery. It had been built as a pleasure pier, allowing visitors to access the sea view, without having to traipse across the sand or get their feet wet. She recalled the wonderful sight of the paddle steamers as they docked regularly at the end of the pier, their huge chimney stacks spewing out smoke as they stopped at the T-shaped landing head. Tourists would wait there for trips to Southwold, Gorleston and Great Yarmouth, and for only seven shillings or so, but it was a whole different world back then, a world of peace and happiness. As the threat of a German invasion became more credible, the royal engineers were instructed to blast a hole in the pier, just in case, because there was always a chance it would be considered a useful landing spot for the German navy.

Ellen stopped her reminiscing about the past and suddenly remembered why she was out, walking along the seafront in the middle of the night, in such frightful weather. She was searching for her missing daughter and her inner panic surged again, those dreadful images springing to the forefront of her mind once more, and immediately she was spurred on, walking more briskly along the promenade and towards the South Pier.

The sporadic sound of fog horns resonated around her and the atmosphere turned more cold and bleak than she could ever remember. The forlorn wailing of the sirens seemed to match her mood which was becoming more melancholy by the minute. Intuitively she sensed her daughter had already come this way, perhaps earlier on in the evening, some sixth sense seemed to be guiding her towards the north end of town but she couldn't really understand why, as all the dances and youthful gatherings would surely be taking place in the town centre. And anyway, she realised, all the dance halls would surely be closed by now, it was long past midnight, the normal time for closing, but still she followed her intuition and continued heading in a northerly direction, hoping that she might stumble across her daughter along the way.

As Ellen arrived at the South Pier she leant over the wall, searching the beach for any sign of a gathering. She looked across the wide expanse of sand, which had only recently been cleared of all the barbed wire defences and 'Keep Out' signs. It was now a large clear area for people to use. She noticed someone had put out a small row of deckchairs, bright stripy seats that sat snug against the wall, enticing people to come down there, a hopeful and reassuring sign that the area was now safe to use and at long last residents and visitors could enjoy the seaside once more.

She wondered if Punch and Judy's stripy show tent would return, she really hoped so, her girls had always loved to sit on the sand and watch the puppet show. They used to cry with laughter at the crazy antics of Punch and his long suffering wife Judy, and of course the scary crocodile, always coming up after the sausages! She wiped away a nostalgic tear with her gloved hand, so many happy memories from a time when the children were small, and she hoped and prayed there would be many more good times to come.

As she walked away from the South Pier, she headed off towards the swing bridge, looking through the mist towards Lake Lothing when suddenly she caught sight of a solitary figure walking steadily across the bridge towards her, head down and hunched against the cold, the figure was gradually getting nearer. Ellen stopped still and caught her breath, as her heart began to thump loudly in her chest, surely it must be Alice? And then, yes, suddenly she knew it, it was her daughter! As tears began to prick behind her eyes she clasped her hands together in a silent prayer of thanks, before running, as fast as she could, towards her daughter, calling out her name in the ever thickening fog.

'Alice, Alice' she called, and suddenly Alice heard her desperate cry and looked up, her unhappy mood lifting a notch as she watched her mother's form coming towards her in the distance. Ellen's anxious voice was carried to her across the muted airwaves and in that moment Alice knew her mother was the lifeline she so desperately needed. She clung to the thought of her mother's arms soon to be wrapped tightly around her and it was with a relief and happiness she'd never realised before. Alice waved a cheery hand, which wasn't at all how she felt, but she wanted to alleviate her mother's fear which she knew would be considerable for it was almost tangible. As her mother's distraught face came into view she knew, shamefully, how worried her mother must have been for her safety at this time of night.

As soon as they came together, they hugged each other tight, both doing their best to control their emotions. As they separated Ellen took one long look at her daughter's face and knew something was seriously wrong. She hugged her daughter again and then she held up the bag she'd been carrying which contained some warm boots and mittens that she'd placed by the fire before leaving the house and which she knew her daughter would need after being out so long in the cold. She got them out of her bag and insisted that Alice put them on. Alice admitted she was cold, in fact she was shivering quite violently, and Ellen could see that her daughter was in dire need of some serious maternal cosseting.

Alice began to feel better as soon as she'd placed the boots on her feet and the warm mittens on her hands and her whole body started to thaw instantly. She hugged her mother close, whilst at the same time trying to hide the tears which were suddenly sliding down her face, as the reality of her ordeal finally began to hit home.

She realised now with hindsight that she'd been swept up on some sort of crusade. She'd really wanted to help Stefan out of his predicament but she realised now just how much danger she'd put herself in. There was no way she could tell her mother what had really happened that night and she knew she was going to have to make up some story. There was no way round it; she was going to have to lie!

As they walked along the road, back towards home, Ellen comforted her daughter, offering soothing words and sounds as she continued to rub the warmth back into her. Ellen wouldn't ask Alice any questions tonight, she decided, not now, not yet. She was just relieved to know that her daughter was alive and well and safely back in her arms again, there would be plenty of time for questions, she decided, but only after a good night's sleep.

CHAPTER TWENTY EIGHT

Stefan had remained in his hiding place, dutifully concealed behind the wooden crates, just as Alice had instructed him. He'd overheard the conversation between Alice and her friend, the sailor, and initially he was excited at the thought that the ship could definitely be his way back home. However, the more he thought about it the more he realised he had a problem! Firstly he was aware that he was putting Alice into grave danger, which he definitely did not want to do, he'd become fond of Alice, she'd been a true friend to him and he didn't want her to end up in prison if they were discovered. Secondly, and probably rather more incredulously, he suddenly assumed a strong sense of duty towards his fellow comrade, Hans.

After they'd left the wreck, Stefan had mulled over what he'd seen inside the cabin. The socks that were hanging over the end of the unmade bed were a dead giveaway; he'd recognised them straight away as one of the few items handed out to prisoners at the camp. His relief at this revelation was immense for it solved a puzzle which Stefan had been pondering over for many months. Even at night it had invaded his dreams and on and off during the interminable days, he'd contemplated the conundrum, unable to stop himself fretting about what on earth had happened to Hans? Now, at last, he knew! Stefan had swiftly concluded that the old abandoned trawler must have proved a very satisfactory bolthole for his ex-comrade. Indeed, Hans had obviously done very well for himself; he'd been perfectly safe all this time, hidden away inside the old wreck.

Strangely, upon this discovery Stefan become aware of a sense of responsibility towards his comrade. Why should he escape himself and leave his friend behind? He suddenly felt an urgent need to find his fellow countryman and yes, he thought to himself, he would like to think of Hans as his friend after all they'd been through together. Somehow he needed to find the strength to row back to the wreck, to find him, involve him in the plan, and let him know that after all this time there was indeed a credible escape route back home to Germany. He'd pieced together the conversation between Alice and her sailor friend and was overjoyed when he learned the ship was headed for Zeebrugge and then on to Hamburg the very next morning. How fortuitous, he thought, not caring that it would mean a long and difficult voyage, stowed away in a lifeboat. He would happily undergo any form of torture in order to return home to his loved ones.

He reckoned they'd have enough time to get back and sneak on board the frigate overnight whilst it lay quietly berthed at Lake Lothing. He'd not seen any guards on duty at the dockside and he was convinced it could be done easily. Stefan became resolute; there was no need to involve anyone else, he just needed to find Hans and persuade him to come back with him, collect a few provisions from the wreck, and with luck they could be hidden on board the ship before dawn. Hopefully, they would then be able to remain undiscovered until the ship docked on the other side of the channel.

In no time at all he found himself climbing down the ladder at the harbour wall and securing himself inside the rowing boat once more. Using the oar as a lever he pushed the boat away from the wooden decking, allowing it to float away from the rest of the boats, and into the centre of the harbour. An eerie silence had settled in the gloom, even the hollow moaning of the horns seemed to have stopped for a while, and all was peaceful within the foggy darkness. Unseen, Stefan rowed in the direction of the harbour mouth, smoothly and efficiently, he steered the craft out to sea once more, the only sound heard was the slapping and shushing of the waves being swept aside by the bow.

Suddenly the solitude and silence was broken by a noisy onslaught of sirens and bells! Stefan looked up and watched as a row of lights seemed to be coming his way, heading towards the harbour. In a matter of seconds a cavalcade of cars and motorbikes came into view, rushing along the road and carrying with them a cacophony of sound which signified they were emergency vehicles, apparently in a desperate race against time. Stefan's heart thumped loudly in his chest as he watched them coming nearer and with baited breath he crouched as low as he could inside the small craft for fear of being seen. He waited patiently, not daring to move, keeping a covert eye on the noisy procession as it continued its journey over the bridge, before finally moving away from him, towards the town centre. As the noise of the sirens gradually reduced to a distant hum, he relaxed, and as he picked up the oars once more he found he could breathe again, deeply, in and out, with utter relief. It seemed, at least for now, they were not looking for him.

He picked up the oars and started to row. This time he got into his stride more easily, moving the oars swiftly, backwards and forwards in a smooth motion, heading speedily towards the harbour mouth and out to sea again. However, he reflected sadly, this time he was alone, there was no Alice by his side, to guide him.

With only his thoughts for company he focused on the task in hand and headed north once more, back towards the wreck.

CHAPTER TWENTY NINE

Over the winter Hans had often thought about Stefan, but it was never in a kind-hearted way. He blamed Stefan for his present predicament and considered his fellow escapee nothing more than an out and out coward. The way he'd had to cajole and persuade him to do anything vaguely risky had told him that. He was sure Stefan would have been happy to just sit and rot in that prison camp for all eternity!

As soon as they'd arrived in Lowestoft, Hans had felt constrained by Stefan's warped view of right and wrong, and quickly decided it was best for them to separate and for him to go his own way. His reasoning behind the split had been clear, in his mind anyway, he needed to get away from Stefan, for his own survival! He was repulsed by Stefan's spineless attitude and it had finally pushed him to the limits of his patience. The farmer's rifle had been lying there, abandoned in the cart, with no one around to see them take it, and in Hans' mind the weapon had been a godsend, too fortuitous to ignore, but Stefan had talked him out of it, pulling him away earnestly until he'd persuaded Hans to leave it where it lay. This had grated on Hans until eventually he'd come to the conclusion that Stefan was a fool. They could have been back in Germany by now. If Stefan thought they could get away from this place on a ship, without a weapon, he was seriously deranged. In fact he was sure they would need either weapons or money to be able to threaten or bribe their way out of there. And of course those were the two things they didn't have.

From that moment on he decided he would make his own decisions, he would be better off, he thought, and so he'd left his friend in the dead of night and entered Lowestoft town alone. But soon he'd realised, apart from a few fishing vessels heading to Iceland, there were no ships leaving port for Europe and it was then that his own hunt for a hiding place began.

As he'd jogged along the sea front one cold night, stealthily crossing the swing bridge and limping onwards towards the north end of town he'd looked around furtively for somewhere to hide.

In the darkness, on a quiet stretch of shore just beyond the beach village, a ship's mast had loomed up in the darkness. He'd walked further along the sea wall to get a better look and there he'd found it, washed up on the beach and leaning to one side was the wreck of an old fishing trawler, which appeared to have been left stranded on the sand. The wreck was almost obscured behind swathes of swirling barbed wire which looked virtually impenetrable but Hans knew that if he could find a way through the tangled mess the discarded wreck would prove an ideal bolt-hole, safely hidden away from prying eyes

Hans surveyed the concertina wire, his keen eyes searching for a possible way through. He was not put off by the impossible task, he was desperate and daring and more than that he was willing to take a chance and, jumping swiftly down on to the sand, he began to weave his way through it. With persistence and determination he fought his way through the spiky enclosure, using a stick and a pocketful of stones, he laid a safe trail as he went, eventually finding his way through to the old trawler by pure luck and fortitude.

After clambering on board the vessel, he crossed the deck to the hatch, heading down the steps into the gloomy crew's quarters. He was not hopeful of much being found down there and had been amazed to find a dry bed, a kitchen of sorts, a few crates of salted fish, a supply of canned food plus more than a dozen large bottles of stout. He couldn't believe his luck, convinced that providence must have smiled down on him yet again, playing her part in his fortunate find, and not forgetting of course, his Adler tag motif. The badge of honour, handed to him by the fuehrer himself, which had always brought him luck. He would touch the badge daily, repeatedly reverently, thankful that it had helped him find this temporary home, and knowing the old trawler would serve him well through the cold winter months to come.

However, after a while, the store of tinned food began to run low and Hans had no choice but to head into town. He tried to avoid going out in the day for fear of being seen but in the dead of night he'd surface from his hiding place and carefully worm his memorized pathway through the barbed wire barricade and out into the silent streets. Recently he'd begun to remain outside the wreck for longer and longer periods of time, in his search for decent provisions, and this had put him in grave danger of being caught. There had been minimal clothing on board the old wreck apart from a few sou'westers and oilskins, but these protective garments had served him well on his trips into town. They'd shielded him not only from the spiky barbed wire but also from the relentless icy rain which lashed down on him frequently from the low brooding clouds above. Under the cover of darkness his face was successfully obscured from view beneath the sou'wester and this had allowed him to scuttle around the town pretty much unnoticed, while he pilfered from rubbish bins, just as his comrade Stefan was doing, only at the other end of town.

In the dead of winter, lonely and hungry, he'd occasionally regretted his split from Stefan. He could feel himself withdrawing as a person! Without human contact he was gradually becoming a lost soul, a lone wolf, and he and Stefan, well they just had different points of view, that's all. He had no idea where Stefan might be now, perhaps they should have stuck it out, and found a way to arrive back home together, as heroes.

But there were other darker times when he'd recall his friend's pathetic attitude and he'd blame Stefan and Stefan alone for their plight, if only he'd bothered to check the fuel on that plane before they'd taken off, there'd been other planes on the strip; it could all have turned out so differently.

He contemplated whether Stefan might have handed himself back in to the authorities and was sitting in some warm cell right now, with food in his belly. But the worst times were those nagging moments of doubt and despair when he thought perhaps Stefan had been the lucky one, that he'd managed to escape, and was already back home in Germany.

CHAPTER THIRTY

When the police vehicles had pulled up outside the house in Kirkley Cliff Road, they were followed swiftly by an ambulance. Their arrival was announced to all and sundry by bells and sirens, ringing and wailing at full pelt. The noise enticed many neighbours to spill out from their front doors to join the handful of onlookers who'd already congregated curiously outside the impressive abode, whispering and wondering what on earth might have happened to their esteemed and noble neighbours, the Algars.

In abject shock and disbelief they observed Tom Algar being carefully stretchered out of his house, his head bandaged and his body covered in blankets, while his wife Peggy was hunched over the stretcher walking along slowly beside him. Her weeping and wailing alone would have alerted the locals as she continued her noisy lament all the way across the street, holding on to his hand for dear life, not daring to let it slip from hers for a moment, even as he was being carefully loaded onto the waiting ambulance she held on tight. After Peggy was helped into the ambulance herself, she continued to sit and sob beside him, clinging on to his hand as though it were her only lifeline, while they sped along on their brief journey through the streets of Lowestoft towards the hospital at Tennyson Road. An escort of two police officers on motorbikes followed on behind, keen young officers anxious to take down witness statements from the victims, as soon as they were well enough, to try and get to the bottom of this nasty business.

Chief Inspector Taylor stood watching the proceedings from the doorway of the large town house in Kirkley Cliff Road. He stayed motionless in the murky shadows of the top step, a surly, solitary figure with a serious and thoughtful expression on his fifty nine year old face. He was snug and warm in his long belted overcoat of dark grey wool, his flat-brimmed trilby positioned securely upon his balding, brylcreemed head. He waited   alone,   except   for   the   companionable   and contemplative cigarette he'd allowed himself, before going back inside. Not long after the emergency vehicles had left the premises he'd watched the last of the neighbours, still agitated about the strange goings on, return reluctantly to the comparative safety of their homes. Only when all was quiet, did he stamp out his cigarette and step back inside the large hallway, shutting the door behind him.

He stood silently on the elegant fringed mat, just inside the front door, his keen eyes assessing the entire area around him. The aftermath of a crime scene held potency somehow, an aura, an impression of what had gone before, if only the walls could talk he thought to himself wryly. He tried to envisage what had happened there earlier that night. There were no signs of a break in, which was rather strange in itself, he thought, and he wondered if Mrs Algar had unwittingly let the man in. He knew he needed to find a clue or a piece of evidence that the intruder might have inadvertently left behind, to help him find and identify this scoundrel. There had been serious wrongdoing in that bedroom upstairs, Taylor knew it, and it turned him cold at the thought. Mrs Algar's pale face had said it all, she didn't have to say a word, her wide frightened eyes and bloodless pallor had given it away. Verbally she had been almost incoherent, a gibbering wreck, but he could tell, he'd seen enough trauma throughout the war. God only knows what had transpired in that bedroom and he hoped Mrs Algar would receive all the appropriate care and attention she needed at the hospital.

He hadn't yet got to the bottom of which crime had actually been committed here. Of course aggravated burglary had immediately sprung to mind but he'd managed to decipher from Mrs Algar's gibberish that the blackguard had made off with Tom's shotgun. When he took into account the fact that Tom's nasty injury was most likely incurred by the scoundrel hitting him with the butt of it, suddenly that deed alone catapulted the crime into an entirely different category, so that now he feared he was dealing with a violent armed robbery. It had quickly become imperative that the culprit was captured very soon, before he killed someone.

He couldn't help wishing they'd taken a bit more interest in Tom Algar's earlier report of an intruder entering his premises, the one he'd lodged only a few days before, for it was indeed a known fact that after one successful burglary an intruder is highly likely to come back and target the same house again. Taylor took a deep breath and went slowly up the stairs, step by step, searching every corner and every crevice along the way for anything the intruder might have dropped in his rush to get out of the house, but he could see nothing.

He walked across the landing and entered the bedroom carefully. He bent down to examine the blood stained floor just inside the doorway which was almost certainly from Tom's head wound where he'd been struck initially. He walked over to examine the blood stained bedcovers where apparently Tom had managed to set his wife free from her bondage before summarily falling unconscious for the second time, sprawled across the bed, right next to her!

Luckily because Mrs Algar had been freed she'd been able to make her way across the room and open the bedroom window, managing to lean out over the windowsill and call for help or rather 'scream at the top of her lungs' so he'd been told, which instantly raised the alarm.

As Taylor surveyed the obvious disarray around him, he trod carefully over the debris, trying not to disturb anything as he continued to look for clues. The soft silken tie from Mrs's Algar's robe was still attached to the headboard and hung down from the bed post. The gossamer scarves lay together in a heap on the bed, one of which had apparently been used sadistically and cruelly to cram inside the poor woman's mouth, and now there it sat, soft and wet, on top of one of the pillows. Many jewellery boxes were scattered about, some were strewn across the dressing table and others sat on various cabinets and shelves, but all of them were lying open and empty. As Taylor peered inside the wardrobe he saw the small safe-like cupboard which now stood open and empty with the door ajar. The intruder had literally ransacked the place; his desperation and intent was written all over the scene, he must have covered every inch in his search for jewels and cash, whoever this guy was he was a wild one, an evil villain, willing to take risks. His frenzied attack had left Tom Algar unconscious and his poor wife traumatised.

Bending down once more, he searched avidly under the bed, not touching anything, just using his eyes, sweeping them from side to side as he scrutinised the luxurious Oriental rug which covered the expansive floor beneath it. His eyes swept around the rug's fringed border and he examined the wooden flooring within each strand until suddenly something caught his attention. He reached out to retrieve a small object. As he picked it up he placed it carefully on to the palm of his hand to examine it. It appeared to be a stitched motif, a badge of some kind, depicting an eagle, but what startled him most as he studied it closely was that the eagle held something in its talons. His stomach churned as he realised what it was, it was a swastika, and immediately he recognised the motif as an insignia from a German uniform, and more precisely a Luftwaffe uniform? What on earth was it doing here in this room he pondered, feeling increasingly uneasy, whilst also becoming more and more fearful as to what kind of criminal they were dealing with here? Who on earth had invaded this house on two occasions that very week?

CHAPTER THIRTY ONE

Stefan continued to row the small wooden boat slowly and deliberately towards the wreck, even though his arms were beginning to give out, he carried on relentlessly. The mist remained dense but the tilley lamp had proved a godsend, its orange glow lighting up the immediate surroundings, radiating a warm comforting atmosphere within the boat and surprisingly the abandoned wreck came into view much sooner than Stefan had anticipated. Once more the hull rose up before him and he manoeuvred the small craft into the same position beneath it. When it had been moored securely he pulled out the small haversack from the centre of the boat, it was the only bag he had left after deciding to dispose of the others. He'd weighed the rest down with rocks, and tipped them over the side of the boat into the sea, hoping they'd never be found. With luck he wouldn't need any of it any more.

He decided to leave the Tilley lamp in the boat, hoping fervently that Hans would be back at the wreck by now and they would be leaving together very soon. He moved softly and stealthily across the sand-pebbled beach to the opposite side of the trawler before attempting to heave himself up once more through the railings.

He found it much harder this time as he had no friendly companion to assist him and when he thought of Alice and all they'd been through together he became quite emotional, sad and ashamed that their friendship had had to end in this way, without a proper goodbye.

He was pretty exhausted, he realised, his arms had virtually no strength left in them, but eventually he managed to haul himself up through the railings and stood on the deck once more.

Picking up his small haversack, he slung it carefully over his shoulder, proceeding across the slippery deck towards the hatch.

At the top of the steps he stopped, wondering whether he ought to call out a warning to Hans, but swiftly deciding he didn't want to draw attention from any passersby. He laughed at the irony, as he proceeded to look across each side of the wreck and inland over the mass of barbed wire. Nothing stirred of any consequence and all around was deathly quiet, apart from the dissonant chimes of the rigging. He doubted whether any person would be mad enough to venture out at this time of night, in such god awful weather, if they didn't have to. The wreck was well hidden behind the density of the barbed wire, the only part of the vessel showing clearly above the rusty forest were its masts and the woodbine stack, still standing tall and proud, if a little lopsided. At this unearthly hour of the night it seemed the north beach was utterly devoid of people.

As Stefan looked up, across the grassy cliffs, everything in sight was coated in the grey murky mist but strange shapes were vaguely visible just below the brow line. He recognised them as a row of gun emplacements, abandoned and ghostlike and he realised that on a clear day the men sheltering inside them would have seen for miles out to sea from that vantage point. His mind conjured up images of the young men, their anxious faces fixed on the horizon as they stood watch, staring out avidly across the vastness of the ocean, watching and waiting for the enemy to approach. As Stefan's eyes adjusted to the greyness of the landscape he saw a further row of huge rectangular blocks at the brow of the hill, probably hastily installed, and what would have been an extremely effective defence against German tanks if they had ever landed at this point. The English had certainly been ready for an invasion, which of course had never taken place, and suddenly Stefan decided he was glad about that.

Bringing his mind swiftly back to the present, Stefan proceeded down the steps, slowly and cautiously, into the cabin below. As he reached the bottom step, a sudden loud noise rang out, catching him completely off guard. He heard and felt the blast almost simultaneously as it impacted his left shoulder, the shock and force knocked him right off his feet, so that in a split second he was lying stricken across the steps.

As he lay there, prostrate, stunned, and not daring to move, it dawned on him, of course, that he had been shot. Strangely, he felt no pain, and he began to wonder if this is what happened before death, that one's mind shuts down on the pain from this life, ready to be reborn, unscathed, into the next!

He slowly raised his hand to his shoulder where the blast had struck. He discovered a hole in the shoulder stitching of his heavy trench coat and was aware of a small amount of smoke escaping from it. As he prodded and pressed around the edges of the hole he could feel just a slight soreness coming from his skin underneath. A sensation of pain was slowly emerging but it was only mild and with a great sense of relief he realised he was not going to die. He'd obviously had a lucky escape for it seemed the shot had missed its mark and he'd not suffered any serious injury. Quickly gathering his senses, he realised that another shot might be heading his way very soon, and so he called out urgently into the darkness.

'Hans, Hans, ich bin es Stefan.'

Hans was waiting silently inside the gloom of the cabin. He had heard the sound of footsteps above him whilst sitting in the semi darkness, counting his stolen money and admiring the array of glittering treasure he'd successfully confiscated from the house at Kirkley Cliff Road. Realising the sound was definitely akin to someone coming on board, he was of course startled into action, sweeping everything off the wooden bench and into the velvet bag quickly. He feared the worst, for no one had ever approached the wreck in all the months he'd been living there. He quickly grabbed his gun, or rather Tom's gun, the one he'd taken along with all the money and jewels, and then he stood and waited, just out of sight, ready for what was to come.

As he watched the unwelcome visitor descending the steps towards him, he became certain he'd been discovered. Fearing the authorities were about to arrest him and take him back into custody, he pulled the trigger, deciding to fire the first shot, for there was no way he would let that happen, he would never surrender, to be incarcerated again? No, he'd rather die!

In the silence, and the growing affirmation that whoever he'd shot must surely be dead, he began to make plans as to how he might dispose of the body but then the urgent voice of his friend rang out to him from the darkness.

All his feigned bravado evaporated as an overwhelming feeling of relief overcame him. Still cautious though, he began to move forwards warily to check on his injured compatriot, to discover whether he'd injured him fatally but also, in a cynical vein of mistrust, to be reassured that Stefan had come alone. Hans looked down at his prostrate buddy and Stefan looked up at him warily but Hans stepped over his friend and with gun at the ready he moved swiftly past him and on up to the top of the steps to check that the deck and surrounding area was clear. When he was sure this was the case and there was no one else in tow he returned to Stefan bending down to check on his friend for any signs of injury.

'Est is ok Hans, mir geht es gut.... you missed!' Stefan gasped with a wry grin.

Before Stefan could speak again Hans grabbed him and dragged him roughly back inside the cabin. Heaving Stefan up onto the bed, he proceeded to yell into his face, *'Du Idiot! Was tun Sie hier?'* he demanded.

Stefan struggled to free himself from his friend's firm grip but his arms were pinned beneath him and Hans was holding him down using the entire weight of his body. Stefan could feel the power and strength of the man above him and realised, with some irritability, that Hans had apparently been surviving a lot better than he had. Hans' familiar face was a mere two inches away from his own, his eyes bulging with fear and irritation at Stefan's impromptu arrival. Stefan began pushing and shoving at Hans, using all of his remaining strength, to free himself from this madman oppressor, his so called friend, who had seemingly turned into someone else entirely while they'd been apart, a wild man he didn't recognise, and he continued to struggle for breath.

Eventually Hans released his hold and stood back but he continued to scowl rudely at his intruder. His privacy had been invaded, after so many months alone, and it was frightening to him. He was effectively a caged animal, alone in his dark den, aggressive and mistrustful, away from humankind for so long and he found himself unable to slip back into the way he once was.

Stefan sat up in disgust, feeling utterly affronted, drawing in deep ragged breaths and trying desperately to recover his senses. He'd come here to help his friend and he'd almost been killed for the favour! He looked down at the shotgun still gripped tightly in his hand, appalled that Hans had managed to appropriate such a weapon after all, and that he'd apparently been prepared to use it on impulse, to kill him in fact, without a second thought.

'I'm here to help you, *Du Idiot!*' English words came out of Stefan's mouth naturally, almost without realising it, he'd obviously been in England too long, he thought mournfully, but then he swiftly reverted to his mother tongue, *'willst du nach Deutschland?'*

Hans considered the question, of course he wanted to go home, and he quickly nodded his head sheepishly, his demeanour becoming less hostile. Stefan spoke again, more urgently this time, *'gut, ich habe einen plan! Funktioniert der funkmast?'*

At Hans' blank expression Stefan reached out and grabbed the khaki coloured haversack which still lay where it had fallen at the bottom of the steps. He carefully unbuckled the leather straps and opened up the canvas bag, taking out the radio telephone equipment hidden inside. He pointed up in the air, 'the radio mast, is it still working?' he asked Hans, but this time he didn't even bother to wait for an answer, there just wasn't time, and so he stood up and walked straight over to the radio apparatus, the small unit he'd spied on his earlier visit with Alice. The pieces of the jigsaw were finally falling into place, he told himself, as he pulled over the small stool and sat down before the ship's radio, which consisted of a transmitter and a receiver all tucked neatly into the corner of the cabin, beneath the ship's mast!

CHAPTER THIRTY TWO

In the hospital Tom was tucked up in a pristine white bed on a side ward and he seemed to be responding well to treatment. He was gradually recovering his ability to speak and to comprehend what people were saying to him. He'd suffered a serious concussion and several stitches had been required at the back of his head but now his headache seemed to be easing and he was feeling a whole lot better. Peggy sat on a firm chair beside his bed, gradually recovering from her own ordeal and getting off rather lightly in comparison. She appeared to have escaped without too much injury. Her mouth was still slightly swollen though, where Hans had tied the scarves so tightly they'd cut into the soft fleshy tissue, and around both her wrists dark bruises were forming.

'I'm fine' she kept insisting, apparently more worried about Tom than she was about herself. And while the Doctors kept trying to persuade her to have a full examination she responded very matter of fact and downbeat, 'no, honestly, there's no need' she kept repeating over and over again, until eventually they gave up asking.

The tables had suddenly turned between husband and wife. It was now Tom who kept reaching for his wife, continually seeking out her hand for comfort and support. When she lent it to him he gripped on to her for dear life, he couldn't describe the guilt he felt.

All through that evening, while his wife was undergoing such trauma, he'd been off pursuing another woman, a woman who was clearly not interested in him and never had been, and all the while his wife had been lying there, tied up on their bed, having to go through that horrific ordeal alone. He hated himself for not being there for her.

The door to the single ward suddenly opened and Inspector Taylor was shown into the room by the nurse. He thanked her and sat down on the spare seat next to Peggy.

'Are you able to answer a few questions Mrs Algar' he asked her, as he took out his notebook and rested it on his knee, retrieving a small pencil from his breast pocket. 'I'm sorry but there is no time to lose. I have of course seen your initial statements, both yours and your husband's, but I just have a few questions of my own'.

Peggy kept her eyes averted, but nodded her head slowly, while gripping even tighter to her husband's hand.

'Can you give me a description of the man who was in your bedroom?' he asked her pointedly.

Peggy had been given a small dose of barbiturates to calm her nerves and this had definitely helped with her emotional state, although the shock of the ordeal was still raw, particularly now she was completely sober. Since arriving at the hospital she'd been doing her best to block out everything that had happened to her during that awful nightmare and yet now she was being asked to relive it. As she stared down at the bed she tried to resist those terrifying images, focusing her mind only on the cotton twill of the hospital bedding. Its geometric design was helping to distract her from the stark reality of her ordeal and the fact that she'd managed to survive the longest, most appalling hour of her life. She couldn't believe she'd lived to tell the tale and yet now here she was, and it seemed that is exactly what she was being asked to do.

As she continued to stare at the coverlet's design, it began to morph into a distinct pattern, a man's face, and suddenly the face of that evil villain was conjured up before her. She could visualise him easily within the weave, as clear as day. He was there again, before her, and a shudder began to ripple down her spine as she fought against the memory. But she wanted the police to catch him, they must apprehend that monster as soon as possible and of course they needed her help to do it. As her mouth began to form the words they came out oddly, in a rather erratic, staccato form.

'He was dirty, I mean his face, it was filthy!' she began, 'I couldn't see his features well, but his eyes were dark, black or brown, I think, and the whites, they were so white, so vividly white, but the light was dim, I only had one lamp on in the room, but all I could see were his eyes, they were intense and menacing. He was desperate, on some kind of adrenaline fuelled mission. He wore oilskins and he had a dark sou'wester on his head, like a fisherman, in fact he smelt of fish, and he kept walking around the room, helping himself to everything, filling my beautiful velvet bag with all my jewellery. I don't think he left a ring or a necklace anywhere in the place. And then when he found the safe, he had such a strange look on his face. He looked round at me with that horrible smile, like he'd caught me out, like I'd known it was there all the time and I was just keeping quiet about it, but I didn't know it was there, I really didn't, and then he just took it, he took all of it, helping himself to all that money and I couldn't do anything, I just sat on the bed watching him fill his pockets and, oh Tom, he took all our money and ......I couldn't stop him!'

Suddenly she started sobbing again and, while Tom shushed and spoke soothingly to her, Inspector Taylor pulled out from his pocket a pure white handkerchief, lovingly pressed for him by Mrs Taylor, which he offered to Mrs Algar and which Peggy took from him gratefully.

'Thank you Inspector,' she said on a sob, whilst at the same time blowing her nose into it, noisily.

'That's very good Mrs Algar, now please, just take your time, you've been very helpful indeed, but try to stay calm, I don't want you to become over anxious in any way at all, but if you can think back again, do you remember if the man said anything to you?'

He paused, allowing her time to recover and gather her thoughts. He knew he needed to tread carefully. The key in these circumstances was to persuade and cajole the victims in a gentle tentative manner. He could see that her panic was very near the surface and that it could rise up again uncontrollably and then he would get nowhere. He knew that the nurse standing in the corner of the room was watching the proceedings closely and that she would soon steer him out of there if he went too far.

Peggy's mind was carried back again into the bedroom, it was as though she was there once more, tied to those bed posts and the intruder was standing in front of her, the frightening man in the black sou'wester with the cruel dirty face beneath it, suddenly she could feel the nausea rising again and she was visibly shaking as she recalled the intruder's strange voice.

'He did say something to me', she whispered, as she reached out again for Tom's comforting hand suddenly needing his support as the nightmare became real once more, and he squeezed her own hand for encouragement as she continued, 'it sounded like *'bitte sei stille'* she said, 'stay still?' Somehow I knew what he was saying and so I did try to become very still. I didn't want to antagonise him in any way but I started crying and he seemed to get all fired up and then he grabbed me and I'm afraid I did start to scream then. I couldn't stop myself and that was when he clamped his hand over my mouth and said something like *'die klappe halten'*, I think he was telling me to shut up and so I did, and then he began to shout at me, 'Gold, money!' but I couldn't answer him, I couldn't speak, my brain seemed to shut down and I couldn't function in any way.

I think he knew then that I would be of no help to him and that was when he put the scarf inside my mouth, pushing and shoving it inside, it was so horrible, it made me gag. At the time it was almost unbearable, I thought I was going to die from lack of air, but I knew I wanted to stay alive and so I just went limp and then I let him do whatever he wanted'.

Taylor watched her distraught face as she suddenly let go of her husband's hand and turned away from them both, groping around for the borrowed white handkerchief, which she found, proceeding to open it up to smother her face with it, almost as though she was hiding from them, or the truth, as she sobbed again, more loudly this time. No one said a word, almost as if they'd been transported into that room with her, sensing her fear and dread which had suddenly become blatantly real, but then Peggy sniffed long and hard, as though she were steadying her nerves and she continued.

'Once he had tied me up, he left me alone, and instantly I was glad. I didn't care how much money or jewellery he took, he could have it all! What is money, or jewellery, they're not important are they? They have no meaning, do they, not when you're dead!'

Tom was stunned to hear his wife speaking in this way. He'd always considered her to be materialistic and vain, almost taking it for granted she would remain like that her whole life, but something had changed and tonight he saw a different side to her.

Inspector Taylor placed his notebook and pencil carefully on the end of Tom's bed and released the shiny brass button on his left pocket lapel. He reached inside for the badge he'd found and, taking it out gingerly, he placed it onto his open palm, holding it towards them, to show them what he'd found. They both leaned forwards simultaneously to have a closer look.

'Do either of you recognise this badge,' Taylor asked, as he watched their faces for any reaction?

With quizzical expressions they both denied any knowledge of it, 'no inspector,' Tom spoke firmly and with conviction, 'I have never seen that before, what is it and where did you find it?'

'I found it under your bed, sir,' answered Taylor, 'and after doing a little research I fear the intruder must have inadvertently dropped it. I have to tell you that this style of badge was worn by the Luftwaffe. The words Adler Tag translate to Eagle Day which occurred on the 13th August 1940. It was a day hailed by Hitler as the start of the Battle of Britain, a day when the Luftwaffe mounted over fourteen hundred missions. The aim was to severely impede our RAF airfields and equipment. If Adler Tag or Eagle Day had been successful then Hitler's plan to invade Britain by sea, 'Operation Sea Lion' as it was called, would probably have taken place. Thankfully the Eagle Day mission failed, mainly because the Germans were disorganised and unprepared, which was very lucky for us indeed! The outcome of the war might have been completely different if that assault had been successful.

Anyway, bringing us swiftly back to the present, I believe our man could well be an escaped prisoner of war, a German Luftwaffe pilot, possibly one of the men who escaped from Island Farm Camp in Wales last year, and who has presumably been on the run ever since.'

The Inspector paused to let the news sink in and then he sat quietly for a moment, watching the couple embrace each other yet again, for reassurance and comfort. Taylor deduced something palpable between the pair. He considered something ostensibly insurmountable had happened to this couple once, a long time ago, and he reckoned that whatever they'd been through, whatever they'd lost, it had now inadvertently been found.

He began to wonder whether this traumatic event, devastating though it might be, could perhaps prove a catalyst for them, a means of wiping away past sadness and enabling them to come together again to start anew. 'Every cloud .....' he concluded magnanimously, as he stood up, unnoticed, and left the room.

CHAPTER THIRTY THREE

Stefan sat in the gloomy cabin and explained the details of the plan to Hans and his idea, or rather Alice's idea, to hide in the lifeboats on board the naval frigate. He told Hans excitedly about the ship, originally named HMS Lowestoft, now a mercantile, renamed 'Milaflores', which was fortuitously docked at the inner harbour of Lake Lothing overnight. Stefan looked at his wristwatch and realised they would need to get moving very soon. Hopefully they would be climbing on board the ship in the early hours, when no one was around, and could be concealed ready for its departure the following day to Zeebrugge. After that, hopefully they would be able to remain hidden for its onward journey to Hamburg.

His successful radio transmission to Germany from the wreck had resulted in confirmation that they would be met in Hamburg, at a secretly coded location, upon arrival. Luckily his contact was still active within the Radio Defence Corps, a counterintelligence agency attached to the Wehrmacht, which had operated throughout the war to monitor illicit broadcasts. The agent had told him that if they could get to Hamburg he would be able to arrange for someone to meet them there for debrief and after that they would be able to return to their homes and their loved ones.

Hans suddenly beamed a wide smile, the widest it had been for many months, relieved to know that at last there was a way home and once there he would be considered a hero by his fellow countrymen! He stood up and wrapped his arms around Stefan in delight.

'Wir wollen Essen für dei Reise', Hans told Stefan excitedly, 'I have food, much food for the journey!' he added in English cheerily, pleased that he was able to contribute in some small way to the venture and after walking over to the small cupboard at the back of the kitchen, he proceeded to bring out all of the ham, cheese, bread and milk, in fact most of the rations he'd stolen recently from the Algar house.

Stefan was amazed at how well Hans seem to have been coping on his own, far better than he, obviously, but then he stopped to think. He realised that in fact he'd received his own piece of luck recently in the form of his true and loyal friend Alice. Without her he wouldn't be here.

A sudden lump rose up in his throat at the thought of how he'd left her, how confused she must have been when she discovered he had gone. He wondered how long had she'd searched for him after she'd hidden him so safe and secure behind that pile of crates nearby? He felt bad deserting her like that, knowingly causing her so much upset, and also that he was now effectively passing off her escape plan as his own. But he'd done it for a reason, he reassured himself. It was all for the greater good. He'd made the decision to leave because he didn't want her to be involved. He couldn't bear the thought of her getting caught and going to prison as a traitor because she'd helped him escape. He hoped now, above everything else, that she was home safe and sound with her family and out of harm's way. He wasn't sure about the sailor though? He could tell from his conversation with Alice that they'd been more than just friends but would he call the authorities? Stefan hoped not? He seemed a wily character and probably involved in some sort of illicit dealings. If he was smuggling goods then he wouldn't want to draw any attention to himself.

Hans and Stefan quickly collected what they needed for the journey, leaving most of Hans' possessions behind; hopefully the quantity of old tin pots and variety of hotch potch clothing garnered during his long months as a fugitive would not be required any longer! Stefan had not been able to dissuade

Hans from bringing the shotgun along though, primarily for the very same reasons as before, and Stefan still felt this was a bad idea, but this time he chose not to pursue it. He just prayed there would be no trouble and the gun would remain hidden and silent. His shoulder was still smarting from where he'd been hit and he knew he'd had a lucky escape.

After jumping off the old wreck for the last time, Stefan made his way towards the small rowing boat. He kept just one small bag with him, the radio haversack, which might come in useful when they reached the other side. He needed nothing now except his own small supply of Hans' food and drink and the warm gloves he'd kept in his pocket, remembering the life saver they'd been for him and Alice.

'Nein, nein' said Hans, pointing away from the boat, and towards his own pathway, the one he'd created valiantly the first time he'd advanced through the barbed wire. Stefan looked across to where his friend was pointing, realising with admiration, mixed with incredulity, that Hans must have been able to set up his own safe trail. It all made sense now, Stefan understood immediately, registering the distinct line of stones that Hans had laid down. He had made for himself a safe pathway into town and one Hans always followed whenever he went to and from the wreck. He was one crazy bastard, Stefan thought to himself, to put his life in danger like that, but of course, that was so typical of Hans.

But instantly Stefan thought of Alice and of the small boat which belonged to her grandfather. If it was left here, the authorities would find it and it wouldn't take them long to find out who owned it. They would interrogate Alice and her family and they would immediately suspect she had something to do with their escape. No, he wouldn't put her through that, he must return it safely back to harbour where he'd found it and so he ignored Hans' continual pleas and futile questions; 'who is this girl, why do you care about her, *sie ist der feind*?' But Stefan shook his head, 'no Hans she is not my enemy, she is my friend' and he continued to place their emergency rations inside the small boat. Stefan pushed the boat away from shore so that Hans eventually complied and followed his 'idiot' friend into the water. He certainly didn't want to upset Stefan again and risk another falling out and so he jumped into the small boat and sat down ready to head back across the waves once more. As he watched Stefan struggling with the oars, Hans insisted wisely that he should do the rowing, and Stefan complied readily. He knew he was beat and needed a well earned rest, and so, after relinquishing the oars, he lay his body back against the bow, his weary arms over the sides of the boat, and utterly exhausted, he was lulled into a brief sleep by the soothing rhythm of the waves while the boat rocked gently once more on the calm sea.

He roused himself to guide Hans into the harbour mouth and in next to no time they were docking once more amongst the row of small boats which bobbed about gently against the wooden decking. The harbour was still and quiet apart from the gentle chinking of masts on the various boats and trawlers which were tied up for the night around the edge of the harbour. The mist hung delicately in the air but Stefan sensed a warmer dawn was fast approaching and hoped that milder weather might well be on its way, it definitely didn't seem as cold now as it had been on his earlier trip that night with Alice. Stefan wondered what the following day might bring, if it was a warm one with the sun high above them and a calm sea he imagined their journey would be a lot easier, the thought of a pleasant warm spell could bode well for their channel crossing. He determined there and then to think more positively about the outcome of their mission.

He reckoned the time was probably around 3 am and on checking his wristwatch he realised he was pretty spot on, it was imperative they should not delay. Now was a good time to head straight for the ship and attempt to get on board before daylight. He hoped there would be no-one about, just like before, when he and Alice were hidden behind the crates earlier, it had seemed pretty deserted then, with no one on guard, and so he prayed for the same scenario, wishing fervently that there would be no last minute delays and that the ship would leave on time.

Before long he and Hans were ensconced behind the same pile of crates not far from the railway lines and within sight of the industrial building where Alice's friend had emerged only a few hours before.

It seemed even more deathly quiet at this time of the morning but when Stefan felt Hans pulling urgently on his coat, evidently on the verge of voicing an opinion, Stefan quickly turned round and placed a finger firmly on his lips, effectively silencing his companion instantly, *'pssst, stille',* he whispered earnestly with eyes full of unease. It was imperative they did nothing to raise the alarm and from then on, using gestures only, Stefan pointed towards the gangway which remained unoccupied as before, still apparently unguarded! Hans nodded his agreement and they both picked up their belongings, moving silently towards the ramp.

As they walked in single file up the ramp, slowly and furtively, moving closer towards the deck, the gangway beneath their feet began to swing ever so slightly under their weight, making a slight creaking noise as it rocked to and fro, and so they stopped for a moment, allowing it to become still and quiet, all the while looking around for any sign of life, but when nothing stirred they continued on their way.

Once they were on board, they kept their heads bowed low, making their way stealthily along the deck towards the lifeboats which were clearly positioned at the back of the ship. They had agreed earlier to separate and that each would take a different lifeboat to hide in, the premise being that they would not be tempted to talk on the journey. They had divided enough food between them for the voyage and each carried their own belongings though Stefan had very little to carry after disposing of his accumulated junk earlier on.   Hans seemed very protective about one of his bags, keeping it constantly hidden away from Stefan, but Stefan decided he didn't want to know what his comrade had in that bag; in fact it was just as well he knew nothing about it, the thought that it might be more weapons or ammunition filled him with dread. He hoped and prayed that Hans would not be tempted to use any of it. All they needed to do now was to keep their cool and remain silent for around twenty four hours and after that they would have safely reached the other side of the channel.

Stefan dared to dream of his arrival back home, of walking into the arms of his family once more, but he wondered what he might find there, he dared not even imagine what state his country might be in.

The tarpaulin on the lifeboats lifted up easily and both men climbed silently into their hiding places, tucking the covers back into place so that no one would be any the wiser.

Inside his own lifeboat Stefan quickly laid down, stretching out his long legs along the bottom of the timber-framed craft so that he was as comfortable as possible in the confined space. After a few minutes, with his own small bag forming a pillow of sorts, he gradually became accustomed to the darkness.

As he looked around the area beneath the tarpaulin, he was surprised to see that it was actually quite extensive. At the very far end of the lifeboat he saw a pile of several boxes and crates, which puzzled him slightly as to what might be inside them? He hoped and prayed that whatever was in those boxes would not be needed until after they'd arrived in Germany, perhaps they were merely lifeboat provisions he thought hopefully.

CHAPTER THIRTY FOUR

Alice woke in her bed a little later than usual that morning and beneath the warm covers she stretched out her sore slim frame so that it reached every corner of the bed, everything seemed to ache, her arms, her back, her neck, in fact just about every part of her seemed to have been affected in some way. She came to the blissful realisation of safety and warmth inside the comfortable cocoon of her bed. But then a distant dream full of events and trauma from the previous day suddenly tumbled back into her consciousness. She gasped once more as she remembered the disappointing end to those tumultuous few days with Stefan and once again she tried to rationalise why on earth he had left her so unexpectedly. Was it something she'd said or done? What could possibly have been the reason for him vanishing like that and where was he now? She just couldn't understand why he had just upped and left, especially when he was so close to returning home. For him to desert her like that, without explanation, her being his one and only ally, surely the only person he could rely on and who'd helped him get that far, she just couldn't fathom it? She'd suffered so much anguish and pain for him and then he'd just left her? Why?

'Alice' a voice called out from the other side of the door. Oh lord, it was her mother!

Alice took in a deep breath and quickly yanked the bedcovers up and over her head once more. She hid beneath them, pretending to be asleep, in the certain knowledge that a ton of questions, and mostly ones she wasn't prepared to answer, were about to come her way.

Ellen opened the door tentatively and walked into the room with a tray of tea and toast in her hands which she then carefully placed on to Alice's bedside cupboard. 'There now', she spoke in the same soothing tones she'd used the previous night, 'you have something to eat and then you can tell me all about it.'

Alice pulled down the covers knowing straight away that she couldn't avoid her mother's questions for ever. She might as well get it over and done with.

'There's nothing to tell' she answered her mother rather abruptly, 'I just stayed out late that's all, I'm sorry if you were worried.'

'Well, of course I was worried; you've never stayed out that late before. I didn't know where you were or who you were with and then to top it all I had Tom Algar banging on my door last night warning me about down and outs, and robbers and thieves, all up to no good in the area. He said they've been breaking into people's houses and stealing food Alice! I've seen our own food and drink going missing and I thought perhaps it was you, that you'd taken it, and that you were giving it to someone. Yes, young lady, you're right, I was worried!'

Alice chewed on her lip, feeling ashamed now for putting her mother through such anxiety, and for the lies that she was going to have to tell. She really didn't want to treat her mother this way but she couldn't tell her the truth, the full facts were too awful to contemplate, weren't they? Alice had no option but to continue with her deceit. If she told her mother what had happened she would call the police and then they'd find Stefan and he would be taken into custody and Lord knows what would happen to him after that.

'I'm sorry mum for worrying you', Alice spoke to her in calmer tones, 'I truly am, but I promise you I've done nothing wrong,' and in that statement she felt she was justified, she was being truthful, for she'd merely been helping a stranger hadn't she? Stefan was no longer the enemy, not in her mind anyway, and what she'd done had been to follow the right path, the path espoused in the bible story that she'd heard preached many times from the chapel pulpit, the one told by Jesus in Luke's gospel. A parable that was all about helping someone in need, and more importantly, the act of helping someone that no one else would deign to help, someone who was, in fact, an outcast. Suddenly she felt very virtuous, for in this particular case Stefan was certainly the outcast and so surely, in God's eyes, she was, in fact, the Good Samaritan?

Ellen sighed deeply, deciding that she would have to leave it for now, she was sure there was much more to know and to be worried about, but for the time being all was well and she was just mightily glad to have her daughter back home, safe and sound. She knew Alice would tell her what happened in her own good time but for now she would leave her be, and to be honest she had more worrying things on her mind, and she changed the subject rather abruptly.

'I'm assuming you are not working today dear?' she asked Alice, checking her watch, 'only Gramps is a bit poorly and I'm rather worried about him. I need to get round there to meet with the Doctor this morning'.

'Oh dear, poor Gramps,' Alice gasped, instantly contrite, 'its fine mum, of course, you go, I'm off work today, so don't worry about anything. I'll take Trix for a walk on the beach if you like, it looks like a nice morning and I feel like a bit of fresh air. You should go straight round there and look after him. Wish him better from me won't you?'

Alice could tell from her mother's troubled expression that she was very concerned about her grandfather but surely it couldn't be anything too serious, he always seemed so well and full of life, she really hoped the Doctor would be able to cure whatever ailment he had.

CHAPTER THIRTY FIVE

Inspector Taylor walked out of the hospital, convinced that his theory was correct, he was certain the villain was an escaped prisoner of war and that he must be apprehended with the greatest possible speed. To that effect he had already contacted the Royal Military Police at Kensington Palace to inform them of his suspicions. He'd realised this was not a straightforward case of a thief on the run; this was a trapped and desperate man, a world war two fighter pilot and worse still, he now had a weapon

The Royal Military Police, or the 'red berets' as they were better known, were the army experts in the capture and interrogation of prisoners of war and although much of their war operation had been 'stood down' since VE Day, the department had been galvanised into action by the Inspector's unexpected phone call. They had quickly agreed to send an army Lieutenant and two members of the military police, without delay, to help the Inspector co-ordinate a search party to hunt down the intruder. They should arrive in Lowestoft within a couple of hours they informed him. Two hours, thought Taylor, in dismay! A lot could happen in two hours!

During the telephone call he'd been able to give them a description of the intruder, hoping it might match any reports among their records of an escaped prisoner of war. It would be helpful to know a little bit more about the man, his character, and exactly what they might be up against? He'd told them he'd not seen the man himself but, to the best of his knowledge, the sketch from Mrs Algar was a good description and taken from the only eye witness. He relayed to them that the man was of slight to medium build with a dirty face, dark hair and dark eyes, he was approximately 5'10" in height and he was wearing a black fishermen's oilskin and sou'wester, he also wore surprisingly sturdy leather boots, possibly of German origin, but more importantly he had a distinct German accent. The Adler Tag badge which Taylor had found under the Algars' bed was the clue he'd needed to tip the balance in favour of his theory and to instigate much more interest from the red berets than would normally be the case.

In his frustration at the unnecessary delay, he decided to organise his own search party but he stressed to his men that if the culprit was found they should sound a whistle, to be blown three times – short and sharp! He'd instructed forcefully that the criminal should not be approached but merely observed from a distance. The German POW was armed, desperate, and potentially extremely dangerous.

As several uniformed officers spread out along the seafront, Taylor watched them moving forwards silently, across the bridge and towards town, whilst two men stayed behind with him to check the South Pier and the harbour area. Taylor walked behind his men, listening avidly for any short whistle blasts.

He was pleased with his decision to carry on and not wait for the MPs to arrive, convinced that he was still the man in charge here, and that they would just have to catch up when they arrived. He'd done his duty by informing them but this was his watch, his patch, and he knew the town like the back of his hand. If that measly skunk had found somewhere to hide, if he'd slithered back down into the dark hole he'd come from, then Taylor was the wily ferret to drag him out of it. If he managed to arrest that German vagrant and take him back into custody, personally, and without incident, well, he thought eagerly, this could turn out to be the pinnacle of his career.

Taylor paused at the harbour for a moment or two and then he stood thoughtfully, watching his men as they spread out across the town. As he gazed out to sea, he saw a thin streak of light appearing at the far edge of the horizon and he realised it was the yellow crack of dawn. He suddenly felt optimistic! This was going to be a good day, he thought to himself, as he watched the sun begin its upward journey, soon it would shimmer and shine its yellow warmth and light over the seaside town of Lowestoft. And here he stood, at the most easterly point in the land, and by golly he was going to be there, to see and enjoy it all!

He dipped his hand into his pocket and pulled out his cigarettes and lighter. As he lit one of the cigarettes he took in a deep drag and then he exhaled the smoke into the heavy morning mist. He dropped the silver lighter back into the darkness of his heavy coat pocket, whilst continuing to survey the area for inspiration.

What would I do, he thought to himself, if I were in his shoes? And why would a German POW need all that money and jewellery? He turned to look across the road and beyond, to see what lay on the other side of the bridge, and it was then that he caught sight of the naval frigate in the distance, silently berthed upon the dark waters of Lake Lothing, it sat strangely still and ethereal, within the gloomy atmosphere.

The ship loomed up before him, moored and motionless, waiting patiently to leave port after its layover at the dockside, and suddenly a seed was planted, an impulsive thought which flourished and quickly began to take root! He called out urgently to the two men scouting nearby at the outer harbour, one of whom seemed engrossed in a small rowing boat, convinced as he leant over it that an element of warmth was coming from the small red tilley lamp, making him wonder if it had been used recently. But, however fleeting that thought was, he quickly abandoned it, for as soon as he heard his master's voice calling him, he stood up instantly and sprinted back along the wooden platform, climbing quickly up the ladder, eager to join his team once more.

'Come with me,' Taylor said, giving his instructions to the men assertively as they arrived by his side and then he took the lead, walking briskly across the road and over to the other side of the bridge, while they followed close behind, all three heading speedily in the direction of Lake Lothing.

CHAPTER THIRTY SIX

Ellen had become worried about Cyril after their trip to the pictures and their long walk back from town. She'd noticed his complexion was looking a little grey and she'd become anxious about his breathing which seemed heavy and laboured. She decided to ask him into the house for a cup of tea so that he could have a rest before heading home.

After Cyril had winced painfully for the duration of those last few steps into the house, finally flopping into the wing-backed armchair with obvious relief, Ellen insisted that something was seriously wrong and he must tell her what the problem was. Eventually he was persuaded to come clean and slowly he lifted up his trouser legs to show her his ankles. Straight away she could see how swollen and red they were, almost purple in places, and they were also covered in dry flaky patches.

'Oh Gramps, you definitely shouldn't have walked all that way home, we could just as easily have caught the bus!' she admonished him soundly, 'why didn't you say something before? You must have been in agony!'

'Oh hush now, stop your fussing Ellen, it's only a bit of swelling. I'll just raise them up here for a little while and they'll be fine'

Ellen swiftly pulled towards him the pretty four legged footstool, formed from solid oak and made for her by Frank as a Christmas present. She carefully lifted both of Cyril's legs over the stool, lowering them gently down on top of it, so that his feet were resting on the soft padded cushion, which she'd embroidered herself in a bright yellow sunflower pattern.

She knew his symptoms were far from normal, his laboured breathing was a bad sign and his grey pallor was very concerning, so she swiftly declared that a visit from the Doctor was urgently required. Cyril complained instantly that this was not necessary and a lengthy argument followed whereby he insisted the Doctor should not be bothered with a little bit of swelling. Dr Hewitt would have many other, far more sickly, patients than him to be dealing with. All he needed was a nice long rest, he insisted. However Ellen was not to be put off and finally she won the argument and Doctor Hewitt was called. When the Doctor visited Cyril at home the very next day he ordered Cyril straight to bed and gave him a fortnight's worth of medicine.

After several days though, it seemed the medicine wasn't helping, Cyril's legs were getting steadily worse and in fact his whole body was puffing out, even his face and hands were bloated. In addition he now had a dreadful pain in his back and so Ellen called round again to the Doctor who promised he would visit Gramps later that morning.

The elderly, overweight Doctor arrived, as promised, and Ellen took him huffing and puffing up the stairs and into the bedroom to see Cyril. After examining his patient, Doctor Hewitt came clomping down the wooden staircase, his stethoscope still in position round his neck and a rather solemn expression on his face. He walked slowly into the small sitting room where the two women, Ellen and Joan, were sitting in front of the warm fire, waiting for him. Dr Hewitt sat down heavily on the green hessian armchair, plonking down his leather medical bag next to him onto the rug, while keeping it close by. Joan sat timidly on the edge of the armchair opposite him, while Ellen excused herself and went off to make them all a cup of tea.

After bringing in the tray and handing round the dainty cups and saucers, she too, sat herself down on the small stool next to Joan, ready to listen attentively to what the Doctor had to say.

Dr Hewitt's brow remained furrowed, while he slowly slurped his tea, and Ellen sensed he was using that activity to delay the inevitable bad news. He was obviously trying to find enough soothing words to lessen the pain for them, although of course none existed, and as they sat listening to the fire crackling in the grate, an expectant silence ensued.

Finally the Doctor replaced his empty tea cup back into its saucer and, leaning forward, he returned it to the tray. After drawing in a deep breath and wiping his mouth with a patterned handkerchief, one he seemed rather surprised to find slightly crumpled in the pocket of his corduroy jacket, he sat up to deliver his verdict.

'I'm afraid your husband is very ill' he spoke directly to Joan in a strangely deliberate manner which came across as rather matter of fact. His words would only tell her the truth; there would be no sugar coating from him.

'Cyril's kidneys are not working at all well and toxins are now flooding through his body. I'm afraid that is the cause of all the swelling. Sadly, there is no cure. Any operation is out of the question because his heart is too weak and to be honest it would be inadvisable to 'open him up' merely to identify something we already know, only to stitch him back up again, with absolutely no benefit. Indeed, I fear that to put him through all of that would be an extremely unkind and inhumane course of action. All you can do for him now is to make him feel as comfortable as possible.'

Ellen covered her face with her hands and stifled a sob. She'd known it was coming and yet the shock of it was so profound she couldn't believe it at first. She breathed in deeply and tried to recover her composure enough to thank the Doctor for his time and trouble.

She stood up from the small stool and moved towards Joan to place a comforting arm around her thin shoulders. Joan said nothing, she just sat very still, in a strange trance-like state, and her only movement was to wring a small lacy handkerchief through her fingers repeatedly. Ellen wasn't sure whether Joan had fully understood the Doctor's prognosis. Her husband was dying and yet there she sat, not uttering a sound, rigid, immobile, and seemingly emotionally detached.

Now that the bad news had been delivered, the doctor stood up, showing immense relief that this, his unkindest of chores, was over and he bent down to retrieve his briefcase. He opened up the catch and returned his stethoscope to its rightful position, taking out a prescription at the same time. It was obviously one he'd already written up so that Ellen couldn't help but suspect he knew what the outcome would be today. The prescription was for a double pack of 5 syrettes of morphine and he took Ellen over to one side to describe to her how the needle should be injected. He told her it that it should not be stabbed into the arm but inserted slowly and at a shallow angle and he also told her that it could take up to thirty minutes to take effect. The thought of administering the drug frightened Ellen. She was not medically trained. The very idea of Gramps being in pain and of her being the only one who could alleviate that pain, was very upsetting but also the notion that she could help him in his hour of need made her position practical and real.

Ellen took the prescription from the Doctor and showed him to the door. She thanked him politely again for his time and trouble and just before he left, he turned and gently squeezed her shoulder, 'you're a good woman Ellen, Cyril couldn't have wished for a better nurse'.

Ellen decided not to share the Doctor's prognosis with the girls or in fact anyone and it was very difficult for her to keep the sad news to herself but in a way it also meant that she didn't have to give up hope. Kind words and pity was something she couldn't cope with at the moment. She sent a wire to Frank immediately, urging him to come home as his father was seriously ill, and then after that, every day, she prayed for a miracle. The girls remained unaware, they just thought Gramps was poorly, they brought him flowers and took Trix in to him, to show him how big he was growing, and of course this made Cyril smile.

Everyone outside the sick room carried on with their lives and even Joan remained oblivious to the seriousness of the situation and its eventual consequences, still managing to find something within her own small world to complain about. Ellen decided that Joan was either in denial or, alternatively, she wondered whether perhaps an element of senility had crept in, that blissful state where one lives in the moment and nothing that happens, before or after, really matters a jot. She wondered whether she ought to sit down with Joan and make her listen, make her understand what the Doctor had told them, but in the end she decided not to. Why do that to her, if Joan preferred to live in blissful ignorance, then let her. Surely nature would take its course and when that time came Joan would know the truth. It would happen soon enough and with her mother in law's neurotic nature any confusion now might only make matters worse.

Ellen thought back to the autumn of the previous year when her father-in-law had decided to write a codicil to his will. Had he known then she wondered? Had he felt some sixth sense that his time on earth was coming to an end? He'd been happy these last few weeks, so full of life, and the puppy he'd brought for the girls had given the whole family so much joy and pleasure, and Gramps had loved watching it.

The next few days were full of suppressed emotion as Ellen tried to carry on with daily living. Alice had gone back to work but she was still not herself and she hadn't said a word about the strange foggy night when Ellen had met her at the swing bridge.

CHAPTER THIRTY SEVEN

Suddenly, the news was all around town that the scoundrel had been caught! This news had brought immense pleasure and relief to Ellen, for it meant that finally she could relax, and not be constantly on her guard for an intruder. She'd heard through the grapevine that the man had been found by the police, hiding on board a naval frigate, docked at the inner harbour on a layover, and incredibly it transpired that he'd also been an escaped German prisoner of war! Golly! Who would have thought it? A German running around their town for goodness knows how long. The town's rumour mill was of course at full throttle. The awful goings on at the Algar house were embellished and embroidered until nobody really knew the truth of it. The fact that this was the villain's second break-in was astonishing, it seemed on the first occasion he'd run off with almost all of the Algar's food rations, but to have the audacity to go back a second time was truly alarming. He'd obviously not been satisfied with mere food and drink and had returned for something much more lucrative.

Ellen was shocked to think of the unfortunate Algars and what they'd been through. Such a dreadful ordeal, she reflected soberly, unable to stop herself from imagining that awful scenario in her mind. She felt instantly ashamed for all her bad thoughts about her landlord and his poor wife. She'd not seen Tom Algar since that very night, when he'd come to visit her, to warn her about the vagabond, but after hearing all the terrible stories of what had gone on she realised he must now be taking time to recover and comfort his poor wife who'd been affected quite badly it seemed. According to the grapevine, Mrs Algar had been all alone in the house when the German intruder had broken in. What a dreadful business, Ellen thought to herself, but she thanked the lord that no one had been seriously hurt. At least the police had caught up with the villain quickly and he was now under lock and key.

Alice's reaction to this news was dramatically different to her mother's. When she first heard that a prisoner of war had been captured in the town she became immediately distraught! No, she thought, it couldn't be? Not Stefan?

But it was true, and she heard it first from Beryl, Katy's friend, who told her the whole story rather nonchalantly, with a big grin on her face, which made Alice feel quite sick to her stomach. But she tried not to show her true feelings and eventually she made her escape, running upstairs to her room, away from all their grinning faces, hiding under the bedcovers. And after that, she just sobbed and sobbed, her face buried in the pillow, for well over an hour, her heart pounding, and tears streaming down her face, but she did it as quietly as possible under the covers. She didn't want her mother coming upstairs and asking awkward questions again.

Over the next few days, she feared what the police might do to Stefan. She'd heard the red berets had arrived from London but apparently they'd returned soon after, realising the job had effectively been done and with very little effort on their part. She now needed to make a supreme effort to keep all she knew about him to herself, though she was sorely tempted to go to the police station and plead for his freedom. But she knew it would only cause trouble for herself and her family, for aiding and abetting the 'enemy,' and so she tried to hide her emotions from her mother's prying eyes. In the end all Alice could hope for, after everything Stefan had been through, was that he would be looked after decently by the authorities and that eventually, hopefully, they would arrange for him to go home.

The rumours of the break-ins had confounded her though! She knew in her heart that Stefan would surely be incapable of inflicting so much pain on anyone and all she could hope was that someone had made a terrible mistake. But when information was leaked that the man had been found hiding in one of the lifeboats on board the naval frigate while it was berthed at Lake Lothing, that seemed the final straw which meant she must believe the stories, and that the young man they'd found had never really been her friend at all, perhaps she'd never really known him? She'd fallen for his charms, hook line and sinker, taken in by those soulful eyes of his, radiating goodness and compassion. Was his goodness only skin deep? Had she really been that much of a fool? She couldn't help but remember his kind deeds, the offer of that gentle massage, the warm gloves he'd given her, the way he'd taken over the rowing so she could rest, his whole demeanour told her he was a good person. As her thoughts and emotions became more and more conflicted, they only brought forth more tears and sobbing, until she railed against her own confusion and stupidity.

After receiving Ellen's wire about Cyril, Frank had explained the situation to his boss and had managed to get time off to come home and see his father.

When he saw his father's ashen face, looking almost as pale as the clean white pillow around it, he knew instantly that Cyril was lying on his death bed. He realised he must contact his brothers straight away to let them know the sad situation. It was obvious Cyril was not going to make it through the week and Ellen and Frank feared the worst would soon be upon them.

Joan had finally been convinced that her husband had only a short time to live and it was time to say goodbye to her husband of forty six years. She realised there'd never been anyone else for her, but perhaps she should have told him that before now. They'd had their ups and downs, they'd argued a lot, but he'd always been there, by her side, and deep down she knew she would always love him. Frank's brothers, Joe and Bill, called in to see Cyril with flowers and good wishes, anxious to know how their parents were getting on. It was their first visit to the house in almost a year, Ellen realised, thinking how sad it was that imminent death was often the only reason to spur people on to make a long overdue visit.

Ellen baked every day, producing a plentiful supply of patties and cakes for any visitors that came to the house and, although Cyril was not eating, she often caught him smiling weakly at her across the room, whenever she brought in tea or sustenance for his visitors. She decided that she wouldn't put any pressure on him to eat, but she did make him drink a little, just water, to cool his parched lips and mouth. She'd only administered the morphine three times so far, and she was glad to say that it had worked extremely well, calming him and sending him off into a land of dreams very soon after.

Frank would often sit next to his father, pulling up a chair at the top of the bed, so that Cyril wouldn't have to move a muscle in order to see him. Frank would hold his hand while he slept, telling him about all the plans he had for the garden at Walmer Road, and all the fruit and vegetables he was going to plant that spring. He was in the middle of telling Cyril about his crop of Ulster Chieftains, his sprouting runner beans and a new variety of red radishes he was going to try, when he felt his father's hand loosen its hold. As he looked up into his father's restful face he thought he caught Cyril smiling, as though he were in the middle of a very satisfying dream, in a place where someone he loved and who loved him in return, had suddenly arrived to greet him. And then Frank watched as his father drew in his last deep breath before finally slipping away to eternal peace.

CHAPTER THIRTY EIGHT

When Alice heard the news of her grandfather's passing, she sobbed for a different reason and she made a supreme effort to push all other swirling, unanswered thoughts into the farthest reaches of her mind. She decided to lock them away in an imaginary box called 'lessons in life' because this present tragedy, the sudden and unexpected death of her beloved grandfather, was all-encompassing. It outweighed all other important events in her life. This was a final goodbye to someone who was never coming back. She would never again see his special smile, his revealing nostril flare, or enjoy the smell of his warm overcoat with its distinct but familiar blend of tar and smoke. Gramps was the only person she'd ever felt close to, the only person who had believed in her totally, who always had her back, she'd miss his funny quips, his words of wisdom, and suddenly she realised how fleeting time is and how every moment should be grasped with both hands, appreciated and cherished.

And, for now, she must wipe away all thoughts of Stefan, all her daily imaginings about his whereabouts and the possible plight he might have found himself in, must cease! If he was a 'wrong 'un' as Gramps would say, she had been lucky to get away from the encounter pretty much unscathed.

She must now play her part to help her parents with the funeral arrangements and that included running around town to let everyone know.

The list of those to call on seemed never-ending; the first was Reverend Slaughter at the chapel, and then there was Mr Raven, the undertaker who'd brought the coffin round to the house, so swiftly in fact, that it was almost as though he'd had it ready! Ellen had been to Dr Hewitt's office to collect the death certificate and from there she'd gone straight round to the Registrar in Brown Street. Many relatives and friends had to be contacted and Alice and Katy were worn out from running around, knocking on all the doors of the various people Gramps knew; his sister-in-law Celia, Cousin Nellie and Uncle Will. And then of course the wreaths had to be ordered from Mr Law, sympathy cards had to be written for the wreaths, and then once written they were taken straight away up to Elm Tree Road. Suitable hats were purchased from Tuttles and Robinsons and finally, in addition to all the running around, extra baking was required to produce the numerous buns and tarts, ready for the funeral wake.

At last, at the end of all that commotion, everything went off very well on the day, it rained a little for the funeral procession, which apparently was lucky, but lucky for whom, Alice wasn't quite sure? The chapel itself was full to bursting which Alice presumed was what most people would wish for at their own funeral and when it was all over everyone came back to the house for tea by 3 o'clock in the afternoon. Joan did amazingly well, quietly shedding a few silent tears, whilst also enjoying the attention and comfort of her two granddaughters who sat either side of her, on the front pew.

After the guests had left, Ellen, Joan and the girls walked along to the cemetery to take another leisurely look at the wreaths and to read the handwritten cards.

It was truly over at last, realised Alice, and suddenly her life seemed empty. Gramps had gone and so had Stefan, two people so different and from such diverse backgrounds that of course there could be no comparison, and yet both had had a major impact on her young life. Now it seemed they had been plucked away from her and she felt bereft, as though a great big hole had been left in the place where her heart used to be.

CHAPTER THIRTY NINE

As always though, life goes on, it always finds a way to do that, Alice realised, and eventually the house at Walmer Road was ready for them all to move back in.

Her mother had of course done a sterling job. She'd scrubbed every surface, painted and decorated every room from top to bottom, she'd hung curtains, laid lino, and of course the new green wool carpet was now in pride of place, covering the spotlessly clean stairs. The carpet was luxuriously soft and had been laid all the way down from top to bottom in a long line, clipped into place with decorative rods on each step, but still showing the polished dark wood either side. It all looked very smart and Ellen was extremely proud of her achievement. But she couldn't and wouldn't compare it to the Algar residence. In fact she stopped feeling envious of their lifestyle completely, hoping and praying that her wicked thoughts had not somehow conjured up all their bad luck.

They had transferred their furniture, bit by bit, so that everything was now set for the final move and surprisingly, on their last day in London Road, Tom Algar called round to see them.

Ellen watched him advancing up the path to the front door of the small terraced house in London Road. She admitted her stomach still fluttered with trepidation as she watched him approaching. She had not seen him since the last time he'd visited, on that fateful night, when he'd walked away from her along the very same path, seemingly angered by her question about the money. Had it only been a few weeks ago? So much had happened since then, changing all of their lives forever.

However, today Tom Algar seemed in an ebullient mood and she noticed no twitching of his whiskers or sneering smile at all. He had merely come to wish them all well, he explained in a cheery voice, and Ellen noticed he did seem much more at ease than in all the time she'd known him. It was a strange thing, but because of his relaxed manner, she immediately felt more comfortable in his company too. She still addressed him as Mr Algar though; she couldn't stop herself, but for now he seemed to have lost interest in that little game. At last their relationship had found some common ground and when he took from his side pocket some official papers for her to sign; she smiled, supremely happy to sign off on their time there.

Finally, it seemed they were back to a business footing once more, just as it should be.

The best news of all was that Frank had managed to find a job locally in Kessingland and from now on he would be coming home to Walmer Road every night and of course every weekend he would be there, in his garden. Everything in their lives seemed to be returning to normal, the way it used to be before the war!

Those awful war years were gradually diminishing in Ellen's memory, becoming just a large blot on the landscape, shrinking every day as they moved further and further away from it. There was no doubt it had been a time of great hardship and courage and of course it should never be forgotten. It had taught people many different lessons, to stand them in good stead for the future. It had taught them about teamwork, about looking after each other, how to make do with very little, and most importantly, self-reliance and how much can be accomplished by every single individual by using their own initiative and drive. The country seemed to have grown a backbone again!

Of course there was no doubt Ellen was the happiest member of the family, her elation at being back in her old home was the ultimate gift, the cherry on the cake, her daily pleasure every morning when she woke, with Frank beside her, in their new floral bedroom, knew no bounds, and she felt sure it was a feeling that would never fade.

There were just two small clouds on her horizon. Firstly, her joy was tinged with a distinct sense of loss and regret that Cyril was no longer there with them and that he would never play a part in their new found happiness. She felt moved that he had bequeathed a surprise gift to her of £500, acknowledging that she'd held a special place in his heart. Secondly, Ellen realised a keen sense of loss for Alice! Of course, Alice was still there with them, but where had the old Alice gone, the daughter she used to complain and worry about? The daughter who used to flutter her eyelashes at every young man who walked by, who preened and paraded in front of the mirror, regularly showing off her latest fashion purchases for all to see? Where was that vibrant young girl?

CHAPTER FORTY

Peggy stood, gazing at her reflection in the full length bedroom mirror, hardly recognising the woman staring back at her. She used both hands to support her swelling abdomen whilst various emotions flooded, unrestrained, across her mind. She didn't know which stood out more than the next, there were so many, intermingling, juggling for position; hope, gratitude, shame, regret, all co-existing in the one space.

Since that dreadful night she had not touched a drop of alcohol. The withdrawal had been hard, the tremors lasting well over a week, and even now, after all these months, every unexpected sound around her, the clock chiming, a loud knock at the door, a raised voice, the slightest thing could send her into a fevered expectation of imminent danger. She couldn't remember feeling like this in her life before, her senses and thoughts were sharp and clear, but it helped to know that Tom was always with her, never straying far from her side. He'd transformed into the most kind, considerate and loving husband she could ever have wished for, constantly doing his best to help her forget her nightmare.

When Inspector Taylor had knocked on their door, a few weeks after the event, to return her velvet bag to her personally, she'd taken it from him gratefully. The rest of the money had also been recovered and returned to Tom, and so financially they were back where they always had been, but to tell the truth she didn't want any of it. She kept looking at the bag, sitting unopened, on the small corner table beneath the clock. Of course she knew what it contained, all the things she used to yearn for, gold, jewellery, money, but she decided all of that meant nothing to her now.

One particular bright morning she gathered it up from its place on the table and took it out with her on a stroll along the prom. She walked quite far in the mid-morning sunshine and with a gentle breeze behind her she managed to wander all the way down to the Beach Village. She knew that she was looking for someone. She wanted to find the little girl who'd come to her door earlier on in the year, begging for help, the one she'd been so rude to, feeling ashamed now to think that she'd sent that poor little mite away from her house with nothing, when they had so much to give, but of course she had been a different person back then.

Now she realised that she wanted to find her, she wanted to try and help the people from 'the grit'. As she walked along the derelict streets she searched in all the doorways and side alleys until she spied a small group of children standing together on the corner of the street. In the midst of them she saw the little girl, instantly recognising the same ragged dress, the bedraggled hair, and her small shoeless feet.

Peggy walked over to the young girl and held out the velvet bag.

'Here, dearie, take this will you, I'm very sorry I didn't give it to you before, when you came to my door in the spring.'

The girl looked up into the face of the woman. She recognised her instantly as the lady who was mean to her when she'd stood on the marble doorstep outside the big house before sending her away empty handed. But today, as she shaded her eyes in the glinting sunlight, she saw a different face looking down at her. She saw the face of someone who was sorry and who wanted to make amends. And so she reached up and took the bag from the grand lady.

'Thank you miss', she said politely, remembering her manners.

'It's Peggy,' she smiled, 'please call me Peggy. And what is your name?'

'I'm Florence,' the little girl answered proudly, 'Flo for short, I was named after Florence Nightingale!' she explained with a shy little laugh and then, clutching her prize, she ran off to find her mother.

When Tom had made love to Peggy only a few weeks after that fateful night he'd afforded her such kindness, such tenderness, one might almost say reverence, as though he were trying to make up for all those years of distance and neglect. In those few moments of sheer bliss her mind had been wiped clean of the dreadful memories from her night of terror and the anxiety she'd suffered ever since.

The traumatic event had also changed Tom. He now looked at his wife in a completely different way. He was attentiveness itself, indeed he couldn't do enough for her, his guilt and shame were his cross to bear. It had become his fervent wish to protect his wife from any future harm and he vowed that he would spend the rest of his life doing just that.

Peggy did her best to push that awful night to the very back of her mind, to try to forget how she'd been defiled by that brute.

After Tom had freed her from her bonds and collapsed on the bed beside her, she'd had a few moments to gather her senses. She'd managed to raise the alarm by calling out for help at the window and then she knew she'd have just enough time, she hoped, to wash her most intimate area, to wash away the smell of him, before they came. She could still remember the disgusting odour of that foul being who'd forced himself upon her so cruelly, at a time when she was at her most vulnerable, who'd taken advantage of her damaged drunken state, and which she now realised was to be her own degradation.

But no one need ever know the full story of what happened in that room for she'd decided to keep it to herself. She was determined never to share it with anyone and there was nothing anyone could do or say that would shift her from that path. This was her penance, the price she must pay for her deeds, the child growing within her was her only hope for salvation, a gift to herself, and she would pay any price for that gift. Everyone said the pregnancy was a miracle and how lucky they were after their earlier loss and so many years of trying, and of course after their terrible ordeal. Yes, of course, it was a miracle, Peggy agreed, and no one need ever know the truth, she would take that secret to the grave.

It seemed Hans had taken everything from her, her old life had been ravaged and left in ruins, but he'd left her with a small parting gift, a German seed he'd planted inside her, which had flourished.

Hans was still in England, unbroken and unrepentant. After his capture he was put to good use, working with other German prisoners along the coastline, helping to clear the hazardous minefields laid in haste at the beginning of the war.

He laughed at the thought of what he'd got away with in town, the possibility of the rumours being true, and how appropriate it would be if he'd left that lucky lady with a little German baby inside her, a small German infiltrator ready to fill her empty cot. At least that sad little nursery would get some use he thought, in bitter irony, and then he smiled with a sense of smug satisfaction that perhaps all had not been lost in the war.

Hans supposed he ought to be pretty content with his lot. Perhaps it wasn't so bad here in England, working side by side with many of his German comrades. It could be a lot worse, he reflected, he might even be content to stay on for a while longer. A little hard work wouldn't kill him and after all he was being fed and watered at the enemy's cost. He was pretty sure that once all the mines were cleared he'd be sent back home to his motherland.

The east coast of Britain was truly a beautiful part of the world he conceded, as he stopped for a minute to enjoy it, to breathe in the salty sea air and take time to survey one of the most beautiful beaches he'd ever seen.

His eyes swept across the expanse of golden sand and rested on the mounds of soft grassy dunes which had sprouted at the back of the beach. He couldn't help but admire those cleverly crafted tufts of protection which afforded a natural shelter from the cold north easterly breeze. His dark eyes skipped again across the vastness of the ocean and off towards the horizon, where rows of rippling waves shimmered in the slowly ebbing sunshine, stretching layer upon layer, far out to sea.

Hans hardly registered the small almost insignificant sound below his foot. He had only seconds to understand what it meant as the round and solid piece of metal clunked hard and unyielding against the underside of his sturdy German boot. With urgency he dragged his scrutiny back from the vastness of the ocean to look down for just one glimpse of the brown rusty biscuit-tin shape which was protruding through the softly shifting sand. There was no time to run, no time to shout, no time to call out to his fellow comrades who were still searching further up the beach, because the mine beneath his foot suddenly detonated, and Hans was blown, swiftly and decisively, to kingdom come!

CHAPTER FORTY ONE

Ellen tried not to but she couldn't help watching over Alice constantly, anxious to see any sign of her old self resurfacing, whilst, at the same time, realising that her daughter had never been the same since the night she'd found her, down at the seafront, in the fog. She knew her daughter was holding out on her, she was keeping something deep inside her that for some reason she just couldn't share, not even with her own mother. Ellen discussed her worries with Frank but all he'd said was to give Alice a bit more time, she'd come round right enough, and so in the end he'd managed to reassure her. Ellen knew Alice was holding on to a secret and she wanted desperately to delve into her daughter's mind to find out the cause of her trauma, because whatever that secret was, it had changed her. But as with all secrets, and Ellen agreed with Frank on this, the key to unlocking them was to wait. And so she must wait, for as long as it took, until the time was right, and then she'd listen to her daughter without judgement.

And sure enough, one day, out of the blue, something happened that changed everything!

The postman delivered the post one Saturday morning when everyone was at home, neither of the girls was working, which was actually quite rare, and Frank was out in the garden. Ellen was busy, rolling out some dough in the kitchen, while the girls were quietly reading their new magazines in the front room; both were snuggled up comfortably in the two big armchairs. When no one made a move towards the door, Ellen sighed and clapped her hands together over the sink, shaking off a large amount of excess flour, before walking slowly along the hallway towards the front door.

She bent down to pick up the letters which had landed on the new front door mat. They were in a muddled heap but right on the top of the pile was a letter addressed to Alice. Ellen frowned, turning it over a couple of times, wondering what it might be, and who it might be from, whilst registering inexplicably the strange foreign stamp stuck on the front of it. How strange, thought Ellen, as she sifted through the rest of the post with her floury hands, quickly realising that all the other letters consisted merely of tiresome bills. She entered the sitting room and walked over to Alice who'd obviously become rather bored of her fashion magazine and had exchanged it for a lazy and compliant Trix, whom she'd lifted up from the warm rug and positioned on her lap, stroking him repetitively in a strange, thoughtful, almost meditative manner which Ellen had noticed her daughter slipping into rather a lot recently.

Alice looked up at her mother with an inquisitive frown, as Ellen held out the strange looking letter, feeling rather bemused by it herself.

Ellen walked away from the girls, leaving the room quietly, feeling somehow this might be a private matter for her daughter to deal with and also wondering whether it could possibly have something to do with the secret Alice had been keeping from her all these months, and so she quietly retraced her steps back into the kitchen and continued to knead the dough she'd left sitting on the work surface.

After placing the dough in a bowl and covering it with muslin ready to prove, Ellen turned away from the counter and stood for a while, staring out through the window and into the garden. She loved watching Frank tilling the soil with his rake and all of a sudden she was overcome with contentment, mixed with a feeling of excitement that all her dreams had finally come true and they were all together again, here at last, in their proper home.

Unexpectedly, she heard a commotion which disturbed her reverie and as she turned she caught sight of Alice suddenly rushing out of the sitting room and bounding up the stairs in a state of apparent agitation, presumably heading towards her bedroom. Ellen walked slowly towards the bottom of the stairs, exchanging expressive looks with Katy, who simply shrugged her shoulders in a gesture that spoke volumes, and revealing that her sister's strange behaviour was now becoming quite commonplace! As Ellen looked up the stairs, waiting for she knew not what, silence seemed to reign for a while, but after a few moments there was a rash of opening and closing of doors and drawers. Her recently quiet and morose daughter seemed to be making a bit of a din up there. She must be looking for something, thought Ellen, wondering what on earth it could be. She made a sudden move to go upstairs and help her daughter in a bid to find out what on earth was going on. But then, abruptly, she stopped herself, she must not interfere! No, she would leave her daughter to it, and wait, maybe all would become clear eventually, but for now she would head back into the kitchen and pound her frustration into the dough instead?

Upstairs, sitting on her bed, Alice read and re-read the letter, again and again, several times in fact, before it finally started to sink in and she could grasp its meaning. Now she sat on her bed in complete shock at the letter's revelation.

It was unbelievable, but the letter was from Stefan. Stefan! After all this time, she'd heard from him and he was home apparently, safe and sound, in Germany! She read the letter again,

'*Liebe Alice,*

I have wanted to write to you for so many months but such a lot has happened to me since the last time I saw you and it has taken all of this time for me to be in a calm place and to be able to sit down and write to you this letter. I am now settled at last, and peaceful, and I have finally been able to stop looking over my shoulder.

I wanted to explain to you why I left you so suddenly that night.

Before I could hide on board the ship there was something I needed to do. I had to go back to the wreck to find my friend Hans. I couldn't tell you about him at the time but we had been comrades through all our time in the prison camp and afterwards when we made our escape from that place. But we decided to split up from the rest of the prisoners and follow our own plan. Sadly our plan failed and when we arrived in your town we argued and then we went our separate ways.

When you and I entered the cabin quarters on the wreck, I came to the conclusion that it was my friend Hans who was living there. I couldn't tell you about him at the time and then afterwards when you were talking to your sailor friend at the dock, I had a sudden feeling that I couldn't leave him behind, and so I decided to go back to the wreck and find him. But I want you to know that it was also my way to protect you, my friend Alice, from any involvement in our escape.

I fetched him, using your rowing boat once more, but I made sure it was returned safely back where it belonged so no one would be any the wiser.

We managed to get on board the ship without being seen, or that is what I thought, and then once on board we hid in separate lifeboats, just as we'd arranged, and there we had planned to remain for the whole voyage. The plan seemed to be going well, and of course this was your plan Alice, and without you I would probably still be stuck somewhere in Lowestoft, somewhere not dissimilar to the small shelter where you found me, at the end of your garden.

Everything seemed to be quiet for a while on board the ship and I really thought we'd made it and that at last we were on our way home. If we could just remain in our hiding places until the ship left port we would be home and dry. But suddenly I heard the sound of running feet coming up the gangplank, there was a lot of shouting, and I knew straight away that the authorities had come on board. I heard them searching up and down the deck, they seemed to be everywhere and I thought my time was up. I became frozen with fear. They were calling out for us to give ourselves up as though they knew we were there and I thought perhaps they'd been tipped off, but I just couldn't move, I shrunk into the dark space of the lifeboat, as small as I could, and I just stayed there, rigid, waiting for the inevitable.

Suddenly a cheer went up and I could hear Hans' voice shouting and cursing in German but they must have wrestled him to the ground and overpowered him and then I suppose after that they must have taken him away, down the gangplank and off the ship, because I could still hear him shouting and cursing way off into the distance.

It dawned on me then, that they were not looking for me, they were only looking for him, and so I just stayed where I was. I feared that they would come back for me at any moment. I was worried that Hans might tell them about me and where I was, maybe out of spite, I don't know, but he didn't and so the ship remained quiet, and finally I realised they had stopped searching. Apparently they had found what they were looking for and it certainly wasn't me. They only wanted Hans.

Later on though, in the early hours of the morning, someone did come on board. The tarpaulin was lifted up above my head and a face peered inside. It was your friend the sailor, Alice, he saw me hiding there in the lifeboat but he never said a word. As soon as he saw me looking up at him I could see the surprise on his face but he gave me a strange smile and put a finger to his lips and then he just pulled the cover back down. He helped me Alice, your friend, he gave me his protection.

When the ship finally left harbour the next morning, as planned, I can't tell you the relief I felt and from then on the trip was trouble-free. The sea was calm and so soothing that I managed to sleep most of the way and I ended up in Hamburg feeling quite remarkably refreshed.

I have to tell you though that it is very bad here in my country. The place is in ruins and my family has suffered terribly in my absence. Our home was shelled several times and sections of the rooms have been virtually destroyed but luckily there are parts of the house which are still fit for human habitation. My father and brother were both lost to the war and my heart aches for their loss but my mother and sister are both here, alive and well, and at least what is left of our family is now together and in one place. Of course there is also Elsa, mas madchen, my love, my liebling, soon to be die Ehefrau, my wife.

I enclose a photo of myself and Elsa and I thank you from the bottom of my heart for all your kindness and your help. In lending me the hand of friendship, as you did, I was able to return home and now I can be of great comfort and use to my beloved Elsa, and of course my mother and my little sister.

Everything they told me about you English was a damn lie. You have been a true friend and at a time when I needed one the most, and for that I will be forever in your debt.

Danke dir, thank you,
Stefan

Alice read the letter again and again and then she looked more closely at the photograph which Stefan had enclosed with the letter. His happy face was there, smiling up at her, and it made her heart glad to see him again and this time he looked better, cleaner and healthier, as though he was enjoying being home and eating his mother's home cooked food again. When she looked at the pretty face next to his, she saw the face of his sweetheart, Elsa.

As she looked down at Elsa's face once more she felt a sharp stab of recognition. In front of her was a face she knew, but slightly different, older somehow, but with the same blonde curly hair, the slight up-slant to the eyes and those rosebud lips which were still plump and full. She looked wiser somehow, as though she'd been through something dreadful, and her innocence had been taken away from her.

Alice felt a sudden jolt as the knowledge of where she'd seen that face before came back to her?

Quickly Alice ran to her wardrobe and wrenched open the doors, pulling the drawers open inside at random, searching avidly for her box of souvenirs.

She began to ransack all of her possessions. She was searching for something and that something might be the missing link, the key to all the events which had unfolded in her life recently.

At last she found what she was looking for as she retrieved the box of war memorabilia from the back of her wardrobe. She placed the box carefully on to her bed and opened the lid. As she began to rummage around amongst its contents, she pushed aside several items of shrapnel, eventually deciding to lift everything out of the box; the rolled up wartime posters, the spent shells, three small wooden animals each handmade and left behind by the kinder transport children, but still she desperately sought that small keepsake, the photograph she'd found tucked at the back of the pilot's seat in the abandoned plane at Fressingfield.

And suddenly there it was!

She lifted out the small crumpled photograph from the bottom of the box and brushed off the dusty surface. She smoothed it out on top of her bedcovers before carefully placing it side by side with the one Stefan had sent her.

She felt a tingling down her spine as she recognised the face instantly. They were one and the same, they matched! It was the exact same girl in both photographs. The pretty girl smiling up at her from the photograph, the one she'd found in that deserted fighter plane, was Stefan's girl! He must have been the pilot of that plane! And she knew now there'd been two of them, someone else had been sitting in the seat behind him, that dreadful man who'd broken in to the Algar's house and caused them all that grief.

Now she knew the full story, she began mull over the implications in her mind, until finally a strange sense of destiny overcame her. She now had indisputable proof that their paths had crossed for a reason and she knew, without a doubt, that she had done the right thing by him. Because of her, he was now safely home with his family.

She felt a weight suddenly lifted from her shoulders, and she released a long pent up sigh of pure relief, knowing that, at last, she could rest easy.

With her head held high Alice left her bedroom and walked slowly down the newly carpeted staircase to find her mother. She owed her mother an explanation and now she was ready to give it. She would tell her family everything and she would do so without fear or shame. Indeed, she would tell them the whole story with a certain amount of dignity and pride!

The End

Printed in Great Britain
by Amazon

34368290R00145